Love Not Poison

Mary Andrea Clarke

They love not poison that do poison need

– William Shakespeare, Richard II

First published in 2009
by Crème de la Crime
P O Box 523, Chesterfield, S40 9AT

Typesetting by Yvette Warren
Cover design by Yvette Warren
Front cover image by Peter Roman

ISBN 978-0-9560566-0-3
A CIP catalogue reference for this book
is available from the British Library

Printed and bound in Great Britain by
CPI Cox & Wyman, Reading, Berkshire

www.cremedelacrime.com

About the author:
Currently working in the Civil Service, Mary Andrea Clarke has been a regular delegate at crime fiction conferences and a member of Mystery Women since 1998. She has reviewed historical fiction for the Historical Novel Society and crime fiction for Sherlock Magazine, Shots Ezine and Mystery Women. Mary lives in Surrey with her cat, Alice.

www.maryandreaclarke.com

A huge thank-you must go to my nephew, Stephen Clarke, for his interest and enthusiasm – and the hard work he put into creating my website.

Thanks are due to Gillian Haslam, Lorraine Hayes, Jason Perrott and Roz Southey for reading, and to Adrian Magson and Linda Regan for ongoing support and helpful advice.

I would like to thank Lynne Patrick for her sound judgement and useful feedback in editing. I would also like to express my gratitude to Lynne, Jeff, Yvette and the rest of the team at Crème de la Crime for their help in enabling the Crimson Cavalier to ride again.

To my family,
Kevin, Peter, Linda, Alice and Stephen.
Thanks for your support and encouragement.

1

The Crimson Cavalier had had a successful evening, with hopes of still more profit before it had to end. The oaths uttered by the last traveller seemed to linger in the still night air. It was clear and cool, and there had been a sense of peace in the stillness, even when the pistol had pointed straight at the near-apoplectic man. His ruddy cheeks had looked ready to burst with outrage, which escalated when the fair haired young lady who addressed him as 'uncle' looked coyly under her lashes at the highway robber who demanded her jewellery.

Yet, like so many, the gentleman had made no attempt to defend the girl, but had handed over his watch and fob with a poor grace and a mouthful of empty threats. The corpulence of his little finger had defied all attempts to remove the ring which encircled it, and with a bow of defeat, the Crimson Cavalier had bidden the traveller keep it. This incensed the gentleman further, a condition not aided by the sudden complaints of his niece over his failure to protect her. Their bickering was clearly audible along the road as the carriage drew away.

With a shake of the head, the Crimson Cavalier put away the treasures contributed by the apoplectic gentleman.

"That girl's no more his niece than I am."

This was no surprise, though it would be astonishing if the girl were allowed to complete her journey in the carriage. Sir Thomas would not be above putting her out on the road if her complaints grew too vociferous, assuming she did not herself lose patience and demand to walk.

A casual glance at the horizon dashed all hope of further

profit for the evening. The Cavalier's deep emerald eyes widened between the securely tied mask and the tricorne sporting its distinctive red kerchief.

There was no mistake. Despite the late hour, the sky further along the road was unnervingly light. A red glow flickered through a thick haze of smoke.

The Crimson Cavalier thought quickly. It was clearly impossible to remain on the road. The alarm should be raised, and quickly. Murmured endearments kept the horse calm, one hand firm on the reins while the other stroked the animal's neck lest the fire spread quickly enough to frighten the beast before help could be found.

Plans for holding up any more carriages abandoned, the Cavalier turned the horse and urged her on along the empty road.

The dark sky began to seem heavy as the gentle breeze carried smoke through the night air. The rider began to feel it, eyes stinging as they tried to focus on the road. The horse seemed in discomfort as well, giving an occasional uneasy whinny and shaking her head.

"Easy, Princess, it's all right."

The soothing tones calmed the horse and the journey continued at a steady pace, though smoke and soot thickened the atmosphere further. The rider's own eyes were smarting and tinged with red by the time Princess recognised their destination and slowed to a walk. In the stable, concern over the fire allowed for no more than a brief pause to throw a blanket over the horse's lathered back.

The Crimson Cavalier stepped silently around the back wall of the darkened house, pulled open an unlocked door and entered with unceremonious haste. A mane of vivid auburn hair tumbled down as a hand tore off the crimson-adorned hat. The other hand removed the mask – and a breathless young lady stood facing the occupants of the room, a man and woman of similar age. Both rose from their seats at the kitchen table, wearing startled expressions.

"Miss Georgiana," the girl began, but was interrupted immediately by the panting newcomer.

"There's a fire," said Georgiana Grey, in businesslike fashion, standing straight in her highway robber clothes as though it were nothing out of the ordinary. She ran her hand through her auburn hair. "I saw the smoke from the road. It looks like it's coming from the direction of Marpley Manor. James, get some men and see if you can do anything to help. You'd better rouse the Watch if you can."

The footman nodded and was on his feet, moving into action before his mistress had finished speaking. Georgiana turned to his sister.

"Help me out of these clothes, Emily." Already untying her cravat, Georgiana turned towards the back stairs, her maid directly behind her. They walked quickly but silently until they reached the sanctuary of Georgiana's bedroom. As the door closed, she removed a small black velvet bag from her belt and handed it to her maid. "Lock that away, please, would you, Emily?" said Georgiana. "There's little this evening, just a few coins from Sir Thomas Drysdale. Still, it may do someone some good."

Emily grimaced as she took the bag. "Was his wife with him?"

"No, a niece."

Emily offered no reply, putting the bag with its few coins and pieces of jewellery carefully in the drawer of the night table. Turning to see her mistress rifling through her wardrobe, she frowned.

"What are you looking for, miss?"

"Something more suitable to wear," said Georgiana.

3

She gestured towards her highway robber's attire. "It's a cursed nuisance, they're more practical for fast riding than anything else I've got." She pulled out a dark green riding habit. "This will have to do."

Emily took it from her, looking doubtful.

"You're going to Marpley Manor, miss? I'm sure there's no need. James can raise the alarm."

"I'm going to Lady Bertram's first, in case that wretched party is still going on."

"The one you left because you had a headache?"

"Yes. Lady Wickerston might still be there." Georgiana grew solemn. "She will need to be told what is happening in her home. Everyone will be busy fighting this fire. No one will have time to go to her."

"No," said Emily slowly. "But how are you going to explain how you know about the fire?"

"I'll think of something," said Georgiana, as she and Emily hastily fastened the buttons on the riding habit. "Don't bother about the hat. I haven't time to waste."

"What about your hair, miss? You can't just ride across country with it loose."

Georgiana admitted the truth of this. It would be impractical, apart from anything else. "Fetch a riband and tie it back. That will have to suffice."

It was not many minutes before Georgiana was back out on the road, bent hell for leather towards the dull party from which she had excused herself such a short time earlier. James had thoughtfully left another horse ready and had put a bowl of water in front of the still-lathered Princess.

Georgiana urged Diamond on as fast as she dared, feeling all the awkwardness of having to ride side-saddle when she was in a hurry. She was relieved to see the collection of carriages still outside Lady Bertram's white-stoned home.

Ignoring the startled expression of the groom to whom she gave charge of her horse, she ran lightly up the front stairs and raised the brass knocker to seek admittance of the equally startled butler.

"I will see if her ladyship can be disturbed, miss."

"No need," said Georgiana, brushing past him. "I must speak to my brother urgently. You need not trouble to announce me."

"But, miss…" The butler's strangled accents revealed all too clearly his shock: an unaccompanied young lady, albeit one of her ladyship's acquaintance, barging into the house, in riding dress, interrupting her ladyship's dinner party. Had Georgiana been in less of a hurry, she would have been highly amused by his expression.

She headed purposefully for the drawing room, the door of which was opened by a footman who realised straight away that it would be unwise to argue with her. Georgiana paused on the threshold, scanning the room. She saw twenty pairs of eyes trained on her. It was easy to pick out those of her brother, their pale green more horror-stricken than any of the others.

"Georgiana!" The weight of Edward Grey's mortification came through in the one word.

"My dear Miss Grey." Lady Bertram came forward to greet her returning guest. "Is anything wrong? Are you unwell?"

For the first time, Georgiana became aware of the dishevelled appearance she must present. She felt strands of hair fluttering around her face. The riband had slipped down, and her thick, hatless locks were barely secure. She raised a hand to brush them back. Her cheeks were hot and, she was certain, glowing red.

"Miss Grey." A calm masculine voice addressed her. "Please, take a glass of wine. And won't you sit down?"

Georgiana accepted the glass held out to her by the polite,

dark-haired young man. She recognised him as Lady Wickerston's brother, Sir Anthony Dixon, to whom she had been introduced earlier in the evening.

"No, thank you, Sir Anthony. I am well enough. I beg your pardon but it is a matter of some urgency. I've seen a fire. It looks as if it's at Marpley Manor. I've sent my footman to raise the alarm but he will need help."

Lady Wickerston paled. Georgiana's sister-in-law Amanda Grey was at her ladyship's side instantly, offering support. Edward Grey glanced towards them in concern, but a nod from his wife sent him immediately to join the other men, most of who were already on their feet and making for the door. Edward turned and met his sister's eyes, then drew in his breath and strode purposefully towards the door, pausing only as he realised Georgiana intended to join them. She tossed back her wine in a most unladylike fashion, and set off towards the door just as Edward reached it.

"What do you think you're doing?" he demanded.

"Going with you. I've sent James on ahead to get help. He should be there by now."

"Are you mad, Georgiana? A fire is no place for a lady."

"Don't be absurd, Edward. I can be of far more use there than here. What would you have me do?" She lowered her voice. "Stay here and hold your mistress's hand while her house is burning? Your wife already seems to have that under control."

Edward's colour had risen at the last part of this speech but he was not to be deflected. "The fact remains, Georgiana…"

"These are not normal circumstances," Georgiana snapped. "Do stop being so tedious, Edward. You are wasting time."

"You've already been of enormous help in warning us, Miss Grey," came the approaching voice of Sir Anthony Dixon. "I'm sure we should not wish for you to put yourself to further trouble, not to say danger."

"I am very well able to take care of myself," said Georgiana coolly, walking out the door to prevent further argument.

The front of Lady Bertram's house was frenetic activity. Horses were being brought round from the stables; others, already between the shafts of their owners' carriages in preparation for departure, were being released to provide extra mounts. Several men had already departed. As Georgiana slid a foot into Diamond's stirrup, she felt a hand lightly touch her shoulder.

"Will you not at least take a fresh horse, Miss Grey?" said Sir Anthony. "Your own must be tired out with the ride here."

Georgiana glanced at Diamond. His chestnut shoulders were beginning to glisten. It would be hard work for him to be pushed further at an urgent pace.

"Thank you," she said with genuine gratitude. "I would appreciate that."

Georgiana was glad to see a decent mount led up to her, rather than something deemed appropriate for a lady, which in her experience had no greater use than a gentle canter around the park. She accepted Sir Anthony's assistance in mounting and ignored the disapproving eyes of her brother as she turned the horse in the direction of Marpley Manor.

The red glow which Georgiana had noticed while she was in the guise of the Crimson Cavalier intensified as she approached the imposing stone manor house. The thickening smoke billowed across the night sky and blocked out the thin light afforded by the moon and stars, and without the protection of the Crimson Cavalier's mask, Georgiana had to battle the stinging sensation which limited her vision. She arrived at the scene of the fire to see every imaginable kind of receptacle being passed from hand to hand, filled with water in an attempt to douse the flames. Georgiana swiftly dismounted, her eyes searching the line for James. She was anxious that exposure to the smoke might aggravate the cough which had been a constant feature of his life since a spell in Newgate prison when he was unjustly convicted of poaching. She blinked away the continued assault of smoke and ash, concerned that there was no sign of him among the water handlers.

A shout went up, capturing her attention. She turned towards the house, and was astonished by the sight of James emerging from what remained of the front of it, accompanied by a gentleman in well-cut coat and knee breeches. Georgiana recognised Maxwell Lakesby with some surprise; she had understood he was accompanying his aunt and cousin into the country. The two men walked sideways, each holding an end of a long, heavy-looking object. Georgiana's eyes were growing accustomed to the thick dark; it was clear someone had not been fortunate enough to escape the fire.

Georgiana quickly joined her footman and his companion as they gently deposited their burden on the ground. James laid down the feet as Lakesby moved one of his hands from the neck to support the head as he followed suit. The grim looks they exchanged told her all she needed to know.

"Is he dead?" she asked.

"I'm afraid so," replied Lakesby. "He was dead when we found him." He took out his handkerchief and bent to wipe the soot from the face of the victim, revealing the coarsened features of Lord Wickerston, owner of Marpley Manor.

"Lady Wickerston will have to be informed," came Edward's voice behind Georgiana.

Lakesby looked up at Edward. "Yes," Lakesby said slowly. "I'm sure it will come as a shock to her."

"I will see that my sister is told." Sir Anthony Dixon joined the group around his brother-in-law's body. "Grey, would you

8

be so good as to assist me in moving Wickerston. I think Lakesby and –" Sir Anthony looked inquiringly at James.

"Cooper, sir," the footman supplied.

"Cooper. I think Lakesby and Cooper here have already done more than could be expected. Besides, I should not wish to inflict such a distressing sight on your sister longer than necessary."

Georgiana refrained from volunteering the information that Lord Wickerston's was not the first dead body she had seen. She remained silently watching with Lakesby and James as Edward acquiesced to Sir Anthony's plan to carry his late lordship to a nearby cart. She nodded absently as James expressed his intention of remaining to help fight the flames which were set fair to swallow the remains of the building. She was lost in her own thoughts about Edward's possible feelings over the death of his mistress's husband.

Georgiana had almost forgotten Lakesby's presence when she felt a light touch on her arm.

"Come," he said, beginning to steer her forward. "We should move away from here. The building may collapse."

"Oh. Yes, of course." Georgiana allowed herself to be led away from the still smoking ruins of what had been a distinguished residence. She found herself wondering how the fire had started, and why Lord Wickerston had not escaped the building in time to save his own life. Perhaps he was drunk, she thought; it certainly wouldn't be the first time.

"What the devil are you doing here, anyway?" demanded Lakesby.

Georgiana sighed. "I had hoped to do something useful."

"From what your footman tells me, you've been useful enough, sending him along to raise help. How did you know?"

Something of the quizzical note in Lakesby's voice caught Georgiana's attention. "I saw the light and the smoke."

"From your window?"

"I went for a walk. I needed some air."

"Even so, you must have deuced good eyesight."

"Exceptional," responded Georgiana gravely.

"Is that the tale you mean to give your brother when he asks?"

"I left Lady Bertram's dinner party early with a headache. I needed some air."

"I see. I trust your headache was profitable?"

Georgiana threw him a sharp glance. She might have known Lakesby would suspect that her evening had not been quite as she described it. It had been some time since he had confronted her with his belief that she was the Crimson Cavalier. She had never confirmed his suspicions, however, and did not intend to do so now.

"How do you come to be here?" she asked him. "I understood from your cousin that you were out of town."

"Only to escort her and my esteemed aunt to visit some aged relative in the country," Lakesby replied. "You didn't imagine I planned to stay there, did you?"

"I'm sure you would find it very restful," Georgiana said solemnly, the barest hint of mischief in her tone.

"Give me strength! Louisa the chatterbox and a couple of dowager harridans. Do you wish to hear that I have done away with myself?"

"No, indeed." Unthinkingly, she took a handkerchief from her sleeve and began to wipe smudges of soot from his cheek. Her hand froze as she realised what she was doing, and she felt the colour slowly creep into her own face.

Grinning, Lakesby took the handkerchief from her and thanked her gravely as he continued the task. He spoke casually as he did so.

"I was at White's with a party of friends when some street urchin came screaming that there was a house on fire. I understand he'd tried to alert the Watch, but would have had more success waking the dead."

"Yes, I told James to rouse the Watch but I don't suppose he fared any better."

"No matter. The boy who dragged us out of White's made enough noise to bring half the town running. We'd already started putting water on the flames when your footman arrived with reinforcements. Very grateful we were to have them." He looked closely at her. "For goodness sake, Georgiana, let me escort you home. Headache or no, you've had a long evening."

"Yes. No. All right," she said, too preoccupied to notice Lakesby's use of her Christian name.

"Well, which is it to be?" he demanded.

Georgiana blinked and looked properly at Lakesby. "I'm sorry. It's just that I feel I should go back to Lady Bertram's."

"Do you think that's wise?" said Lakesby. "I'm sure Lady Wickerston will have enough people to tend her. I really can't see you as one of a parcel of women clucking about her, not to mention the attention she will be getting from her brother and – "

"And mine?" Georgiana asked with a smile.

"Well – "

"It is my sister-in-law who concerns me, Mr Lakesby. When I left Lady Bertram's she was trying to comfort Lady Wickerston."

"Good grief," said Lakesby. "All the more reason for you to leave it well alone, my dear girl. Go home and count your profits. I'll take you driving tomorrow."

Georgiana bristled at his tone. "I am not your dear girl,

Mr Lakesby. And I am going to Lady Bertram's. If you care to come with me I should be glad of your company, but I beg you won't put yourself to any trouble." She walked purposefully towards the horse she had tethered to a tree, mounting unassisted as Lakesby came up behind her to offer some help.

"Don't be so high and mighty," he said. "Of course I mean to accompany you. I assume you've left your pistol at home. I don't hold with unarmed females riding about the country alone."

Georgiana ignored the jibe and waited as Lakesby mounted his own horse before turning her animal back in the direction of Lady Bertram's. Lakesby's hand reached out and took hold of her bridle before she had moved two steps.

"Come, why are we quarrelling?" he said. "I daresay we are both tired, but are we not still friends?"

Georgiana looked at the blue eyes seeking forgiveness in her green ones and found she was not proof against the plea. She smiled.

"Indeed, I have no wish to quarrel, Mr Lakesby, but this evening has been – has been…"

"Exactly."

Georgiana held out her hand. "Friends?" she said.

Lakesby stretched out his own hand to take hers and surprised Georgiana by raising it briefly to his lips.

"Friends," he affirmed.

Georgiana quickly withdrew her hand. "We should go," she said, urging her horse forward. "My brother and Sir Anthony have already gone ahead with Lord Wickerston's body."

"Only just. But you are right; there is no reason to tarry here."

The two rode in silence for a few moments, alone with their thoughts. Georgiana was first to speak.

"It was very sad that Lord Wickerston should have died in the fire."

"Yes. I suppose so," said Lakesby. "Though I'm not sure for whom."

Georgiana looked sharply at him.

"Come, Miss Grey, the man was a drunkard, very poor company, coarse, rude. He was only ever accepted in society on account of his wife, whom he treated quite abominably."

"Yes," said Georgiana. She recalled her own shock when Edward told her Lady Wickerston had been beaten by her husband, and her shame that she had not noticed this herself. She became aware of Lakesby speaking again.

"It was not only your brother who was angry over this," he said. "A number of gentlemen of my acquaintance were ready to take Wickerston to task."

"I see," said Georgiana. "Perhaps one of them did?"

"By setting fire to the Wickerstons' home?" Lakesby said with a frown. "It seems a rather extreme course of action."

Georgiana did not speak immediately. She knew Lakesby was right. No matter how angry any gentleman was about the treatment Lord Wickerston meted out to his wife, setting fire to a house was not the action one would expect from a civilised person. More than likely it would be thought improper to interfere. Yet something troubled her.

"Miss Grey?"

Georgiana blinked. "I beg your pardon. You are quite correct, Mr Lakesby. No right thinking person would do such a thing."

Lakesby continued watching her, his eyes solemn.

"Yet you sense something wrong?"

"Something," she said. "I hardly know why. There is no reason to imagine the fire is anything other than an accident."

"No."

Georgiana continued in thoughtful silence.

"Perhaps…" Lakesby ventured. "Perhaps I provoked your uneasiness with my suggestion that the cause of Lord Wickerston's death may have been less simple than it appeared."

Georgiana glanced towards him, her expression perplexed.

"Forgive me," he said. "It was hardly charitable and I certainly had no wish to worry you."

"There is no need to apologise for it," said Georgiana. The thought, however, once planted in her mind, refused to go away.

"His body did not seem very badly burnt," she said slowly. "Would you not have expected it to be?"

"A gruesome thought. I don't think the fire had been going long before the first help arrived," said Lakesby.

"Surely he would have called out, or tried to escape, unless he was unconscious. Is that possible? Perhaps something could have fallen on his head."

"I saw no indication of a head injury."

"Perhaps he was drunk," said Georgiana. "That would not be unusual."

"True. I could certainly smell wine on him." Lakesby paused, frowning. "Although it could not have been on his breath."

"No," said Georgiana.

"Perhaps you should speak to your footman. He seems an intelligent, observant fellow. He may have noticed something I missed."

Georgiana doubted this. While she did not underrate James's intelligence, she knew Lakesby was no fool. He had, after all, penetrated her disguise and identified her as the Crimson Cavalier after relatively short acquaintance. Georgiana remained silent, conscious of a sense of uneasiness as she twisted the reins around her fingers.

The scene at Lady Bertram's home was quiet. Lord Wickerston's body was on the cart where Edward and Sir Anthony had laid it, respectfully covered by a blanket and guarded by two servants. Of Edward and Sir Anthony there was no sign, but a brief inquiry of a servant elicited the information that the gentlemen had only just arrived. Georgiana entered the house ahead of Lakesby, her increasingly windswept appearance occasioning less reaction than on her preceding visit. Nevertheless, she brushed back her hair, a gesture which drew a smile from Lakesby.

"You look enchanting," he said in an excess of gallantry.

"And you, Mr Lakesby, should look to the problem of your eyesight."

"I assure you, there is no problem with my eyesight."

Georgiana preceded Lakesby into the drawing room. Lady Wickerston was seated in an armchair close to the fire. Sir Anthony knelt in front of her, clasping her hands between his own. Her ladyship's blonde head was bowed slightly, the pallor of her fair complexion even more pronounced than when Georgiana had burst in with news of the fire.

Most of the guests had left. Edward stood by the window, looking at the newly widowed woman with a degree of concern which could not have been more evident had he made a formal announcement that Lady Wickerston was his mistress. Georgiana's gaze travelled to Amanda, who stood at her ladyship's side. Her worst fears were realised. Amanda maintained her accustomed air of quiet dignity, but to one who knew her well there could be no mistaking the suspicion and hurt in her eyes. Amanda had a more trusting nature than Georgiana, but she was no fool. Georgiana wished she had the same certainty about Edward, at least as far as Lady Wickerston was concerned.

Just behind her, Georgiana heard Lakesby quietly ask a

servant to fetch some brandy. He walked straight to Lady Wickerston with the glass which was brought to him.

"Drink this," Lakesby commanded her.

"No, no… thank you. I don't want it," Lady Wickerston said weakly.

"Drink it," he said more forcefully. "Trust me, you'll feel better."

Edward began to protest, eyeing Lakesby with dislike. "If Lady Wickerston doesn't want it…"

Lakesby returned Edward's gaze with one of pure indifference. "Lady Wickerston is in no condition to know what is best for her," he said. "You tell her, Dixon."

"Mr Lakesby is right." Sir Anthony's tone was calm as he took the glass from the tray. "Drink it, Theresa. You have had a nasty shock."

Her ladyship accepted the brandy with apparent reluctance. After a tentative sip, she screwed up her face and tried to push it back into her brother's hand.

"No, please, I really don't like it."

"Just a little more," Sir Anthony coaxed.

Lady Wickerston complied, and those around her were rewarded with the sight of a tinge of colour returning to her cheeks.

"Perhaps you would like to lie down, my dear?" asked Lady Bertram solicitously.

"Yes, yes, thank you. I would, if you don't mind."

Lady Wickerston rose a little unsteadily, reaching out for her brother's supporting arm. She smiled wanly.

"Thank you, Anthony. I shall be well enough." She paused, nibbling her underlip before she spoke again. "May I see him?"

"I don't think that's wise, Theresa," said Sir Anthony.

"Just for a moment, to say goodbye?"

"You will get an opportunity to do that later. Dr Masters will need to examine him first."

"What?" Lady Wickerston looked at her brother in alarm. "Why? He's dead. Why can't he be left in peace?"

"Hush, Theresa. There's nothing to worry about," said Sir Anthony. "It's perfectly regular in cases of sudden death."

"But I don't understand. Surely it's obvious? The fire…" Lady Wickerston's voice trailed off as her distress increased.

"It has to be checked, Theresa. No matter how unlikely that anything else will be found."

Georgiana felt rather than saw Lakesby's eyes on her. She did not dare shift her own to meet them. She focused on the scene between the newly widowed Lady Wickerston and Sir Anthony.

"Now, you must go and lie down. I think someone has sent for Dr Masters." Sir Anthony looked inquiringly around. It was Amanda who nodded confirmation. "We will ask him to give you a sleeping draught. All right?"

Lady Wickerston nodded. Sir Anthony smiled, gave his sister a kiss on the cheek and stepped back as Lady Bertram came forward to lead her out of the drawing room. Amanda followed, not looking at Edward as she walked from the room. What concerned Georgiana most was that he did not even seem to notice.

Georgiana suddenly found the room oppressive and wanted desperately to be out in the fresh air. It was clear nothing more could be done, and the headache she had pleaded to effect her earlier escape was beginning to form in reality. Involuntarily, she glanced towards Lakesby who smiled. Georgiana sensed he could read her thoughts as he crossed the room towards her.

"I should return home," Georgiana said, beginning to draw on her gloves.

Edward suddenly seemed to become aware of her existence. "Wait, I shall escort you."

"There's no need, Edward."

"No, indeed," interposed Lakesby. "I shall be happy to see your sister safely home, Grey. I've no doubt you will want to wait for your wife."

"I can come back for Amanda," responded Edward through gritted teeth.

"But why put yourself to that trouble?" said Lakesby with easy friendliness. "I am on my way home anyway. It is perfectly convenient for me to escort your sister."

It was apparent Edward was inclined to argue the matter but a look from Georgiana silenced him. She accepted Lakesby's offer and was on the point of departure when her attention was claimed by another.

"Miss Grey." Sir Anthony Dixon stepped forward. "Miss Grey, I want to thank you for bringing us word of the fire. It's been a tragedy, of course, but I'm very grateful for the effort you made on my sister's behalf."

"Indeed, anyone would have done the same, sir."

"No, I don't think so," Sir Anthony said seriously, shaking his head. "Particularly as you were feeling unwell. I must not detain you and I must go myself. There are arrangements to be made. However, will you allow me to call on you, to thank you properly?"

Georgiana felt the eyes of both her brother and Lakesby fully focused on her. Uncharacteristically, she found herself faltering over her words.

"You make too much of it, sir, though of course you are most welcome to call if you wish."

Sir Anthony gave her a smile warm with charm. Bowing slightly, he said, "Thank you. I shall look forward to it."

With a brief nod in the direction of her brother, Georgiana

followed the footman out of the drawing room and towards the front door. Lakesby was close behind her, and took the now rested Diamond's reins from the groom who was waiting outside. He helped her to mount, and she waited in patient silence as he settled himself on his own horse.

"Well," Lakesby said as they moved to ride off, "you seem to have made a conquest."

Georgiana was hardly listening. Something was still worrying her about Lord Wickerston's death. If she could only think what...

2

Georgiana breakfasted late the next day. Although her way of life made early hours a rarity, the events of the previous night had been exceptional even by her own standards. It was not her first experience of sudden death, but the whole circumstance of the fire, along with Edward's close involvement in the situation, combined to make her uneasy.

Matters were not helped by Lakesby's strange attitude as he escorted her home. Georgiana did not know what was the matter with the man. She could swear he was growing as critical as Edward. First he had made that absurd comment about her having made a conquest of Sir Anthony Dixon. A spell of silence followed, broken only by one or two remarks about how surprised he was to see her encouraging someone as tame as Sir Anthony. Encouraging Sir Anthony indeed! As if there was anything to encourage, just because he had indicated a desire to call and express gratitude. Not that it was any of Lakesby's concern. Although they had not parted company on ill terms, Georgiana had certainly lost patience with him, informing him roundly that she was not his unfortunate cousin and had no need of a guardian.

Georgiana's reflections were interrupted by a discreet cough from her butler.

"I beg your pardon, miss, but Sir Anthony Dixon has called and is desirous of seeing you. I said I would ascertain whether you were at home to visitors."

Georgiana looked in some surprise at the card resting on the small silver tray which Horton held out to her. Sir Anthony had wasted no time in paying the promised call. Georgiana supposed him to be a gentleman particular in observing the proprieties, and could only imagine he considered it correct form to ensure his social obligations were discharged as soon as possible. She saw no reason to delay speaking with him and rose from the table. Horton opened the door for her and she preceded him out of the room.

"Drawing room?" Georgiana tossed over her shoulder.

"Yes, miss," said Horton, moving ahead to open the door for her.

Her visitor turned to greet her as she entered. "Good morning, Sir Anthony," she said pleasantly, hand outstretched. "I am so sorry to have kept you waiting. Please, won't you be seated?"

Sir Anthony ended his contemplation of the fireplace and gave her a smile which lent a warmth to his already personable features.

There could be no denying he was good-looking. His dark, wavy locks were well-regulated but not stiff; his brown eyes held an intensity which could draw earnest attention. He was slim and of good bearing, carrying himself with ease and confidence. It was also clear that he patronised the best tailors and wore his clothes with comfortable assurance. He accepted Georgiana's invitation with apparent pleasure, seating himself with respectful attention once his hostess had chosen a chair for herself.

"As I said last night, Miss Grey, I wanted to call and properly express my thanks for the service you rendered my sister."

"Please, Sir Anthony, there is no need. I am only sorry for your sister's loss and wish I could have been of more help. Tell me, how is she?"

"Very upset, naturally," said Sir Anthony seriously. "It has been a tremendous shock to her, to us all."

"Yes, of course."

"Your brother's wife has been very kind and attentive.

I believe she sat with Theresa for a large part of the night, certainly until Dr Masters came."

"Yes, Amanda is the best of creatures," said Georgiana with feeling. She had always been genuinely fond of her brother's wife, different though Amanda was from herself. She knew how loyal and caring her sister-in-law was, how willing to put herself to trouble for those in need. Knowing her brother had married Amanda Richardson for love rather than convenience, Georgiana had been astounded to learn of his liaison with Lady Wickerston, despite her knowledge of gentlemen's 'indiscretions'.

Rousing herself from her thoughts, Georgiana became aware her visitor was speaking.

"I am so sorry, Sir Anthony, I am afraid last night's tragedy has left me rather abstracted."

"I understand, Miss Grey. I feel rather that way myself. I was just inquiring whether you would care to come for a short drive in the park. We cannot proceed with arrangements for my brother-in-law's funeral until he has been properly examined, and I feel the need for some fresh air. Would you object to bearing me company?"

"No, indeed, I should be glad to," Georgiana responded. She found herself wondering if she dared ask about the examination of Lord Wickerston's body. It was likely Sir Anthony would be shocked, since such matters were not normally discussed with ladies. However, the uneasy feelings which had sprung on the previous night refused to be banished. Georgiana could not help but believe that the removal of Lord Wickerston would make life easier for more than one person, including her brother.

Georgiana excused herself to fetch a bonnet and pelisse, and was back in the drawing room not many minutes later, smoothing out the grey kid gloves on her hands. She gave her escort a smile, and received a glance of warm approval in return as he moved to hold open the door for her.

Georgiana accepted Sir Anthony's assistance into his phaeton, acknowledging with a smile his desire to assure himself of her comfort. She was appreciative of his concern, which stopped short of fussing. If there was one thing Georgiana could not bear it was fuss.

It was a fine day, and the gentle breeze on her cheeks and through her hair was a refreshing sensation after the activity of the previous night. The fresh night air was one of the things she enjoyed about her career as a highway robber, particularly after being confined in a stuffy ballroom or dinner party.

"You must forgive me, Miss Grey, I had quite forgotten to ask whether you are feeling better."

"Better?" Georgiana looked blankly at her companion. Enlightenment dawned as she recalled just in time the head-ache she had pleaded to escape the dinner party for more important matters. "Oh, indeed, yes, Sir Anthony. It's very kind of you to inquire. I lay down for a little while and then decided to take a turn outside for some air. That was how I came to see the fire."

Sir Anthony accepted this explanation without question, although he did express concern about her being out alone so late. He showed no other inclination to inquire into her behaviour. However, Georgiana knew Edward would and thought it sensible to tell her story sooner rather than later. She looked at Sir Anthony, mulling over a question in her mind. She decided the moment was right to ask it.

"Tell me, Sir Anthony, what you said to your sister about an examination of your brother-in-law's body, is that really the case?"

Sir Anthony looked at her with some surprise. "Why ever do you ask, Miss Grey?"

"Oh, I am merely curious. A shocking fault, I'm afraid. You see, I know so little about these matters."

"I see," he responded. "If you will pardon my saying so, Miss Grey, in this case a *little* knowledge is no bad thing. It is an unpleasant business and not one to which a lady should be subjected."

Although Sir Anthony's tone was firm, it was not unkind. His attitude irked her but it was no less than she had expected, and her mind was relieved to find he accepted her account of herself at face value. It was apparent that he would be astonished to find her anything other than as society imagined. It could be useful to nurture this perception.

"But, Sir Anthony, your sister…"

"Believe me, Miss Grey, I intend to shield my sister as much as possible from the more unpleasant aspects of this business. I'm sure you will have seen last night, Theresa's sensibilities…"

"Of course, I understand," said Georgiana. This portrait of Lady Wickerston concurred with the few details Edward had already let slip: the beatings Lord Wickerston had inflicted on his wife, her fears, her turning to Edward for comfort. Privately, Georgiana was not certain Lady Wickerston's sensibilities were all she would have had Sir Anthony and Edward believe. In her own pursuit of her ladyship's acquaintance, Georgiana had found her extremely reserved, her manner polite but cool. Yet she had even roused the protective instincts of Lakesby, and others too if he was to be believed. It was clear her tragedies enhanced her china blue eyes and creamy porcelain complexion, emphasising an air of sadness which cried out for help. Georgiana was sure the fear of Lord Wickerston was genuine but suspected her ladyship capable of utilising her misfortunes to gain the advantage of others.

Georgiana looked thoughtfully at Sir Anthony, wondering

24

if she could persuade him to satisfy her curiosity. She decided to adopt a slightly different approach. Idly twisting a lock of hair around her forefinger, she gave him a cajoling smile.

"I'm sure your sister must appreciate your concern, Sir Anthony. Indeed, I have no wish to pry but I was wondering… I beg your pardon, I'm sure it's none of my business."

Sir Anthony looked across at Georgiana. "No, please, Miss Grey, what is it? Is something troubling you?"

He seemed so genuinely concerned that Georgiana was conscious of a twinge of guilt. It was insufficient to prevent her from pursuing her objective, however, and she smiled, as if in gratitude at his understanding.

"Well, your sister seemed so distressed about her husband being examined that I was a little uneasy. Is there likely to be any difficulty over your brother-in-law's death?"

Sir Anthony seemed a little surprised by her question and hesitated only briefly before offering her an answer.

"No, I don't think so," he said. "People die in fires. I'm sure it was just an unfortunate accident."

"Is there any reason to imagine otherwise?"

"No, of course not," said Sir Anthony hastily. "How could there be?"

"I'm sure you are right," Georgiana said. "You will let me know if there is anything I can do, won't you?"

"Thank you, Miss Grey," said Sir Anthony. "You have been much too kind already. I should not wish to impose. Although…" He hesitated. "There is something, if I do not ask too much?"

They had arrived back at Georgiana's house and Sir Anthony was helping her to alight. Georgiana felt the intensity of his gaze as his eyes searched her face, seemingly seeking permission to ask his question.

"What is it, Sir Anthony?"

25

"May I be permitted the pleasure of your company to go driving again? My brother-in-law's death makes it difficult to go into society, of course, but if you should not object…?"

"Why, no, I should not object," said Georgiana, her tone betraying just a touch of surprise. "It is most kind of you to ask. I should be glad to bear you company."

Sir Anthony thanked her and took his leave. Georgiana watched the back of the departing carriage for a moment before turning to mount the steps. Horton had the front door open before she reached it.

"Spying on me, Horton?" inquired Georgiana lightly.

"No, indeed, miss," responded the butler in shocked accents. "Though in truth, I have been watching for your return. Mrs Grey has called."

"Oh? Well, surely someone could give her some tea and ask her to wait."

"Yes, miss, it has been attended to."

"Good. Where is she now?"

"In the drawing room, miss. She – ah – I beg your pardon, miss, but – "

"Yes?" Georgiana prompted.

The butler spoke with more confidence. "It is not my place to say so, of course, miss, but Mrs Grey seems somewhat distressed."

"I see. Thank you, Horton. I will go and see her. Would you be good enough to see we are not disturbed? I shall ring for some fresh tea presently."

"Very good, miss."

Georgiana drew off her gloves and walked towards the drawing room. She closed the door behind her as soon as she had entered. Amanda turned away from the window and smiled. Georgiana thought she looked calm but it was apparent tears had been shed. She crossed the room quickly

26

and gave Amanda a kiss on the cheek.

"Oh, Georgiana, I'm so sorry to bother you."

"Nonsense. Amanda, what has happened?" Noticing the bandbox at the door, Georgiana looked intently at her sister-in-law, already suspecting the answer.

Amanda drew a deep breath. "I've left Edward."

3

Georgiana had rung for fresh tea and now sat quietly, waiting until her sister-in-law should feel ready to speak. Amanda sat with her hands folded in her lap, as if considering her words. She seemed more composed after her tea but Georgiana was not about to press her.

"I am sorry to be such a nuisance," said Amanda after a few minutes.

"You're nothing of the sort," said Georgiana. "You should know that, Amanda."

Amanda smiled gratefully at her sister-in-law. "You're kinder than I deserve. I wouldn't want you to think... Georgiana, please don't imagine that I have left Edward for good. But things are not right, and at the moment I can't bear to be in the house with him. It is just that I did not know what else to do and I needed... time to... to think."

"I understand."

"Do you?" said Amanda, her eyes widening as they flew questioningly to search those of her sister-in-law.

Georgiana remained silent. She could not betray her own brother. Furthermore, while she was willing enough to give Amanda whatever help and support proved necessary, she could not come between husband and wife.

Amanda had fallen back into her own thoughts, and did not seem to notice the silence. Her hands began to twist around in her lap.

"It seems," said Amanda slowly, "that Edward and Lady Wickerston are... that is, they..." Her voice faltered and a tear escaped her eye. "Oh, Georgiana, she is his mistress. I am certain of it."

Georgiana waited while Amanda tried to compose herself, observing the war between emotion and dignity. To Georgiana's great admiration, dignity emerged the victor as the tears came under control.

"Have I failed him so badly?" Amanda finally asked in little more than a whisper.

"Good heavens, no!" said Georgiana with feeling, moving to her sister-in-law's side on the sofa and putting an arm about her shoulders.

"Then, why? I know she is very beautiful, and I don't wish to sound vain, but – "

"Vain? You, Amanda? What an idea!"

Amanda smiled. Georgiana looked at her for a moment, weighing her words with some care.

"What did Edward say to you?"

"He said Lord Wickerston used to beat his wife. I own I was very much shocked, but knowing what sort of person Lord Wickerston was, I can believe it to be true. Edward told me he felt sorry for Lady Wickerston and that – that was all."

Georgiana slowly let out a breath. "Well, then…"

"He looked so – so… guilty."

"You can't be certain of that, Amanda."

Amanda shook her head. "No? You saw how he was with her last night. I know gentlemen are prone to… indiscretions… but he didn't even seem to notice I was there."

"He will very soon notice you are not."

"I wonder."

"Certainly."

"It did not seem that way last night." Amanda sighed. "How could I have been so blind?" she said, shaking her head.

"Try not to worry too much. Edward loves you. He may feel compassion for Lady Wickerston because of her difficult circumstances, but I'm sure it is no more than that." Georgiana told herself this was not strictly a lie. It had been compassion which had drawn Edward to her ladyship, whatever else may have happened between them.

Amanda looked steadily at Georgiana. "I am very sorry to impose on you like this, Georgiana. I daresay I am very much in your way."

"Not at all."

"Only I did not know where else to go. My parents – well, they would ask questions, and I don't wish…"

"Of course. Pray don't give it a thought. Why don't you stay here for a while? Selina is away and I shall be glad of your company until you feel ready to return."

"Thank you." Amanda attempted a smile and almost succeeded. "I didn't know what to do," she confessed. "It's just – just that…" She paused, thinking how to frame her words. "It's just that I feel – I feel I need to be away from Edward right now," she finished in a rush.

Georgiana nodded. "That's perfectly understandable."

"In fact," said Amanda, "I would much prefer not to see him if he calls. Would that make difficulties for you?"

"Not at all," said Georgiana. "I shall instruct the servants to say you are not at home. They are very well trained. Horton is the essence of discretion. Emily and James, well, I would trust them with my life."

"I suppose some talk is inevitable," said Amanda. A small frown crumpled her brow and she absently nibbled on her lower lip.

"Don't worry. Selina is visiting a sick friend of her mother, and likely to remain away for some while. No one will think it remarkable that you are here to bear me company."

"I suppose not," said Amanda without conviction.

Georgiana rose and held out her hand to Amanda. "Would you like to freshen up? I could send Emily to help you."

"Oh, no, Georgiana, Emily is your maid. I would not dream of taking her from you. I can manage."

"I have no intention of letting you take Emily away. However, she will not object to helping you while you are here, and finding you anything you need."

Amanda smiled. "Thank you, Georgiana. You are much too good to me."

As they reached the drawing room door, Georgiana's hand paused on the door knob. "What of the children?"

"They are well enough. They have their nanny to look after them, though I know I shall miss them both." The look Amanda gave Georgiana was tinged with guilt. "I am afraid I have not thought beyond how I felt. I know it's selfish of me, but – "

"It's not selfish. The whole situation is enough to shake anyone. I think you are being very sensible," said Georgiana. "A period of calm reflection is what you need. Come, let's get you settled."

Georgiana led Amanda out of the drawing room and they walked towards the stairs. Georgiana noticed James approaching, a folded paper resting on a small silver tray. Georgiana signalled for Amanda to precede her up the stairs and she immediately went to her footman.

"What is it, James?" Georgiana asked in a low voice.

James also spoke in quiet tones.

"Mr Lakesby called while you were closeted with Mrs Grey, miss. He did not wish to disturb you, but asked me to give you this note. I got the impression it was rather important."

"Thank you, James." Georgiana took the paper held out to her. She noticed the footman cast a swift glance towards Amanda.

"Mr Lakesby wondered whether you would be attending Lady Richmond's party this evening," said James. "I understand he plans to be there."

"Oh?" Georgiana was fairly certain Lakesby was not sending messages through James for the purpose of keeping her informed of his social calendar.

"Yes, miss. He suggested if you do go, you might be wise to avoid the road on the Heath because of the highwaymen."

"Most solicitous."

"As you say, miss. He seemed to think it might be particularly dangerous this evening." James's voice was as impassive as his face. "Apparently there was talk of one or two Bow Street Runners lying in wait to trap them and Mr Lakesby thought it possible innocent parties might be hurt."

"I see. Thank you, James."

Georgiana joined her sister-in-law on the stairs and the two proceeded up, chatting about Amanda and Edward's two children. Georgiana was always a favourite with young Edward and his sister Cecily. As the two women walked together, Georgiana noticed Amanda cast a quick, curious glance at the note she held but betrayed no other sign of interest. She had, to Georgiana's relief, a serious respect for the privacy of others.

When they reached the guest bedroom allotted to Amanda, Georgiana rang for Emily. As soon as she was satisfied that Amanda had everything she needed, she left her guest to the expert ministrations of her maid and made for her own bedroom to read Lakesby's note.

Miss Grey,

Rumours are already circulating that the fire at Marpley Manor was not an accident. Dr Henry Masters is irritatingly discreet but happily his brother is not. I shall be dining with him this evening before Lady Richmond's card party. Do you mean to go? Join me in a rubber of picquet and I shall hope to explain it all.

Your servant,
Maxwell Lakesby.

Georgiana tapped Lakesby's note thoughtfully against the palm of her left hand. Like Dr Masters, he was being irritatingly discreet. She had not intended to go to Lady Richmond's. Card parties bored her rigid and were useful only insofar as at least some of the guests could be counted upon to have large sums of money or pieces of jewellery carelessly pledged and lost. However, work for the Crimson Cavalier had been halted for the evening, not only by Lakesby's warning but also by Amanda's presence. Georgiana's companion Selina Knatchbull normally slept soundly, but Georgiana could not take the chance of a possibly wakeful sister-in-law encountering a highwayman in the corridor. The ghost of a smile played around Georgiana's lips. She could not deny the vision had its amusing side, even if she could not indulge it. She held Lakesby's note in front of her, looking thoughtfully at it as if it held the answer. Suddenly making up her mind, Georgiana put the note away in her top drawer and went quickly back to Amanda's room, entering after a brief tap on the door.

"Amanda, have you had an invitation to Lady Richmond's party this evening?"

"Yes, but I had not planned to go," said Amanda. "You do not, do you, Georgiana? I thought you did not like card parties."

"Not usually, no, but this one could be interesting."

Amanda looked doubtful. "Really? Well, you go if you wish, Georgiana, but I think I would rather stay at home. Besides, I believe Edward has already written to decline."

"Even better," said Georgiana. "We shall go together. I'll write Lady Richmond a note immediately."

"I don't know, Georgiana, I'm not feeling very sociable.

Besides, the suppers! Lady Richmond has the most filthy cook in London. I don't know how she puts up with it. The man positively murders the food."

"Yes, I know, that is unfortunate," acknowledged Georgiana, "but we can eat before we go. I daresay we shall not be the only ones."

At length, Amanda allowed herself to be persuaded, even to the point of accepting the loan of one of Georgiana's dresses and the talents of Emily to style her hair. Georgiana was on her way to her study to write the note to Lady Richmond when Horton intercepted her.

"Miss Georgiana, Mr Grey has called. I have put him in the drawing room. I undertook to check if you were at home but he would not be denied and insisted on waiting."

"How very like Edward," said Georgiana wearily. "Did you mention Mrs Grey was here?"

"Mr Grey did not inquire, miss."

Georgiana nodded. "Thank you, Horton. If anyone should ask, Mrs Grey is not at home to visitors."

"Very good, miss."

Georgiana walked to the front parlour to deal with her brother. She found Edward in an agitated state, uncharacteristically pacing the room.

"Hello, Edward," Georgiana said brightly. "What can I do for you?"

Edward halted in his tracks. Georgiana was stunned to see the haggard expression on his face, the fear and loss in his eyes.

"It's Amanda," he said. "Georgiana, she's gone. I don't know where. What am I to do?"

"I should sit down, if I were you," said Georgiana prosaically, taking her own advice. "You are accomplishing nothing by wearing a hole in my carpet."

Edward cast his sister a baleful look but did as she bade him.

"You are a fool, Edward. Whatever did you expect? Amanda's not blind and your behaviour last night all but announced your liaison to the world. I thought you had broken it off."

"I did," he replied, stung into defending himself. "But I told you how it was. Wickerston had a violent temper, and things have been difficult for Ther – his wife."

"A difficulty that seems now to be resolved," said Georgiana, smoothing out her skirts.

"Georgiana!"

His sister raised an eyebrow but gave no other response.

Edward put his hand to his forehead. He seemed unable to speak. Georgiana relented.

"What happened, Edward?" she asked in a gentler tone.

Edward looked up. There was a lost expression on his face, and the words he needed appeared to elude him. Georgiana waited, watching him patiently.

"I told Lady Wickerston it had to end," he said. "I thought she had accepted it. She was very quiet, and said she understood that I had to be loyal to Amanda. Yet she looked so forlorn, so despondent, struggling to be brave." He shook his head. "It wrenched my heart to see her like that, knowing she had to face that bully without protection." His fists clenched, and he stared ahead, moodily.

Georgiana waited. Edward's head drooped forward into his hands. It came as a shock to his sister to see his normally upright posture crumpled and his shoulders hunched as he slumped dejectedly in his chair.

"You knew all the time that she had to face her husband," said Georgiana in a gentle tone. "Did something else happen?"

"No, not as such." Edward spoke slowly. He seemed almost

confused, as if he could not quite remember. He sighed. "She just sat there, hands folded, so still, so silent. I felt unable to leave. I wanted to assure myself she would be all right. Eventually she told me she would be well enough, and I should go. She even gave me a smile, difficult as it clearly was for her. Only..." Edward's voice trailed off.

"Only?" Georgiana prompted.

Edward stared ahead, silent for a further moment. Georgiana continued to wait.

"I felt such a brute, leaving her there," Edward said at last. "All alone, with no one to call upon for help if she needed it."

"I see," said Georgiana. Her tone was sympathetic but her mind was on Lady Wickerston's brother. Surely he could offer some comfort or protection if his sister was in difficulties.

"I was weak," Edward said. "I let myself be drawn back in."

Georgiana thought this was less to do with weakness than compassion, which her ladyship's delicate prettiness seemed able to turn into something which was not quite infatuation but as near as made little difference. Georgiana suspected there was an air of helpless reliance about her ladyship, which Edward would certainly find flattering.

"Anyway, that doesn't matter now," said Edward. "It's Amanda who concerns me. She's not like you, Georgiana, she can't fend for herself. She could be hungry, or hurt, or – or – " He shuddered at the possibilities.

Georgiana found herself in sympathy with his fears but could not help appreciating his involuntary acknowledgement of her own capacity for self-reliance.

"Amanda may be more resourceful than you imagine," she said.

Edward didn't seem to notice his sister's words. "What am I to do?" he asked, looking desperately at her.

In all the years Georgiana had known Edward, she had

never known him to ask for advice. His four years' seniority over her, as well as the advantages of his sex, gave him an authority and conviction that he always knew best. It was the first time Georgiana had seen his faith in himself shaken. She found herself relenting.

"Calm yourself, Edward. Amanda is perfectly well. She is upstairs."

"What?" Edward stared at his sister, his expression a mixture of relief and betrayal. "Upstairs? Amanda is with you? Why could you not tell me sooner? Where is she? I want to talk to her."

Edward had risen and crossed the room, only to be halted by Georgiana's restraining hand.

"No, Edward. She does not wish to see you."

"What? But…"

"No," said Georgiana. "I only told you Amanda was here so you would not worry over her safety. However, she does not wish to see you and I intend to respect that. Now you had better go home. We have plans for the evening and it is not at all convenient for you to be here."

"Plans?" Edward resumed his seat and looked up blankly. "What sort of plans?"

"Nothing that concerns you. Oh, do go away, Edward. In Amanda's position, I should not want to see you either. Give her some time. If you want her back, I suggest you go and put an end to whatever remains of your liaison with Lady Wickerston."

His shoulders sagged once more, and Georgiana hid a smile as she saw something approaching shame flicker across his face.

"Yes, yes. You are right, of course. Georgiana, you will – you will take good care of Amanda, won't you?"

"Of course I shall. Now be off with you."

Georgiana urged her brother out of the door, pausing only to give him a quick parting kiss on the cheek. He went without resistance, an air of bemusement about him which could have made his sister laugh in other circumstances.

Sighing, Georgiana made her way to the study to write her note to Lady Richmond, then rang the bell for James.

"Send Tom to Lady Richmond's with this note, would you, James? Then please arrange to have the horses put to the barouche for eight o'clock. Mrs Grey and I will be going there for the evening."

"Yes, miss. Do you wish Tom to accompany you?"

"Yes, please, assuming he has some suitable clothes as yet undamaged," Georgiana said. Her young page had an unfortunate habit of abusing every item of clothing put on his back, whether by accident or design she had not yet determined.

James grinned. "There may be one or two garments still whole, miss. It's persuading him to wash the back of his neck that's the real problem."

Georgiana laughed and shook her head. Leaving the study in James's wake, she began to mount the stairs. Pausing halfway, she glanced towards the upper landing before continuing. She had committed them to it now, but she found herself wondering whether Lady Richmond's party was such a good idea after all.

4

"My dear Miss Grey." Lady Richmond took Georgiana's hand in both of hers, stepping forward as she effusively greeted her guest. "And Mrs Grey too! My dear, we did not expect to see you. But I suppose…"

"Amanda is bearing me company while my cousin is visiting a sick friend," said Georgiana. She could see her ladyship was about to offer Amanda a dose of patronising sympathy, which indicated that there was gossip about Edward's attentions to Lady Wickerston. Glancing towards Amanda, Georgiana was pleased to see her head high and a smile of unalloyed charm on her face.

"Oh. Yes, of course," said her ladyship. "I'm afraid you've missed supper."

"That is a pity," said Amanda. "We have heard so much about your cook. But I don't think Georgiana's chef would have forgiven us if we had failed to do justice to the dishes he had prepared. I believe he had not realised we were planning to go out and had gone to a great deal of trouble."

Georgiana was surprised at the ease with which the lie slipped off her sister-in-law's tongue. Full of admiration, she continued, "I'm sure we'll have a pleasant evening, in any case. We are looking forward to it."

"Good," said Lady Richmond. "Ah, here is Mr Lakesby. He has pre-empted me in bringing you some wine. Naughty man," she scolded. "You will make me feel an inadequate hostess."

"I do trust not, ma'am. On the contrary, it seemed to me you were in danger of being overwhelmed with demands. I thought you had earned a respite."

Lady Richmond's laugh was of the giggly, schoolgirl variety which prompted Georgiana to raise a quizzical eyebrow in Lakesby's direction. He ignored the silent message, and handed glasses of wine to Georgiana and Amanda before proffering an arm each to lead them into the gathering. Amanda looked as if she was already regretting the impulse which had prompted her to accede to Georgiana's suggestion.

Her attention was soon claimed by an acquaintance, eager to compare stories on the progress of their respective children. As Amanda excused herself, slipping her hand from Lakesby's arm, she cast a quick, almost furtive glance at her two companions. Pleading a lack of interest in or skill at card games, she expressed her intention of having a comfortable cose with her friend, having assured herself that she was leaving Georgiana in safe hands.

"Your sister-in-law seems very well," said Lakesby, leading Georgiana to a table in a well-lit alcove.

"Yes," said Georgiana.

"I do not recall you mentioning she would be visiting you."

"No? Well, I don't feel it necessary to discuss my domestic arrangements with you, Mr Lakesby. However, since my cousin is away, it seemed a good idea."

"Of course."

Lakesby was shuffling a pack of cards and began to deal them without comment. Georgiana picked them up one at a time, her attention apparently absorbed by the hand she had been dealt.

"How long do you expect your cousin to be away?" inquired Lakesby, studying his own cards.

"I'm not certain," said Georgiana. "She is visiting a sick friend so I imagine it rather depends on how well she recovers. Selina is always anxious to be useful. It is unlikely she will return until she is certain her friend is able to manage without her."

"Very commendable," commented Lakesby, "though I daresay your brother is not entirely happy about his wife's absence."

Georgiana looked up from her cards, meeting Lakesby's direct gaze.

"No."

Lakesby offered no further comment, his eyes going back to his cards. Georgiana toyed with hers a moment or two longer before laying them down. She leaned forward, her elbow resting on the table, her hand under her chin.

"So, Mr Lakesby, you said there were some rumours?"

Lakesby cast a quick glance around the room, then laid down his own cards.

"Yes," he acknowledged, his voice low and serious. "It seems Lord Wickerston's death may not have been the accident it appeared."

Although Georgiana had been uneasy about his lordship's death, this nevertheless came as a shock.

"I see," she said at last.

Lakesby looked at her intently. "You suspected something was wrong?"

Georgiana did not answer immediately, her expression thoughtful. "I'm not sure I would go as far as suspicion, though I was uneasy. Did you not think it strange he had no time to escape?"

"When even the horses were rescued," he said thoughtfully. "An excellent point."

"Did anyone hear him call for help?"

"I'm not sure," said Lakesby. "I suppose it was assumed everyone would fend for themselves. However, if his lordship was in the habit of – er – falling asleep when he had been imbibing, it seems odd that no one would think to check whether he had got out safely."

"Yes," said Georgiana. "Unless everyone thought someone else had done it."

"Possibly. Remarkably careless, if that was the case." Lakesby paused, as if considering how next to word his thoughts. "I may have mentioned, Henry Masters's brother, Alfred, is a friend of mine. I ran across him at Jackson's Saloon this morning and we dined together this evening."

"Oh?" said Georgiana expectantly.

Lakesby lowered his voice. "It seems Dr Masters is not satisfied with the circumstances of Lord Wickerston's death. In fact, the good doctor is not certain Wickerston died in the fire at all."

Georgiana blinked, trying to assimilate the implications of this. "I beg your pardon? Are you saying…?" She halted, and met Lakesby's gaze steadily. Her eyebrows creased together. "But then…" She continued to look at Lakesby. "He was dead before the fire started?"

"It certainly seems a possibility. I believe Dr Masters suspects poison. But he is not sharing his suspicions as yet."

Excitement vied with dismay in Georgiana's mind. "How did his brother discover this?"

Lakesby grinned. "Sheer nosiness."

Georgiana was unimpressed at his levity, and threw him a look of disdain. He schooled his face and continued in more serious vein, "Alfred Masters noticed his brother was preoccupied, as if he was worried. Dr Masters had made some notes, largely intelligible only to himself, but his brother understood the general sense of them."

"Looking over his shoulder?" inquired Georgiana.

"When Dr Masters was out of the room. Curiosity is Alfred's abiding vice, as is passing on interesting titbits of information. I'd advise you not to tell him anything you'd prefer kept secret."

"Thank you," said Georgiana coolly. "If that is the case, I must confess myself surprised Dr Masters is not more careful."

Lakesby shrugged. "I believe it is the case with many – er – deep-thinking men. In contemplating what they perceive to be more important matters, they neglect practical considerations."

Georgiana remained silent, her expression thoughtful. Lakesby watched her from under lazy lids, idly shuffling the cards he held.

"I am aware I sound flippant, Miss Grey. Such is not my intention. In all seriousness, Alfred did notice his brother seemed uneasy. It would of course have been improper for Dr Masters to discuss the details of Lord Wickerston's death with him, but I believe he did confide enough for certain conclusions to be drawn."

"Prompting his brother to investigate his notes?"

"Something like that," confirmed Lakesby.

Torn between an uncomfortable disapproval of the inquisitiveness of Dr Masters's brother and her own some-what hypocritical desire to ask what he had discovered, Georgiana fell silent once again. The look she saw in Lakesby's eyes seemed to suggest that he was aware of her quandary. He leaned forward.

"From what I can gather," he said slowly, "Dr Masters saw little evidence his lordship breathed in any smoke."

"Suggesting Lord Wickerston wasn't breathing?"

Lakesby nodded. "Slight evidence, I know. However, Dr Masters is not usually a man who jumps to conclusions. He is also very thorough."

Georgiana pondered on this. "I suppose if his lordship

made no attempt to escape…" A thought occurred to her, making her tone more brisk. "You don't know if the servants tried to rouse him?"

Lakesby shook his head. "No, I'm afraid I don't. I haven't spoken to any of them. They all seemed preoccupied with getting themselves out of the building. However, I would have expected his valet to be concerned, at least. In the event, his lordship was locked in his study. Your footman and I had to force the door to reach him." He glanced around the room to see if they were the subject of unwanted attention, and lowered his voice still further. "He was seated near his desk. Perhaps 'seated' is too generous a term; he had slid some way down the chair. A wine glass lay on the floor, some distance away."

"I see." Georgiana looked steadily at Lakesby. "You saw immediately that he was dead, I suppose?"

Lakesby nodded. "It was fairly apparent. In fact, he was rather cold when Cooper and I carried him out." He frowned. "I own I did not give it much thought at the time. Now it occurs to me he may have been dead longer than we realised."

"I wonder you and James should have taken such risks to carry him out."

Lakesby shrugged. "Lord knows I didn't like Wickerston but anyone deserves a decent burial."

"Yes, of course. Still, it was very courageous of you both, especially when it was clear you couldn't save him."

"The fire had not been going as long as you might imagine. Admittedly it took hold very quickly, but the room was locked and there was little damage to it."

Georgiana nodded. Before she could speak again, a shadow fell over the largely ignored cards which lay scattered on the small table between them. Georgiana glanced up to see the diffident smile of her sister-in-law.

"I do apologise, Georgiana, but if you don't mind I think I shall take the carriage and go home. I have a slight headache. Pray, do not concern yourself," Amanda said, hurriedly stretching out her hand. "I shall do very well and will send the carriage back for you. I have no wish to spoil your evening."

"I'm sure Miss Grey's pleasure is already marred by knowing you are unwell, ma'am," said Lakesby, who had risen at her approach. "Please allow me the honour of escorting you."

"Oh, no, please, I do not wish to be a trouble," protested Amanda.

"I assure you, Mrs Grey, it's not the least trouble in the world. If you will allow me, I will have my own carriage summoned. There is no need to disturb Miss Grey's coachman."

"Nonsense," said Georgiana. "I should have no pleasure in remaining while you are unwell, Amanda."

"Oh dear, I am becoming a dreadful nuisance. I have no wish to tear you away, Georgiana. I hate to be presumptuous but I had hoped to depend on Mr Lakesby to escort you home."

"Most certainly," Lakesby replied. He gestured towards the chair he had vacated. "Please sit down, Mrs Grey. You may feel better for a cup of tea. I suggest you and Miss Grey settle the matter between you while I see if there's some to be had."

He departed, leaving the two women together, and Georgiana eyed her sister-in-law with some concern as Amanda's eyes followed Lakesby before flicking back to Georgiana.

"Poor Amanda, I'm so sorry I dragged you to this wretched affair. We shall both go if you are not feeling quite the thing."

"There's truly no need to worry, Georgiana, it's just..." Amanda's face wore a grimace Georgiana had never seen there before. "It seems that everyone knows! About Edward,

I mean. I've had so many pitying looks it's beyond bearing."

"I see," said Georgiana. "I must say, I was impressed at how well you put Lady Richmond in her place."

Amanda returned her smile, if a little wanly. "Yes, but it's so wearing. Only Mr Lakesby has shown any genuine kindness."

"I can well believe it. Don't let it worry you, Amanda, and rid yourself of any notion you are a rejected wife. No one thinks it, I promise you."

"Everyone thinks it," objected Amanda.

"Nonsense. Lady Richmond and her cronies have nothing better to think about, take no notice of them."

Lakesby reappeared, carrying a steaming teacup which he put down in front of Amanda. He looked from one to the other with a smile.

"What have you decided?"

Georgiana spoke. "We shall both leave, Mr Lakesby. There is no need for you to go to the trouble of escorting us."

Lakesby proved insistent, however, declaring his obligation to them for assisting his escape from such a dull gathering. Judging by the cries of disappointment from Lady Richmond at their departure, Georgiana suspected it was the hostess rather than the gathering from which Lakesby wished to escape. She also had the feeling that there may have been something Lakesby intended to tell her before they were interrupted. Perhaps Dr Masters had found something to support his conjecture that Lord Wickerston had died before the fire.

5

Georgiana had no opportunity for further private conversation with Lakesby that evening. The following morning saw her toying with the notion of paying a condolence call on Lady Wickerston, although she knew she could not ask Amanda to accompany her. Georgiana understood from Sir Anthony that her ladyship was staying with an aunt, and mulled over the idea as she consumed her tea and toast. Amanda arrived for breakfast, giving James a smile as he held out her chair. Georgiana suspected she'd had little sleep. Amanda protested the suggestion but expressed surprise that Georgiana had risen so early and looked remarkably well despite the late hour at which they had retired. Georgiana reflected how more than two years of highway robbery had accustomed her constitution to less sleep than most ladies of her acquaintance.

As Amanda attempted to eat a few mouthfuls of breakfast, Georgiana looked through the morning post and found a letter in the carefully penned hand of her cousin.

"Selina expects to be away for some weeks yet," Georgiana remarked as she cast her eyes down the single page. "It seems her friend is still rather weak, and relies on her for support. Bless her, she is very apologetic and hopes I am able to manage without her. In fact," she continued, a twinkle of amusement in her eyes as she laid down the paper, "she suggests I pay a visit to you and Edward."

"Oh dear."

"Quite. Wouldn't you expect her to realise by now how impractical that is? Edward and I would be at loggerheads within a day." She allowed the smile to reach her lips. "Poor Selina, I daresay she imagines she is promoting harmony between us. However, her absence is the very thing. No one will think it strange that you are here."

"Well, if I am not a bother," Amanda said doubtfully.

"Nothing of the kind," said Georgiana. "You are welcome for as long as you wish, Amanda."

"Thank you, Georgiana. I know I could go to my parents but…" Amanda paused, chewing her lip as she considered how to proceed. "You see, they would ask questions…"

"Which you would rather not answer," Georgiana finished for her. "Perfectly understandable."

The discreet entrance of her footman prevented any development of this theme.

"I beg your pardon, miss, but Mr Grey has called."

Amanda paled. Georgiana kept her composure.

"Where have you put him, James?"

"In the drawing room, miss."

"Very well. Tell him I shall be there directly."

"Yes, miss."

As the door closed behind James, Georgiana laid her napkin on the table and spoke to Amanda as she rose.

"You need not see him if you had rather not."

"I really should prefer it. I should not know what to say. Am I being very cowardly, Georgiana?"

"Not at all."

Bidding her brother a cheery good morning as she entered the drawing room, Georgiana hoped she managed to conceal her shock at his appearance. While his attire was put together with his accustomed neatness, his face was drawn and pale, contrasting with the dark circles which made his light green eyes stand out in a most unflattering manner. He was pacing the room as his sister approached, seeming unable to settle. Georgiana suspected he had had no more sleep than his wife. She made no comment, though suggested he take a seat.

Edward refused her offer of tea with a terse shake of his head. He sat with his hands folded and head bowed, leaving Georgiana to watch him while she contemplated other possibilities to calm him.

"Have you breakfasted?" she asked.

"No. That is, I had some coffee but couldn't swallow any food." Edward looked up, facing his sister for the first time since his arrival. "How is Amanda?"

Georgiana sat thoughtfully for a moment before answering. While she had no wish to keep her brother in suspense, it seemed harsh to blurt out immediately that his wife did not want to see him. However, telling Edward she believed Amanda to be as unhappy as he was could lead him to insist on seeing his wife; this was exactly the type of meeting Georgiana knew her sister-in-law dreaded.

"She is well enough," she said in what she hoped was a reassuring fashion.

Edward gave a weak smile. "I do miss her," he said. "I don't suppose... no, of course she wouldn't wish to see me."

Georgiana was glad she was not expected to answer Edward's question. She waited a moment with her hands folded, her eyes focused on his face, before she thought it right to speak.

"How are the children? I know Amanda misses them."

"They miss her," Edward said with a smile. "I have told them she is keeping you company while Selina is away. I just hope..."

"Yes, that is the tale I have told," said Georgiana briskly.

"Told? To whom?" Edward asked, looking up with the first signs of animation Georgiana had seen in him.

"We went to Lady Richmond's card party last night."

"Georgiana!"

"Would you have your wife remain indoors feeling sorry

49

for herself?" Georgiana asked.

"But the gossip! If anyone were to learn the truth…"

"Why should they?" Georgiana responded in matter of fact manner. "People would talk far more if Amanda were to shut herself away." She smiled. "True enough, Lady Richmond did seem inclined to offer sympathy and probe a little."

Edward groaned.

"However," Georgiana continued, "I must say, Amanda put a stop to it immediately. You would have been proud of her, Edward. Her head was high and she seemed far from melancholy."

"I have always been proud of Amanda," he said with a hint of sadness in his voice.

"Yes, well, perhaps you should have made her more aware of that."

"I know," Edward sighed.

Georgiana continued watching her brother.

"Edward, have you seen anything of Lady Wickerston since this business started?"

Edward stared at Georgiana in horror. "No, of course not," he said, his voice sounding hoarse. "Apart from the impropriety, I have been able to think of nothing but Amanda since she left the house. How could you even think…?"

"Yes, all right." Georgiana paused. "Tell me, did you think there was anything odd about Lord Wickerston's death?"

Georgiana saw genuine astonishment on Edward's face as he answered. "Of course not. It was just a horrible accident."

"When I spoke to Mr Lakesby he mentioned Lord Wickerston was already cold when he and James carried him out of the house. Doesn't that suggest he had been dead for a while?"

Edward shuddered. "Really, Georgiana, is such detail really necessary?"

Even the present circumstance of his wife's absence from

home could not prevent Edward from voicing his disapproval of her outspokenness. For once Georgiana controlled her exasperation; it was a minor point at such a time.

"How does Lakesby come to be such an expert?" said Edward in scorn.

Georgiana ignored the comment about Lakesby. "The house was on fire, Edward. Surely Lord Wickerston would not be cold unless he had been dead for some time," Georgiana pointed out.

"Really, Georgiana."

"Isn't it logical?" she pursued.

"Oh, I don't know," he said. "Ask your friend. Though it sounds to me as if he is out to make mischief."

"What nonsense. Why should he do such a thing?" said Georgiana.

"I don't know," he said impatiently.

"I was thinking of calling on Lady Wickerston," Georgiana said, "to offer my condolences. I believe she's staying with a relative. It did not seem entirely suitable to do so the other night."

Edward paled. "Do you think that's wise?"

"Why ever not?"

Edward gnawed his bottom lip. "I should accompany you."

"Do you think that's wise?"

"Georgiana, you can hardly go alone."

"I wasn't intending to," she responded.

"Surely you don't mean to take Amanda?" He looked aghast.

"No, of course not," she said. "I'll take one of the servants with me. Do be sensible, Edward, how would it look for you to go calling on Lady Wickerston right now? You were hardly discreet on the night of the fire, the way you were comforting her. You think that wasn't enough to cause gossip? Besides," she continued, as he seemed inclined to argue, "if you want Amanda's return soon, you had best not give her yet more reason for staying away."

"Yes, of course. You are right." Edward stood. "I should go. Amanda will be getting anxious for you." He kissed her lightly on the cheek before going to the door. Pausing with it ajar, he turned back. "She needs someone to take care of her, Georgiana. Please make sure she's all right."

"Yes, of course," she smiled. "Goodbye, Edward."

On returning to the dining room, Georgiana found Edward had not been mistaken. Amanda looked considerably paler than when Georgiana had left the room. It was clear she had barely touched any breakfast and had twisted her napkin into an almost unrecognisable shape. Georgiana smiled as she sat down and put her hand to the teapot.

"Shall I send for some fresh tea? You look as if you need some and mine has gone cold."

"No – that is – oh, I don't mind, Georgiana, whatever you wish." Amanda continued twisting her napkin until Georgiana laid a hand on her arm.

"H-how is Edward?" Amanda asked, her eyes looking down at her hands.

"Miserable, he looks dreadful." Amanda looked up quickly. "He is clearly lost without you," Georgiana added. The expression on her sister-in-law's face made her wonder whether she had gone too far.

"Really?" Amanda sounded unsure.

The entrance of the parlourmaid in response to a summons on the bell halted further conversation. Georgiana's mode of life had instilled discretion in her as second nature and she suspected her servants were often frustrated that they picked up fewer morsels of gossip than colleagues in other households. She requested the fresh pot of tea and waited until the door was safely closed before answering Amanda's question.

"Of course," Georgiana said calmly. "What did you expect?"

"I don't know. Are the children well?"

"Fine, though they miss you, of course."

"I miss them," said Amanda sadly. "I wonder if I have done the right thing."

"Nonsense," said Georgiana. "You will not be away long. You are merely keeping me company while Selina is away. That is what Edward has told the children."

"Yes, but –"

"But nothing, Amanda. You have not taken any drastic step."

"Thank you, Georgiana. Truly, I am very confused at present and it's difficult to know what is best."

"That's understandable." Georgiana looked thoughtfully at her sister-in-law, trying to determine how best to frame her next sentence.

"Have you thought about what you would like to do today, Amanda?"

"No, not really, though I do feel I would like to be of use, to make up for imposing on you and putting you in this ghastly position with Edward."

This was perfect. While Georgiana's protestations that Amanda was not imposing were quite sincere, she would be very glad to give her guest some small task which would prevent her from showing interest in her own plans for the day.

"I must admit, I have missed Selina's expertise with the needle. You know I have no patience with sewing myself and a few simple repairs have been left undone."

Amanda was all willingness, and was soon ensconced in

the small saloon with a mending basket and a little pile of linens which constituted her occupation for the next few hours. Georgiana was able to relay her intention of calling on an acquaintance without eliciting awkward questions, satisfying her sister-in-law with the promise to take her groom with her. While there was nothing reprehensible or improper in her decision to pay a condolence call on Lady Wickerston, it was also something she preferred not to discuss with Amanda under the current circumstances. Beyond a casual inquiry as to whether Mr Lakesby had mentioned calling to take Georgiana for a drive, Amanda showed no inclination to pursue the matter. However, she did utter a scandalised exclamation at Georgiana's suggestion that Amanda go driving with him on the chance he called in her absence.

Georgiana changed into a high-necked gown of pale lilac for her visit to the home of Lady Wickerston's aunt. When they arrived at the front door, the groom who accompanied her raised the knocker and they waited for a reply.

The door was answered by a dignified butler who held it for Georgiana in respectful fashion, and asked her to wait in the hall while he inquired for her ladyship. It was not many minutes before he returned and bade her follow him. As they proceeded towards the drawing room, Georgiana found the hushed, bereaved air of the house weighing more heavily upon her. The low sounds of conversation drifted through the door before she entered the room. As the butler drew back after announcing her, she noticed that there were three occupants in addition to Lady Wickerston. Sir Anthony Dixon was present, which Georgiana had expected; there was a small, round-faced woman wearing a cap, whom she took to be their aunt; and a man who was a stranger to her.

It was Sir Anthony who came forward to greet her.

"Miss Grey, how kind of you to call. Isn't it, Theresa? Please, do sit down."

Georgiana accepted the invitation as Lady Wickerston stretched out her hand to her visitor, warmly echoing her brother's expression of Miss Grey's kindness.

Sir Anthony gestured towards the round-faced woman. "Miss Grey, may I make you known to Mrs Hobbs, our aunt? She has taken excellent care of my sister since the accident."

Georgiana had already formed the impression that a strong gust of wind would blow the little woman away.

Sir Anthony held his arm towards the other visitor. "May I present Mr Morris? Mr Morris, this is Miss Grey."

Mr Morris bowed to Georgiana, declaring himself very pleased to make her acquaintance despite the unhappy circumstances. He was taller than Sir Anthony, his face as trim as his figure, its oval length tapering down to his triangular chin, which was saved from sharpness by a gentle curve underneath and a crooked smile. Georgiana received the impression of a man who took care of himself without being overly preoccupied by his appearance. He was well dressed but not dandified, his clothes perfectly cut by a tailor who clearly took a pride in his work. His light brown hair was neatly combed and his hazel eyes clear and friendly. Georgiana was surprised she had not previously encountered him. His name was familiar to her, and though he was not a regular guest at the more popular squeezes of the Season, she had heard hostesses who did persuade him to attend their functions were always grateful for his presence, even if he showed little inclination to change his unmarried state. His manner was pleasant as he shook her hand, friendly but not cloying. After paying his respects, he turned back to Lady Wickerston, his manner solemn, his eyes full of concern.

Lady Wickerston appeared pale as she sat opposite, her

hands folded in her lap and her head tilted a little to the side with her gaze fixed downwards. Her air was subdued, almost reflective and Georgiana could not help thinking that her black mourning gown showed her fair complexion to advantage.

"I came to offer my condolences for the loss of your husband," said Georgiana. "There was no opportunity to do so the other evening. I know it must be a great shock to you."

"Yes," said her ladyship. "Thank you, Miss Grey, you are very kind. I must say, it is difficult to take it in. It still doesn't seem real."

"Time will help," said Morris. He continued in deep, rich tones, "I know that is what everyone will say and perhaps it sounds a little unconvincing at present. However, it is true. You will never forget your husband, of course, but gradually the wound will heal and the pain will lessen."

"Yes – yes, of course," said her ladyship, a hand to her brow. "It just all seems so – so strange."

Georgiana considered what Lady Wickerston had said. *Strange* seemed an odd choice of word for a woman whose husband had died suddenly. It sounded detached, almost disinterested: not at all the reaction of a bereaved wife.

"Have you any idea what could have caused the fire?" she inquired.

Sir Anthony shook his head, taking his sister's hand in one of his own.

"No. Perhaps my brother-in-law fell asleep," he suggested, which Georgiana interpreted as a polite way of referring to the effects of excessive imbibing of alcohol. "If one of the logs fell from the hearth on to the carpet, he wouldn't have noticed, and then, of course…?"

Lady Wickerston gave a small, choking sob, her handkerchief

pressed to her mouth. Her brother looked at her in anguished concern. Morris also looked towards Lady Wickerston, his face a model of silent compassion, before transferring his gaze to Georgiana. As she met his eyes, she became aware of a small smile in her direction. He seemed to be asking her to share in his feelings, as if he was trying to establish a bond of sympathy between them for the newly widowed woman.

"There, there, my dear," said Mrs Hobbs, trotting across to pat Lady Wickerston's hand. "I know it is hard but these things are sent to try us."

Georgiana resisted the temptation to roll her eyes. She had no doubt the sentiment was offered as a sincere attempt at comfort but it seemed to trip off the tongue with too much ease, as if it was a stock phrase held for such an eventuality. Mrs Hobbs was fluttering a fresh handkerchief at her afflicted niece.

"Surely there was a fireplace screen in front of the hearth?" asked Georgiana. "I beg your pardon but it seems such a simple precaution and to avert such a tragedy…"

Sir Anthony looked nonplussed. It was Lady Wickerston who answered.

"My husband was apt to be forgetful."

Georgiana hoped her response conveyed her sense of tragic misfortune. Her brain, meanwhile, told her that any servant would remember to ensure the fireplace screen was in place, even when the master was as difficult as Lord Wickerston must have been.

"We can all be forgetful at times," said Sir Anthony.

"You must not tease yourself, my dear," said Mrs Hobbs, still patting her ladyship's hand. "You could not have prevented it. We can only hope he was taken quickly."

"In a fire?" asked Georgiana, the astonishment in her tone bringing the stares of all the room's occupants fully upon her.

"I beg your pardon," she said in a gentler voice, realising the agitation her outburst must have caused. "I have no wish to cause distress, but I have always thought death in a fire must be… forgive me, rather slow and… painful."

Mrs Hobbs closed her eyes. Lady Wickerston brought her handkerchief back to her nose. Tears could be seen streaming down her cheeks.

"Oh, the poor man," her ladyship whispered.

Georgiana said nothing but sensed something odd about the scene she was witnessing. Lady Wickerston seemed to be demonstrating strong emotion, but there was also an air of detachment about her which was more appropriate to the death of an acquaintance. Either she was too strongly affected to bear her loss with the fortitude she considered appropriate, or something was not right. Perhaps, Georgiana thought, her knowledge of Edward's liaison with Lady Wickerston was causing her to judge her ladyship with undue harshness.

Sir Anthony broke the oppressive silence.

"However one looks at it, the accident was a tragedy. My brother-in-law will be deeply missed."

"Indeed he will," said Morris. "I was fortunate to count Lord Wickerston among my friends. He was a good man and good company."

Georgiana made no comment. She had not known Lord Wickerston well, but her limited experience of his company would not have led her to describe it as good. Of course it was not deemed polite to speak ill of the dead, and Morris would certainly wish to offer respect and comfort to his widow. As for his lordship being a good man, information Georgiana had gleaned from both Edward and Lakesby suggested the truth was otherwise. She knew Lady Wickerston suffered at her husband's hands, was it truly possible she would miss him?

Judging it time to depart, Georgiana smiled sympatheti-cally towards her ladyship, begging the other woman to let her know if she could be of service through this difficult time. As she rose to take her leave, Morris did the same, surprising Georgiana with an offer to escort her home. She hoped this surprise wasn't evident in her acceptance, although she noticed it reflected in Mrs Hobbs's expression; the silent 'O' formed by her lips created a shape which matched that of her face in miniature. The widening and whitening of her little eyes hinted shock and disapproval.

Lady Wickerston herself clasped Georgiana's hand warmly as she raised eyes full of gratitude. "You've been most kind, Miss Grey. I have no words with which to thank you."

"Nonsense," said Georgiana. "I am only sorry I could not be of more help."

Sir Anthony rose to ring for a servant to see the visitors out and made his own farewells as Mr Morris opened the door for Georgiana. She glanced back into the room and was startled to see the warm gratitude in Lady Wickerston's eyes replaced by hot anger.

6

Georgiana's curiosity was piqued. What had prompted such palpable anger in Lady Wickerston at that last moment? In someone whom Georgiana had always found cool and reserved, it was an odd change. Was it to do with Mr Morris's departure with Georgiana? Or was she angry with Georgiana herself for some reason? Despite the calm, well-bred exterior, Georgiana could imagine Lady Wickerston would want to be the focus of attention. In her newly widowed state, she would expect this as a right and perhaps Georgiana's condolence call would cause resentment if it divided the attention of the gentlemen present.

Richard Morris was a courteous escort, attentive and interested: perhaps more so than one would expect at a first meeting. Georgiana soon found that attempts to deflect the conversation away from her and towards himself bore little fruit.

"How are you acquainted with Lady Wickerston?" he inquired.

"My sister-in-law introduced us a few months ago," Georgiana replied, recalling the party where she had first become aware of Edward's interest in her ladyship.

"Indeed?"

"Yes." Georgiana sighed. "I recall she had just lost her uncle. It's dreadful to think of the tragedy which has befallen her now."

"Yes."

"Such a horrible accident," continued Georgiana. She glanced toward her companion. "Tell me, do you think it likely Lord Wickerston fell asleep and didn't wake when the fire started?"

"Very likely."

"You must have known him quite well, then?" said Georgiana.

"Well enough," Morris replied. "We've been members of some of the same clubs for some time. Lord Wickerston could often be found at White's or Watier's when I looked in."

"I see." Georgiana was not surprised by this.

"He was not the most active fellow," Morris continued.

"Odd, for so young a man," Georgiana mused. "He could not have been far from your own age, yet from what I have heard he seems to have acted somewhat older."

"Yes, he had fallen into rather sedentary habits of late."

Georgiana thought of what Edward had told her about Lord Wickerston's treatment of his wife. Sedentary was not a word she would have equated with one of his lordship's violent temper. Her own observations had not included anything so dramatic, but Lord Wickerston had presented the impression of a brooding, permanently angry man. Georgiana suspected Mr Morris had chosen the word as a polite way of referring to Lord Wickerston's drinking. She returned to the point which was of more concern to her.

"How do you think the fire started?"

Morris glanced quickly towards her, his eyes a picture of astonishment. "I really can't imagine, Miss Grey." He paused. "I beg you will try not to think about it. The whole business is a great shock and it can only distress you further."

This was no more than Georgiana expected but it was irritating nevertheless. Lady Wickerston's sudden widowhood and the arrival of Amanda on her doorstep left Edward open to scandalous gossip at best and possible accusations of murder at worst. Georgiana checked herself; wherever had that thought come from? Edward had his faults, but he was no murderer.

Georgiana roused herself as she became aware of Morris addressing her. "I beg your pardon, Mr Morris, I'm afraid my mind was wandering."

"It is no matter, Miss Grey, though I must confess myself intrigued. What is keeping your mind so uncommonly active?"

"I wouldn't say *uncommonly* active," responded Georgiana.

"You are too modest, Miss Grey." He paused. "You seem very concerned. Is it Lord Wickerston's death?"

"It is all very… strange," said Georgiana.

"Tragic, certainly, but I don't know that I'd call it strange. These kinds of accidents do happen."

"Yes," she said slowly. "It's just that I can't understand how it was that no one managed to get into the house and save him."

Morris frowned. "Was the door not locked?"

"Yes, but Mr Lakesby and my footman managed to get through it, although too late to be of use." Georgiana glanced towards him. "One can hardly consider such niceties as damaging the door at such a time."

"Of course. I can see why you are concerned, though I'm sure no one would have left him deliberately."

"Of course not."

Morris continued to look thoughtful. "Perhaps no one was able to get to him. If the fire took hold quickly, perhaps that room was not accessible until Lakesby and your footman went in. I understand men had been fighting the flames for some while by that time."

"Perhaps." Georgiana was not entirely convinced.

"Lady Wickerston will need her friends now," said Morris.

"Yes," said Georgiana. "However, her brother seems very attentive and helpful and she is fortunate to be able to stay with her aunt."

"Indeed she is. Her own house will hardly be habitable. In any case, I'm sure she would find it too distressing." Morris paused. "I believe your own brother and sister-in-law have been good friends to Lady Wickerston."

Georgiana did not answer immediately. She was not certain whether Morris was referring to Edward's friendship rather than Amanda's. She had no wish to fuel gossip, yet sensed he had a reason for mentioning it other than to entertain himself by casting aspersions on the reputations of others.

"Yes, Edward and Amanda were concerned that Lady Wickerston had been going through a difficult time, especially in view of the loss of her uncle as well as this current tragedy. It must be very trying for her." Georgiana shook her sadly. "However will she cope?"

"It will be very difficult for her, of course," said Mr Morris. "We can only hope things will be better for her in the future."

Georgiana, however, was less concerned about Lady Wickerston's future plans than her current situation. Two sudden, unnatural deaths in a family were unfortunate to say the least.

"I have very much enjoyed our conversation, Miss Grey," said Mr Morris as they drew up in front of Georgiana's house, "despite meeting under such sad circumstances. I hope I shall have the opportunity to see more of you."

"Thank you. That would be very agreeable," she responded.

"Perhaps I could call on you?"

"Yes, if you wish," she responded with some surprise.

Georgiana thanked Mr Morris for his assistance as she alighted. He gave her a small bow as they took leave. Georgiana began to mount the front steps, surprised to see the door open before she had progressed beyond the two lowest. It was clear someone had been watching for her. Horton seemed to sense her irritation and spoke before she could challenge him.

"I beg your pardon, miss, but Mr Lakesby is here. He arrived about half an hour ago and requested permission to wait."

"I see. Where is he?"

"In the small saloon," Horton responded. "Mr Lakesby wanted to pay his respects to Mrs Grey."

Georgiana nodded, drawing off her gloves as she walked to the small saloon. Here she found Lakesby, still in his top-coat, seated opposite Amanda, who was busy with the sewing task she had set herself. It was an ironically domestic picture, and one Georgiana knew her brother would not appreciate were he to see it.

Lakesby rose at her entrance.

"I beg your pardon, Mr Lakesby," said Georgiana, hand outstretched. "I have been to call on an acquaintance. I see my sister-in-law has been entertaining you."

"Yes, indeed. However, I fear I have been distracting her from her work."

"Mr Lakesby would not take any refreshment, Georgiana," said Amanda in a tone of some concern.

"No, indeed, it's not necessary," said Lakesby with a smile at Amanda. "Please don't worry, Mrs Grey." He turned towards Georgiana. "I have been trying to persuade your sister-in-law to take a turn in the park in my phaeton. I am sure she would find the fresh air beneficial."

"Yes, indeed," said Georgiana, hiding a smile. Lakesby would be every bit as aware as Amanda of how Edward would view such an expedition. "Why don't you go, Amanda?"

"Alas, she tells me she is too busy," Lakesby responded before Amanda could speak. "Your sister-in-law has been very conscientious."

"I do not make a practice of putting my guests to work, Mr Lakesby," said Georgiana with a twinkle.

"Georgiana, really," said Amanda, her head bent once more to her sewing.

"Perhaps you would care to take a drive with me, Miss Grey?"

"Now that sounds much more sensible," said Amanda.

Georgiana glanced at her sister-in-law in some surprise. In the light of Edward's dislike of Lakesby, this would have been the last thing she expected. Could this be a sign of rebellion in her quiet sister-in-law? The thought aroused Georgiana's sense of mischief and ready sense of humour. Had she not seen how shaken Edward was by his wife's absence, she might have been ready to encourage it.

As Georgiana looked towards Lakesby, who waited in patient expectation, she sensed he had something of import which he wished to relate.

"Very well," Georgiana agreed.

Several minutes later, she was seated beside Mr Lakesby in his phaeton as he set his horses to. She spoke without preamble.

"Have you some news, Mr Lakesby?"

"Possibly," said Lakesby with a slow smile. Seeing Georgiana in no mood for drawn-out games, he spoke more seriously. "Dr Masters is now certain Lord Wickerston was dead before the fire started."

"I see." Georgiana looked thoughtful. "I beg your pardon, Mr Lakesby, but surely that is just confirmation of what we already suspected."

"True," said Lakesby, slightly irritated by her tepid reaction. "However, there is a little more to suggest this is the case." He paused. "Are any of your servants acquainted with those of the Wickerstons?"

Georgiana looked at him in astonishment.

"I have no idea." Georgiana had never considered it her place to inquire into the personal lives of her servants. She scrutinised his face closely. "Why do you ask?"

"Servants can be an excellent source of information." He paused, considering his next words. "I'm sure it will come as no surprise to you that Dr Masters is well acquainted with the local apothecary."

"I had not given the matter much thought, but I can see he would be."

"It appears this person, Gregson, I believe is his name, told him that one of Lady Wickerston's maids recently purchased some arsenic, apparently to despatch some rats in the cellar. I understand from my friend Mr Alfred Masters that his brother was inspired to make some inquiries, and the apothecary showed him the Poison Book."

Georgiana digested this information. "It is an unsettling coincidence, certainly," she said. "But rats are not uncommon. I believe people often have to resort to such measures."

"Do you have them?"

Georgiana laughed. "I confess I would prefer not to know," she said. "I trust there are some matters I can leave to the discretion of my servants."

"Of course. However, I'd be surprised to find that the Wickerstons' maid was acting on her own initiative. The question is who gave her the instruction."

"The fact that it was a maid rather than a footman does suggest it was Lady Wickerston," said Georgiana. "But she would hardly ask the maid to bring it back to her. Surely it would be put somewhere in the kitchens, or given to the person with the task of disposing of the rats."

"Not Lady Wickerston."

Georgiana pictured Lady Wickerston, serenely elegant,

calm, composed. Surely the maid's curiosity would have been piqued if her ladyship had directed that the arsenic be brought back directly to her. Georgiana could not imagine her ladyship presiding over the removal of the rodents herself, nor searching the kitchen at dead of night to locate the arsenic for a more sinister purpose. Nevertheless, Georgiana knew only too well the dangers of judging by appearances, and the thought had often occurred to her that Lady Wickerston was not all she seemed. If her ladyship had planned her husband's death, could there have been an accomplice?

The thought which followed this made Georgiana's blood run cold and she pushed it away immediately.

"Miss Grey?"

Georgiana smiled apologetically for her abstraction. "I beg your pardon, Mr Lakesby."

Georgiana thought she detected some understanding in the look he gave her, and his next remark confirmed this.

"I can't imagine your brother to have been involved in Lord Wickerston's death."

"No," Georgiana replied. She felt uneasy at this turn of the conversation. There was something uncomfortable about hearing uttered aloud a possibility she feared to admit even to herself.

"I beg your pardon," said Lakesby. "It was presumptuous of me to imagine you prey to such a suspicion."

Georgiana did not answer immediately.

"It makes no matter," she said after a few moments. "Does Dr Masters have any other reason for suspecting Lord Wickerston was murdered?"

Lakesby frowned. "I believe on examining Lord Wickerston he detected signs of arsenic."

"Signs?"

Lakesby shook his head. "I had in mind to spare you such

unpleasant details. I ought to have known you would press for the truth." He continued in a more matter of fact tone. "Dr Masters found some grains of arsenic mixed with the wine which stained his lordship's teeth."

"Oh."

It was an inadequate response, but Lakesby's observation was not quite what Georgiana had expected. She did not feel the revulsion expected of a young lady in her position. Yet Dr Masters's findings seemed too straightforward. If the fire was intended to make the murder of Lord Wickerston seem accidental, had the person responsible considered that the arsenic would be discovered so easily?

"He encountered a case of arsenic poisoning a few years ago," explained Lakesby. "I understand there are certain recognisable symptoms, including nausea."

"Which could also be a symptom of excessive drinking," said Georgiana slowly.

"True," said Lakesby. "Although since Lord Wickerston was accustomed to excessive drinking, he may not always have been subject to nausea."

"No," said Georgiana. "Still, surely it would be the conclusion of anyone who witnessed it." She looked up at him. "Or anyone responsible for attending to it."

"Quite."

"That would most likely have been his valet. It would hardly be the maid sent to buy the arsenic for the rats," she mused. "Even if the servants were gossiping, they wouldn't necessarily associate one with the other."

"No, that would more likely be the deduction of someone who suspected all was not as it seemed, and would be looking to prove their theory."

"Yes." Georgiana was pondering her own suspicions.

Lakesby abruptly changed the subject. "Your sister-in-law

seems well."

"Indeed, she is." Georgiana wondered where this could be leading.

"It must be very agreeable to have her company."

"Yes." Georgiana felt her eyes narrow as she looked towards him.

"She decided not to accompany you on your call?"

Now Georgiana understood.

"I went to pay a condolence call on Lady Wickerston. Amanda had already done what she could on the night of Lord Wickerston's death. There was no need for her to visit Lady Wickerston today."

"Of course. Tell me, how was Lady Wickerston?" Lakesby inquired.

"Subdued. She still seemed very shaken. Yet – " Georgiana paused, trying to determine how best to phrase her thoughts.

Lakesby waited.

"It was the oddest thing," Georgiana continued. "Although she did seem rather shocked, in a way she also appeared detached, as if it were happening to someone else."

Lakesby looked thoughtful. "That could be an effect of her bereavement. People don't always react as one might expect."

"True," said Georgiana, "and I imagine the treatment she received from her husband would have made her accustomed to concealing her feelings."

"Very likely. Did you learn anything?"

Georgiana shook her head. "Nothing of significance. The thinking seems to be that Lord Wickerston fell asleep and a log or a piece of coal fell on to the hearth rug."

"What nonsense! That's the purpose of fireplace screens."

"Yes, that was my own thought. However, I am told Lord Wickerston was apt to be forgetful."

"Good grief! Apt to be forgetful, indeed! As if Wickerston

would ever expect to touch the fireplace screen himself. I suspect any servant who forgot would be sent to the rightabout."

"I imagine so," said Georgiana. "Unless..." She paused, and gazed thoughtfully at Lakesby. "Unless that was what they were supposed to do."

7

Lakesby looked thunderstruck. The horses took advantage of his momentary lapse of concentration to pull at the reins, breaking into impatient strides. He apologised to Georgiana, brought them back to a gentle canter and drove in silence for a few minutes.

"So you are saying the fire was deliberate as well as the arsenic?" he said at length.

"The one could conceal the other," she said. "Who would consider looking for arsenic poisoning in such circumstances? It would be seen as a tragic accident."

"In that case, why even bother with the arsenic?" Lakesby objected.

"The fire might not have killed him," Georgiana pointed out.

Lakesby let out a long breath. "We are assuming a great deal."

"Yes, I know," said Georgiana, "but you'll allow it's a possibility."

"It's certainly a possibility." He frowned. "Yes, I can see that an accidental fire at Marpley Manor on the very day Lord Wickerston is murdered by arsenic poisoning is an unlikely coincidence."

Georgiana could not resist throwing him a triumphant glance.

"However," he continued, "it does not necessarily follow that Lady Wickerston murdered her husband."

"Yes, I am aware of that," snapped Georgiana, irritated by his patronising tone. "Yet it is only common sense to consider who could benefit by Lord Wickerston's death. He may have been a surly, unpleasant individual but I cannot imagine a long list of people with something to gain from his death. Indeed, in view of the beatings she suffered, I can immediately think of no one who would gain more than his wife."

"It is true she will be safer out of his presence," said Lakesby, "but she seems to be profiting little otherwise. She has already lost her home, and if Wickerston left anything other than debts I shall be very much surprised. He certainly raced through her inheritance. She will have to marry again."

"After such an experience?" Georgiana shuddered.

Lakesby shrugged. "A second marriage need not follow the pattern of the first."

"No, of course not," said Georgiana impatiently. "However, since Lady Wickerston's first experience has been so distressing, she may view the prospect with some nervousness."

"Perhaps," said Lakesby. "On the other hand, it may have given her another reason to kill her husband."

"True," said Georgiana. Her mind turned unwillingly to Edward.

"I'm sure there will be no shortage of suitors once her mourning period is over," commented Lakesby.

"Yes," said Georgiana. Her mind was not on her companion, but on the visitors she had encountered during her call to Lady Wickerston.

Her thoughts must have occupied her longer than she realised. When Lakesby's voice penetrated them, it carried a note of anxiety. "Miss Grey? Miss Grey, are you quite well?"

Georgiana roused herself.

"What is it?" He looked concerned.

"I beg your pardon. I was just…"

She paused. He waited. She gathered herself and gave him her full attention.

"I'm sorry, Mr Lakesby. Tell me, are you acquainted with Mr Richard Morris?"

"Not well," he responded. "Why?"

"He was visiting Lady Wickerston when I called on her today. He described himself as fortunate to count Lord Wickerston among his friends."

"I see. I'm not aware that Morris has any particular friends. I don't recall seeing him in Wickerston's company, but that doesn't mean he was not speaking the truth." Lakesby paused and frowned. "I have to confess, I could not imagine they had much in common."

"Perhaps not," said Georgiana. "Nevertheless, he does seem concerned that Lady Wickerston should have support at this difficult time."

"Does he?" said Lakesby. "That is interesting. Does he propose to offer it?"

Georgiana smiled. "She has her brother to aid her."

"Ah, yes. Sir Anthony. Was he there?"

Georgiana nodded. "He seems very protective of her." She thought for a moment. "It is odd that he should not have done anything to protect his sister when her husband was alive."

"Perhaps he did."

"Perhaps." Georgiana looked towards Lakesby speculatively. "Do you really imagine Sir Anthony is a murderer?"

"Do you really imagine he is not?"

"I don't know," she replied candidly. "However, it seems rather a risk to despatch one of his sister's maids to fetch some arsenic. Why not use one of his own servants whom he could be sure was trustworthy?"

"He may not have felt completely sure. They would know him better, and at the very least might think it odd. His sister's servant would be less well acquainted with him, and unlikely to think he was being anything other than helpful."

Georgiana considered this. "Then why not do something earlier?"

"Perhaps he did not know what was going on. Or there may have been no opportunity."

"Possibly," said Georgiana slowly. "Nevertheless, it all seems very odd."

Lakesby shrugged. "Murder is hardly commonplace."

Georgiana threw him a baleful look. "I am not seeking to trivialise the matter, Mr Lakesby."

"I was not suggesting you were, Miss Grey." He paused, looking at her more closely. "You have a logical mind." His tone was lighter when he spoke again. "It simply occurs to me that Sir Anthony Dixon must have made quite an impression if you are so reluctant to consider the possibility that he may have killed his brother-in-law."

Georgiana chose to ignore his observation.

"What of Mr Morris?" she said. "I know you said you are not well acquainted with him, but you must have heard something of him."

"Very little," Lakesby said. "He is well to do, of good family, excellent estates."

"None of which precludes his being a murderer."

"Indeed they don't." Lakesby laughed humourlessly. "But I fear I truly know little of his character. You would do better to apply to your brother. Although..." He paused, and appeared to consider his words carefully. "He is unlikely to give you a favourable report."

Georgiana eyed him guardedly.

"Oh?"

Lakesby glanced towards her. He spoke in a measured tone when he continued. "They have never been friends."

"I suppose you mean to tell me Edward has quarrelled with him as well as with you," she said.

"With stronger reason," he said, "assuming what I've been told is true."

"What is that?"

Lakesby gave her a thoughtful look before he responded.

"I have heard one or two whispers to the effect that he once wanted to marry your sister-in-law."

"What?" Georgiana was dumbfounded. "Amanda?"

Lakesby nodded. "You understand I am not in his confidence."

Georgiana nodded slowly, her eyes staring fixedly on the road in front of her, trying to digest what Lakesby had told her. Richard Morris did not seem to her to be at all the type of suitor who would have been interested in Amanda. Be that as it may, since she had chosen to marry Edward, it was fair to assume his regard had not been returned. However, in any case, it would have been a long time ago. Why would Lakesby bring up the subject now?

Georgiana turned towards him, her gaze steady.

"I beg your pardon, Mr Lakesby. This is just something of a surprise. Not that there is any reason Amanda should tell me if she had received another offer of marriage besides Edward's."

"No."

"Though Mr Morris seems rather an unlikely suitor."

"I believe he was considered very eligible, even six years ago," remarked Lakesby.

"I'm sure. However, he and Amanda seem so – so –"

"Incompatible? Well, since she married Edward I imagine they must have been." He took his eyes from the road to meet hers. "Your sister-in-law has many good qualities."

"Yes, I know," said Georgiana, wondering where his trend of thought was taking the conversation.

"I imagine Morris could appreciate that as well as anyone."

"Are you an admirer of my sister-in-law, Mr Lakesby?" she said quizzically.

"Not in the sense you mean," he responded with a slight smile. "I'd be surprised to find Edward has ever considered me a rival. However, I do have a great deal of respect for Mrs Grey. Your brother is a fortunate man."

"More fortunate than he knows," murmured Georgiana.

"Perhaps."

"Mr Lakesby, are you suggesting Amanda is the reason Mr Morris has never married?"

"It is possible," said Lakesby. "Morris is very reserved. If that were the case, he would hardly wish it to become public knowledge."

"It's fantastic," said Georgiana, "to think, all these years." She gave Lakesby a sideways glance. "When I met him today, visiting Lady Wickerston, it occurred to me he might be an admirer of hers."

"That is quite possible," he replied. "As you say, your brother and sister-in-law have been married for some time now."

"No doubt he has had dalliances elsewhere," said Georgiana. Mr Morris's offer to escort her home now appeared in an entirely different light from what she had originally supposed.

"In any case, he seems to have a motive for Lord Wickerston's murder," said Lakesby.

"You think so?" Georgiana looked surprised.

Lakesby nodded. "Certainly. An admirer of Lady Wickerston's would be glad to have her husband removed, and an admirer of your sister-in-law..." He left the sentence unfinished.

Georgiana frowned. "Yes?"

"There are two possibilities," Lakesby suggested. "It might be supposed that with Wickerston eliminated, your brother might leave his wife in favour of his mistress."

Georgiana shook her head vigorously. "Edward would never do that."

"No, it would create a scandal," said Lakesby dryly.

Georgiana chose not to acknowledge Lakesby's observation. She was certain that in this case Edward had stronger, more personal reasons for adhering to society's rules.

Lakesby continued, appearing to choose his words carefully. "However, if the killer *assumed* that Edward might take such action, he would also see the path clear to your sister-in-law."

Georgiana stared at him in astonishment, as though she suspected some wild disease had taken hold of his brain.

"You can't be serious. Do you honestly imagine that Amanda – *Amanda*...?"

"Yes, I realise it is a little far-fetched."

"A little far-fetched?" repeated Georgiana, an unaccustomed faintness in her voice. "What is the second possibility you mentioned?"

"More likely, I think," began Lakesby.

"You surprise me." Her tone was as dry as his had been.

He threw her a scornful look. "It occurs to me that if the killer was someone who held your sister-in-law in high regard, he might be angry over your brother's association with Lady Wickerston."

Georgiana shrugged. "Possibly but I don't see how killing her husband would help."

"Suppose the killer were to arrange matters so that the blame was laid at Edward's door? By way of punishment for his betrayal of his wife?"

Georgiana chewed her bottom lip thoughtfully.

"A severe punishment. He could be hanged."

"Yes."

"You are forgetting that Lord Wickerston's death appeared

to be an accident," Georgiana pointed out. "Edward could hardly be blamed for a mishap which took place when he was elsewhere."

"True," said Lakesby, "but we are working on the assumption that it was not an accident. Whether any killer intended it to be seen as such could have a bearing on how careful he – or she – was in concealing their actions."

"Yes," said Georgiana. "It could have been quite methodically planned and made to look careless."

They had by this time arrived back at Georgiana's home. As Lakesby helped her to alight, the front door opened and Amanda flew down the steps.

"Oh, Georgiana, thank goodness you are home. The most dreadful thing has happened."

"Good gracious, Amanda, what is it?" asked Georgiana, alarmed by her sister-in-law's pale complexion and fraught expression.

"It is Edward. He has been arrested."

8

Devoutly hoping her sister-in-law had missed the expressive look she had cast in Lakesby's direction, Georgiana led Amanda back into the house. Lakesby called for Horton and requested that some brandy be brought with all speed. When it arrived, he ignored the barely suppressed surprise of this normally imperturbable individual that a gentleman should be issuing orders in Miss Grey's house, took hold of decanter and glass and closed the door of the drawing room.

Georgiana knelt before Amanda, her hand covering the trembling ones which her sister-in-law had clasped in her lap. Lakesby held out the glass and gently urged Amanda to drink. She looked up at him doubtfully but he nodded firmly.

"You will feel better," he assured her.

Georgiana smiled reassuringly. Amanda accepted the glass and took a sip. A second followed; she appeared to find Mr Lakesby's prediction correct. She seemed calmer, though it was clear it would take some time for her agitation to disappear fully.

"Now," said Georgiana, taking a seat next to her sister-in-law, "tell us what has happened."

Amanda cast another dubious glance towards Mr Lakesby but apparently decided she had already broken the bounds of discretion by her revelation of Edward's arrest.

"A servant came with a note from Edward. He – he has asked me not to worry." She looked up, her eyes frightened. "How can I not worry, Georgiana? I don't understand. Whatever has happened, Edward is not a killer. How could anyone think that?"

"No." Georgiana's tone was thoughtful.

"I must go to the children," Amanda said hurriedly, looking for somewhere to put her brandy glass as she prepared to rise.

Georgiana gently pushed her back into the armchair. "Amanda, wait. Please finish your brandy. You will feel calmer."

Amanda seemed to accept this; she bent her head forward and brought the glass to her lips. While her expression did not convey enjoyment of it, some colour returned to her cheeks. She took another sip, then looked expectantly at Georgiana and Lakesby.

"What is to be done? Mr Lakesby, is there anything you can do?"

Lakesby's expression of concern was overtaken by swift surprise. He exchanged a glance with Georgiana.

"I? Mrs Grey, I should be pleased to help you in any way I can but I'm not certain what I can do." He paused, with a fleeting glance towards Georgiana. "Nor that your husband would welcome my intervention."

"Please," Amanda said. "I'm sure you could find some way of helping Edward. I cannot bear to think of him in such a place, and if things don't go well, he could... he could..."

"Don't think about that now, Amanda," said Georgiana. She found the image of Edward on a scaffold in her own mind and resolutely pushed it away. "It will not help."

"I can certainly make some inquiries," said Lakesby.

Amanda thanked him, her face emanating gratitude and relief. Georgiana put an arm around her shoulders. Her own mind was on potential inquiries which could be effectively made by the Crimson Cavalier. If Amanda had decided to return home, Georgiana could take these forward more easily.

"What exactly happened?" she asked Amanda in a gentle tone.

Amanda moistened her lips. "Edward said in his note that two Bow Street Runners came to the house and asked to speak to him." She looked up, appeal in her eyes. "He has gone with them to speak to a magistrate. It seems they think Lord Wickerston was deliberately killed." She shook her head slowly. "I don't understand, I know he was… concerned about Lady Wickerston, but he could not have done such a thing." She looked from Georgiana to Lakesby and back again. "Could he?"

Neither answered her immediately. After a pause charged with apprehension, Georgiana was the first to speak. "Did Edward say they actually accused him of murdering Lord Wickerston?"

Amanda shook her head. "No, I don't think so. But it seems they think he might know something about it."

Lakesby frowned. "Have they any particular reason for such an assumption?"

"I don't know," said Amanda. "I really don't understand any of this."

"I imagine the Runners will need to speak to acquaintances of the Wickerstons," said Lakesby. "I understand you were all at the same dinner party on the night of the fire?"

"Yes," said Georgiana.

Amanda nodded in agreement. "But why would two Runners be needed?" she asked. "Surely one would be sufficient."

The same thought had occurred to Georgiana, although neither she nor Lakesby attempted to answer the question. Lakesby attempted to reassure Amanda again, by repeating his offer to make some inquiries if Edward had not returned home by morning.

Georgiana raised no objection when Amanda again mentioned the need to return to her children. Amanda rose to leave the room, and paused with one hand on the door knob.

"Georgiana, I wonder, would you mind coming with me?"

"Yes, of course, Amanda, I shall be there directly. I'll direct Emily to help you get ready," responded Georgiana.

"No, I meant – I meant – home with me."

"I see."

"After all," continued Amanda in a rush, "you should not really be here on your own. Perhaps until Selina returns…"

"We'll talk about it," said Georgiana.

"I should be on my way," said Lakesby. "There is no need to trouble yourselves, I shall see myself out." He paused as he drew level with Amanda. "Please try not to worry too much, Mrs Grey. I shall do what I can."

"Thank you, Mr Lakesby," she said with a small smile.

Lakesby nodded towards Georgiana and departed.

"Come, Amanda, let's go upstairs," said Georgiana when the door had closed behind him.

Georgiana was surprised when the footman brought a message only moments after she entered Amanda's room. Mr Lakesby had returned and begged the favour of an urgent word with her. Excusing herself, she left her sister-in-law contemplating the contents of her wardrobe and descended the stairs to speak to the returning visitor.

She found Lakesby in the hall, tapping his driving whip against his leg. "I beg your pardon," he said, "but I thought you would wish to know, I have just seen Lady Wickerston's carriage turning into this road. I rather gained the impression it was coming here."

"What?" Georgiana cast a horrified glance up the stairs. "Whatever can she want?"

"I daresay her brother is with her," remarked Lakesby in a neutral tone.

Georgiana looked at him in some puzzlement, not sure how this was relevant. She thought it best not to respond and merely shrugged. "Let us hope Amanda keeps to her room." It was not often Georgiana wished for her cousin's presence, but it occurred to her that Selina's help would be invaluable just at this moment. She frowned. "It is not likely she would have heard of Edward being arrested, is it?"

Lakesby shook his head. "I doubt it. Your sister-in-law has only just heard herself, and in a note directly from Edward. I daresay there may have been some speculation among the servants in both households, but I can't imagine rumours would spread quite so quickly."

"No," said Georgiana. "It's just that if Edward sent a note to Amanda, might it not also be possible that he…"

"Sent a note to Lady Wickerston as well?" Lakesby finished for her. It was his turn to shrug. "Possible, but unlikely. Excellent fodder for the scandal sheets. I can't imagine Edward providing such material with alacrity."

"He did not seem so concerned about scandal when he was comforting Lady Wickerston on the night of her husband's death," Georgiana pointed out.

"True," said Lakesby. He turned back towards the door. "I must go. I'll do what I can."

Georgiana nodded, thanked him and returned quickly to Amanda's room to explain that an urgent matter required her attention. With apologies, she undertook to send Emily to her immediately, which she did with a hasty request to her maid to ensure that Amanda remained upstairs.

She then returned to the drawing room, and stood by the window, to await the butler's announcement that another visitor had arrived.

It was not long before it came. Turning towards the open door, Georgiana schooled her expression to one of surprised pleasure. Her visitor came forward with hands outstretched, her expression agitated.

"Oh, Miss Grey, I must beg your pardon for intruding like this."

"It is quite all right, Lady Wickerston," said Georgiana, who had never before seen Lady Wickerston in any other state than collected and self-possessed. "Please won't you sit down? Can I offer you some refreshment?"

"No, no, thank you," said her ladyship, accepting a seat. She clasped her hands together, head bowed forward.

Georgiana sat opposite, watching her ladyship, making no attempt to break the silence. A moment or two later, Lady Wickerston looked up and gave a wan smile.

"I must beg your pardon for bursting in on you in this fashion, Miss Grey. I don't know what you must think of me."

"Please do not concern yourself, Lady Wickerston," said Georgiana. "You have had a considerable shock and this has been a difficult few days for you. It would be surprising if you were not at sixes and sevens. Please tell me what I can do to help."

"You are very kind." Lady Wickerston paused. When she spoke again, her speech was slower, more deliberate. "I feel I must apologise to you. I'm sure I must have appeared very ungrateful when you were kind enough to visit."

Georgiana was surprised. "Good heavens, whatever gave you that idea? I assure you, Lady Wickerston, that was not the case."

"Well, I fear I was not very gracious," said her ladyship in a faltering tone.

"Pray, do not worry about it," said Georgiana. "You have had a bereavement, no one would expect you to act normally."

"That is no excuse," continued her ladyship. "It was kind of you." She paused. "Everyone has been very kind," she said, almost to herself. "I really don't deserve it."

Georgiana's eyes widened. She said nothing, however, thinking it better to wait for her guest to continue when she felt ready. She hoped devoutly that this would not take too long; the last thing Georgiana wanted was Amanda coming in search of her.

Lady Wickerston sighed, then gave her hostess a small smile, as though she had suddenly become aware of her surroundings.

"I'm sorry, I'm being a dreadful bore."

"No, not at all."

"It is just – you see…"

Georgiana leaned forward attentively, her expression encouraging. Tears began to drop from her ladyship's lashes.

"I killed my husband."

Georgiana felt unable to speak for a moment.

"You killed…? Lady Wickerston, I beg your pardon, the fire killed him."

Her ladyship shook her blonde head vigorously. "No, it was supposed to look that way but that wasn't the case. I couldn't bear it any more, it was awful. I was so frightened all the time, so I poisoned him." She paused, her head bowed, eyes focusing on the hands clasped in her lap.

Georgiana waited a moment or two, then stood to ring the bell. When James responded, she excused herself to her visitor and quietly indicated that the footman should leave the room with her. Once they were outside the door, she asked him to arrange some tea, and also to convey a message to her sister-in-law, apologising that the matter which had demanded her attention was taking longer than expected.

"And once the tea is brought, I do not wish to be disturbed."

"Yes, miss."

Georgiana slipped quietly back into the drawing room to see Lady Wickerston in the same position as when she had left. She wondered whether her guest had even noticed her brief absence. She walked softly back to her seat, her eyes never leaving Lady Wickerston. Her ladyship made no attempt to speak. Eventually, Georgiana gently broke the silence.

"Why are you telling me this, Lady Wickerston? It does not seem at all proper."

"I keep thinking about what I've done," said Lady Wickerston, her voice barely above a whisper. "It haunts me. I can't live with myself." She looked towards Georgiana, her eyes pleading, anxious. "Since you were so kind as to visit me to offer condolences, and to go to so much trouble on the night of the fire, I felt I could talk to you."

Georgiana was surprised at this. Her acquaintanceship with Lady Wickerston was slight but she had formed a strong impression of her ladyship's reserve. But before she could speak, the doors opened to admit the parlourmaid, bearing a tea tray. The girl placed it on a low table and left the room noiselessly at a nod from her mistress.

Georgiana moved towards the tray. "Let me pour you some tea, Lady Wickerston."

Lady Wickerston shook her head, her clasped hands raised in front of her, twisting and rubbing them in a manner which reminded Georgiana of Lady Macbeth in a production she had once seen of Shakespeare's play.

When Georgiana held a cup of tea out to her, she accepted it despite her initial refusal, and sipped absently. Georgiana sat down with her own tea and waited.

"I didn't know what else to do," said Lady Wickerston, her voice cracked and high-pitched. "My husband was – was not very kind, you see."

"No," said Georgiana.

"In fact, he could be quite cruel." Tears filled her eyes again, and threatened to overflow.

"I see."

"I didn't know what to do," her ladyship repeated. "I was so frightened, I was desperate." She paused, moistening her lips. "I – I sent my maid to an apothecary to buy some poison, arsenic. I said it was to kill rats in the cellar." She ran her tongue over her lips again. "I'm sure you will have noticed my husband had a tendency to drink more than was wise."

Georgiana nodded.

"I put some arsenic in his wine glass," her ladyship said. "He was in the study, where Mr Lakesby and your footman found him." She shook her head. "I left the house, went for a walk. I needed to talk to a – a friend."

Georgiana thought she had a good idea who this friend was.

"I didn't see my husband when I went home, I didn't go into the study. I went to my room and changed to go to Lady Bertram's dinner party. My husband had not planned to go. My brother called to escort me. I'm afraid I neglected to say goodbye to my husband." She looked up, directly at Georgiana. "I don't know how the fire started, truly, I don't. The first I knew of it was when you came to tell us."

Georgiana was thinking. Her mind was on Edward, apparently under arrest, and Amanda upstairs, fearful and anxious to return to her children. She wondered what Lady Wickerston was not telling her.

"Where did you go, Lady Wickerston? For your walk, I mean."

"What?" Her ladyship looked uneasy.

"Where did you go for your walk?"

"I – I don't know. I don't remember."

Georgiana did not believe her. She was about to pursue the point when came the interruption she had been at pains to avoid.

"Georgiana, I'm sorry to disturb you – oh!" Amanda's elfin face took on a startled expression.

Georgiana saw hurt and confusion in her eyes. Lady Wickerston's expression was nothing short of horrified. Georgiana rose to her feet.

"I beg your pardon, Amanda. It has been shockingly rude of me to keep you waiting so long. I trust Emily has been looking after you." She caught sight of her maid in the hall behind Amanda, shrugging her shoulders in resignation.

"Yes, yes, thank you. Emily has been excellent, she's taken very good care of me." Amanda smiled in what Georgiana considered a brave manner. "You have quite a treasure there."

"Yes, I know." Georgiana wondered if she imagined a hint of reproach that she herself had not taken quite such good care of her guest, or whether this was only in her own mind. She continued, "I'm so sorry I've been neglecting you. Lady Wickerston has just been telling me how she was finding the indoors so oppressive and decided to take some air. When she found herself in this vicinity, she thought it would be civil to call."

"I see," said Amanda in a small voice. Her hands were folded primly in front of her.

Lady Wickerston's own hands were clasped even more tightly in her lap, her knuckles white, her eyes lowered. Her wedding ring glinted gold in the sun shining through the window.

"I knew you were busy and I did not wish to disturb you," said Georgiana.

"Of course. That was very thoughtful," said Amanda.

"I really must be on my way," said Lady Wickerston, rising. "I'm so sorry to have intruded. I did not know you had a guest."

"Amanda came to bear me company while my cousin is away," said Georgiana.

"Yes, well, you must have a thousand things to do," said Lady Wickerston, setting down her cup.

"As must you, Lady Wickerston," said Amanda.

"Yes. Yes," said her ladyship. "Thank you so much for your kindness. Goodbye, Miss Grey. Goodbye, Mrs Grey."

Amanda inclined her head and stood aside to allow Lady Wickerston to leave the room. The bleakness in her eyes was not lost on Georgiana.

9

Georgiana rang for a servant to see Lady Wickerston out. Amanda remained where she was, standing with hands folded. As soon as the drawing room door closed, Georgiana turned to face her sister-in-law.

"I'm so sorry, Amanda. Lady Wickerston's arrival was the last thing I expected. I suppose I should have denied her but I did not expect her to stay so long."

"No, of course you could not deny her," said Amanda, seating herself.

"I had hoped you would not have to meet her," said Georgiana, a touch guiltily.

"It is of no importance. Please don't concern yourself, Georgiana. It was not your fault. Why did Mr Lakesby come back?"

Georgiana saw no reason to hide the truth of this from Amanda.

"He saw Lady Wickerston's carriage approaching and came to warn me. He was as much surprised as we were."

"Oh." Amanda showed little interest. After a brief pause she continued, "I have packed my bandbox. I wondered, do you mean to come with me?"

Georgiana hesitated. She got the impression Amanda wanted her company but she had no wish to uproot herself. It would certainly be difficult for the Crimson Cavalier to operate from an abode that wasn't her own.

She smiled at Amanda. "I'm not sure Edward would be pleased to find me installed in his home on my return."

Amanda began to protest. Georgiana raised her hand and shook her head. "Amanda, Edward's arrest is clearly a mistake.

I'm sure he will be home very shortly." She paused and offered a reassuring smile. "When you and Edward see each other, you will need to talk. I would be very much in the way."

"But…"

Georgiana squeezed Amanda's hand.

"No buts. Come, Amanda, you know I am right."

Amanda looked hesitant. Georgiana took advantage.

"If you are concerned about leaving me on my own, pray do not give it a thought. I shall do well enough, and I don't expect Selina will be away many more days."

"I'm not sure Edward would be happy about me leaving you alone," said Amanda.

"He was much less happy about your departure." Georgiana took both of her sister-in-law's hands in a warm clasp. "Trust me, Amanda, Edward has far too much on his mind at the moment to worry about my affairs."

Amanda nodded slowly. "Very well, if you think so," she capitulated. "I really don't know what to do for the best, except that the children will need me. I do hope no one has told them what has happened to Edward."

"I'm sure no one would be so indiscreet."

Amanda smiled. "Thank you, Georgiana. You have been a great comfort." She glanced towards the clock over the mantelpiece. "I must go. May I impose on you for the use of a carriage?"

"Of course. Good heavens, Amanda, you know it is no imposition." Georgiana rang the bell. "I shall ask James to accompany you."

"Truly, Georgiana, there is no need. "

"I insist. He is one of my most trusted servants. Ah, James, my sister-in-law will be returning home shortly. Would you accompany her, please?"

"Of course, miss. I'll take Tom to carry Mrs Grey's box,

if you've no objection."

"No, none at all." Noticing the look of anxiety which flitted across Amanda's face at the mention of the page she had acquired some months earlier in unconventional circumstances, Georgiana smiled reassuringly. "You need not worry, Amanda, it is a long time since Tom has attempted highway robbery. You have nothing to fear. Isn't that true, James?"

James nodded. "He's actually a good worker, strong too."

This did not surprise Georgiana. As errand boy at the Lucky Bell tavern he was well used to hard work, and the three generous meals a day he received under Georgiana's roof had added some flesh to his bones. Though he no longer enjoyed the thrill of regular contact with highway robbers and footpads who tipped him from their ill-gotten gains, he had quickly become proud of his uniform and was regularly spoiled by Georgiana's housekeeper, Mrs Daniels, who had taken a fancy to him.

"Thank you, James," said Amanda with a smile. She turned to Georgiana. "Perhaps Emily could fetch my cloak?"

"I'll speak to her, ma'am," said James, leaving the room as he spoke.

Georgiana looked seriously at Amanda. "Are you certain you feel ready to return home?"

Amanda nodded. "I must. The children." She leaned forward and embraced Georgiana. "Thank you so much for your kindness and understanding."

"Not at all," said Georgiana. "You know you're always welcome here."

Emily arrived with Amanda's cloak. "The carriage is ready, miss," she said, helping Amanda to slip the garment around her shoulders. Both ladies walked down the front steps, Georgiana's arm about her sister-in-law.

Watching the preparations for Amanda's departure, Georgiana's mind turned to the startling revelations she had heard over the past hour: first Edward's arrest, and then Lady Wickerston's confession that she was responsible for her husband's murder. Georgiana's spirit longed for action but her mind wanted to think through all the information she had received.

As soon as she had seen Amanda safely on her way, Georgiana summoned Emily to her bedchamber. As the door closed, Georgiana beckoned her maid to a seat, while she herself perched on the edge of her bed.

"Lady Wickerston just told me she killed her husband."

Emily's jaw dropped. "What?"

Georgiana nodded. "Unbelievable, isn't it?"

"That she killed him or that she told you?" said Emily. "I'm sorry, miss. No offence meant, it's just – I didn't think…"

"You didn't think we were on such close terms that she would confide in me," finished Georgiana.

"Yes, miss," nodded Emily.

"No, nor did I," said Georgiana, her tone serious. She looked steadily at Emily, moistening her lips. The maid watched her.

"There is something else. The reason my sister-in-law left in such a hurry." She paused, her eyes on Emily. "My brother has been arrested for Lord Wickerston's murder."

"I see. I'm ever so sorry, Miss Georgiana."

"You don't seem very surprised."

Emily lowered her eyes. "I'm sorry, miss. I can't believe your brother is a killer. It's just that, well, I have heard…" She faltered, looking embarrassed.

"About him and Lady Wickerston?" Georgiana asked.

Emily nodded, still apparently unable to look her mistress in the eye. "Begging your pardon, miss, but I've heard some talk."

"Yes," said Georgiana with a sigh. "Fuelled by my sister-in-law's arrival here, no doubt."

"I believe so, miss."

"Oh, dear," said Georgiana. "Oh, well, it can't be helped." She looked at Emily thoughtfully. "Perhaps you should tell me what else you've heard by way of gossip."

Emily nodded, wrinkling her nose as she frowned in an effort of concentration.

"I'm not sure if there's anything that can help, miss. I don't know anyone in Lady Wickerston's household well, though I've heard the odd whisper here and there."

"I understand."

"I believe your brother has sometimes met her ladyship in the park of a morning, though not so much of late."

"Well, that seems innocent enough."

"That's what I thought, miss. Sounded like it was the sort of thing put about by someone wanting to cause trouble."

"Ye-es," said Georgiana slowly, knowing from Edward's own lips the truth about his association with Lady Wickerston.

"But then I saw him myself one day, coming out of the Wickerston house. He looked…"

"Guilty?" suggested Georgiana.

"I suppose so, miss, but it was more than that. He looked around, checking if anyone could see him, I suppose, fair nervous but his face and his eyes…" Emily paused, trying to find the words. "White as a sheet, he was, strained, not like himself at all."

"Really?" said Georgiana. "When was this?"

"A few days before Lord Wickerston died." Emily paused and took a deep breath. "Defeated, that's how he looked, miss," said Emily. "Defeated."

"I see. Did he notice you, Emily?"

Emily shook her head. "Don't think so, Miss Georgiana.

Didn't seem to me he noticed anything, for all his checking along the road."

"Somehow I am not surprised." Georgiana sighed. This piece of information merely served to confirm what she already knew: that Edward's break with Lady Wickerston had not lasted, that he had been drawn back into his liaison with her. Could Edward really be so spellbound? Sufficiently under the woman's spell to... Georgiana resolutely pushed the thought away, and her tone grew brisk.

"Have you noticed anything else, Emily?

The maid shook her head. "Not really, miss. Like I said, I don't know Lady Wickerston's servants well. Anyway, I'm afraid other people's servants don't usually tell me very much because..."

"Because you don't tell them very much?"

Emily nodded, a slight smile appearing.

"I suppose that's to be expected," said Georgiana.

"There is a new maid at Lady Wickerston's, arrived recently."

"Oh?" A sudden thought occurred to Georgiana. "I understand the Wickerstons had a problem with rats in their cellar and Lady Wickerston sent someone to the apothecary for some arsenic to poison them. I don't suppose you know if she was the person?"

"I believe it was, miss. Bit fearful of the rats, she was."

"Did she see any?" asked Georgiana.

"I don't know." Emily tilted her head slightly. "Did you see any rats around during the fire?"

"No, I didn't notice any," responded Georgiana. "However, I suppose if they were in the cellar, they might have been killed."

"Perhaps. Though if they could get in, they might be able to get out as well. I would have thought a fire would send them running."

"Yes, I suppose it would, unless the arsenic had already despatched them."

"If her ladyship gave it to her husband, would she bother holding some back for the rats, assuming there really were any?"

"That's what I'd like to know. The maid would not expect Lady Wickerston to put down the poison herself. However, if there were no rats, surely one of the other servants would have been able to tell the girl that."

"If she was the one who put down the poison," said Emily slowly. She shook her head. "I don't know about that, miss. I can't think this maid would go near the cellar once the rats were mentioned to her. You said her ladyship had the poison, miss?"

Georgiana nodded. "She said she put it in a glass of her husband's wine."

"Well, that would be sure to get him," Emily observed.

Georgiana smiled. "One would imagine so. Emily, do you think you could speak to that maid? Find out a bit more about that arsenic, in particular what she did with it."

"Well, I could, miss, but you might be better to ask James." Emily grinned. "I believe she has a soft spot for him."

"Really? That is interesting. Does James return her regard?"

Emily shrugged. "I don't think so, she's a bit young. Mind, he doesn't discuss his lady-loves with me."

"No, I suppose he wouldn't," said Georgiana. "He may not thank you for volunteering him for this task."

"No, I suppose he won't," laughed Emily.

James, when the proposal was put to him on his return, looked balefully at his sister but expressed himself willing to help Georgiana in any way he could. Emily, for her part, stood with eyes down and hands piously folded, apparently unconcerned about any retribution her brother might wreak later.

The three were closeted in the morning room. Having learned from James, that, as far as he could tell, Edward Grey had not returned home, Georgiana told him of her brother's arrest and Lady Wickerston's confession. James looked very much shocked.

"Unfortunately, my sister-in-law came upon Lady Wickerston and me in the drawing room. It was rather awkward. Lady Wickerston departed a few minutes later."

"I see, miss," said James in a level tone. He frowned. "I beg your pardon, Miss Georgiana, but did you say her ladyship put the poison in a glass of wine?"

"That's what she told me," nodded Georgiana.

James continued to frown, his face an effort of concentration. Emily looked towards Georgiana.

"The thing is," said James slowly. "There was no glass near Lord Wickerston when Mr Lakesby and I found him on the night of the fire."

"What?"

"Are you sure?" asked Emily.

James glanced towards her disdainfully. "Of course I'm sure. Ask Mr Lakesby if you don't believe me."

"Of course we believe you, James," said Georgiana, casting a quelling look at Emily. "What exactly happened?"

"He was in the study. The door was locked, so we had to break it down. He was sitting at his desk, slumped forward."

"At his desk?" asked Georgiana. "It is difficult to imagine Lord Wickerston occupied by anything which would require a desk."

James gave a half smile. "As you say, miss. There was a glass on the floor, now I think of it. But," he continued, glaring at Emily in response to her look of triumph, "it was nowhere

97

near Lord Wickerston. It looked like it had fallen off a small table near the fireplace. It was on the hearthrug. His lordship couldn't have reached it from where he sat."

"How very odd," said Georgiana.

"Perhaps he drank it, dropped it and then collapsed in his chair and died," said Emily.

James shook his head. "It was a pale rug, big red stain on it. If he drank any, it couldn't have been more than a sip or two. Looked like most of the glass was emptied out."

"How much of the poison would it take to kill him?" inquired Emily.

"I don't know," said Georgiana. "I daresay a doctor could advise us. Possibly that friend of Mr Lakesby's, Dr Masters's brother, I'm sure he could find out. Or the surgeon who removed the bullet from my shoulder a few months ago."

Emily looked doubtful. "Difficult to ask a medical man how much arsenic would kill a person. They'd think you were planning a murder yourself."

"Well then, perhaps Dr Masters's brother is the better avenue. From what Mr Lakesby said, the doctor suspected Lord Wickerston had been poisoned, and his brother is something of a gossip."

"Will you speak to Mr Lakesby, then, miss?" asked Emily.

"Yes, I suppose that is the easiest way, though I can't do so immediately. At present, he is trying to find out my brother's situation in Newgate."

"Beg pardon, miss, but I can do that," offered James.

Georgiana looked at him in surprise. "Really?"

"I do know the place, miss. It would be easy enough to ask a few questions."

"Well, yes," said Georgiana doubtfully, recalling the eighteen months James had unjustly spent there for poaching. "It is just that, well…"

"Oh, it's not an experience I'd like to repeat," said James with a smile, apparently aware of what was in his mistress's mind. "But I'd be glad to use my knowledge to help your brother. At least it would be put to some good."

"Thank you, James," said Georgiana warmly. "I'm very grateful and I know my brother will be. My sister-in-law is beside herself with worry." She frowned. "I wonder if I should call on Lady Wickerston."

"But, miss, if it wasn't her ladyship who killed her husband..." said Emily.

"I know," said Georgiana. "But if she is telling the truth, she intended to. I would like to know more from her."

James spoke up, his own face a mask of concentration.

"Begging your pardon, Miss Georgiana, but how did the fire start?"

10

There was silence. Georgiana and Emily looked at each other. It seemed no one knew what to say.

"Couldn't it have been an accident?" said Emily.

"It could have been," said Georgiana, thinking back to her conversation with Mr Lakesby, "though it is rather a strong coincidence that it should occur at the time of Lord Wickerston's death."

Emily nodded.

"Lady Wickerston didn't mention it, miss?" asked James.

Georgiana shook her head. "No, but as I mentioned, we were interrupted." She frowned, thinking back to the night of the fire. She had been so concerned about raising the alarm that Lady Wickerston's reaction had not seemed important. As she recalled her arrival at Lady Bertram's house, Georgiana thought Lady Wickerston had looked shocked at the news of the fire, as had all Lady Bertram's remaining guests. However, Lady Wickerston had also seemed shocked when told of her husband's death, yet she had just confessed to killing him. Was she merely a consummate actress?

"Miss Georgiana?" Emily's voice prompted.

Georgiana roused herself from her reverie and smiled at the two servants, who were both watching her closely.

"I beg your pardon. I was just thinking."

"Yes, miss," said Emily. "Is there something you'd like us to do?"

"We need to know more," said Georgiana. "At present we have only speculation."

"Except for Lady Wickerston's confession," Emily pointed out.

"Yes, but if James is correct, that is not necessarily reliable," said Georgiana.

"No," said Emily, then fell silent.

James was frowning. "Even though her ladyship says she tried to kill him?"

Georgiana nodded. "If she put the arsenic in the wine glass as she said, it appears he could not have consumed it."

"A second glass?" said Emily. She glanced towards her brother. "Though someone would have had to get rid of it, if you and Mr Lakesby didn't see it."

James nodded.

"Perhaps," said Georgiana. "There may have been another purchase of arsenic. The apothecaries keep poison books, don't they?"

"Wouldn't they be under lock and key?" said Emily.

"It would come out for someone who needed to sign it," said Georgiana. She leaned confidentially towards James. "Tell me, have either of you noticed any rats in our cellar?"

He grinned. "Now you mention it, miss, I have heard a bit of scratching," said James.

"We'd best get something to get rid of them," said Emily.

"Excellent notion," Georgiana approved.

"Perhaps Emily had best go, Miss Georgiana," said James. "I assume you'd like me to get off to Newgate and see what can be done for your brother?"

"Yes, that should be done immediately, thank you, James. I must write a note to Mr Lakesby and let him know you intend to visit Newgate and that he needn't go to the trouble." Georgiana turned to Emily. "Do you mind going to the apothecary, Emily?"

"No, miss," said Emily woodenly.

Georgiana glanced from brother to sister and back. There was something they weren't telling her.

"What is it?" she asked.

"I'm sure Emily would have more success with the apothecary, miss," said James, a wicked gleam in his eye. "Old Mr Scott is a bit sweet on her."

"I see." Georgiana was not that well acquainted with him but she knew Mr Scott was sixty if he was a day. "Emily?"

"I'll manage him, miss." The look she cast her brother suggested he would also be subjected to her management.

Georgiana frowned, recalling something she had heard. "Mr Lakesby mentioned that the apothecary's name was Gregson," she said.

"He's Mr Scott's apprentice, I believe," said James.

"Oh, I see." Georgiana looked at James. "Is Tom in the kitchen?"

"I believe so, miss," said James. "I imagine Mrs Daniels had a bit of food for him."

"That's what I thought," said Georgiana.

Emily was shaking her head. "I've never known a boy who could eat so much."

Georgiana smiled. "Well, they didn't give him a lot in the Lucky Bell."

"Suppose not," Emily conceded, accepting her mistress's acquaintance with the highwaymen's tavern without question.

"Anyway," continued Georgiana, "send him to me when I've had a few minutes to write to Mr Lakesby."

The door opened and the solemn figure of Horton stood framed there. He addressed Georgiana.

"I beg your pardon, miss," said Horton. "Mrs Daniels would like to know if you will be dining at home this evening."

"Oh, yes. Thank you, Horton," said Georgiana. She had been so preoccupied with the events of the day that she had not noticed how far the hour had advanced. "By the way,

102

Horton, I have an urgent errand for James. I trust you can manage for a few hours?"

"Very good, miss," replied Horton.

As soon as the butler had departed, Georgiana pressed some money into James's hand, and the footman went to fetch his coat for his visit to Newgate. With James on his way, Emily returned to her duties while Georgiana went back to the morning room to write her note to Mr Lakesby. She apprised him of James's intention to visit Newgate to help Edward. She spent some minutes in thought as she considered how to word her request to approach his friend, Dr Masters's brother.

Georgiana was folding the paper when her page Tom appeared, waiting for his orders. Well scrubbed and well fed, he appeared a different boy from the urchin she had found at the Lucky Bell.

"Tom, I need you to take this note to Mr Lakesby's house right away. I have written his direction."

"Yes, miss." Tom took the note. He did not move.

"Is something wrong?"

"Beg pardon, miss, isn't that the man who could set the law on me?"

Georgiana understood. In Tom's previous encounter with Lakesby, he had been on the wrong side of the law. She did not think it at all likely Lakesby would hand Tom over to the authorities, but recalling his cow-handed attempt at highway robbery, she understood the boy's fear.

"I don't think you need worry, Tom. Mr Lakesby is unlikely to open the door himself. Besides, you are looking very different from the occasion when Mr Lakesby saw you. It is likely he would not recognise you."

Tom set off with chest proudly puffed out, looking pleased with himself. Georgiana smiled to herself, shook her head and went to her bedchamber to seek out Emily. Her own present inactivity irked her. It was time the Crimson Cavalier took some action.

Not for the first time, Emily seemed able to read her mistress's thoughts. Georgiana noticed a hint of suspicion in her eyes.

"Miss Georgiana…"

"There must be something I can do, Emily."

"Wait for James," said Emily promptly, smoothing the creases out of a morning dress.

Georgiana did not respond. There was a faraway look in her eyes as she contemplated what Edward would be experiencing in Newgate. She hoped his place in society would at least afford him a private cell, rather than the communal area shared with countless other prisoners, rats and other vermin. She recalled something the highwayman Harry Smith had once said to her about his own experience of prison; he had mentioned the bribing of a guard. No doubt it was difficult to depend on their all being equally corrupt, but it was unlikely they were well paid, so perhaps it would not be difficult to find one who was open to temptation. Armed with the right information, Georgiana might be able to buy Edward a few advantages. She glanced at the clock on the mantelpiece.

"James hasn't been away that long," said Emily. "He'll not delay."

"No, I know," said Georgiana. "But you know I dislike waiting around."

"Yes, miss, but you know it was sensible for James to go. He knows the place, he'll know who to talk to."

"True," said Georgiana. "At the same time, it must be difficult for him."

"He wouldn't have offered if he hadn't wanted to help," said Emily. "The best thing you can do is get ready for dinner.

James will come straight to you on his return."

Georgiana looked at the clock again. "I suppose so," she sighed. She grew thoughtful again.

"I wonder if one could obtain arsenic at the Lucky Bell," she mused.

"Miss Georgiana!" Emily sounded alarmed.

Georgiana smiled. "I'm sorry, Emily. You needn't worry, I'm not planning to do away with anyone. It just occurred to me that it could be a potential source."

"Have you ever seen Lady Wickerston there?"

"No, of course not." The very thought made Georgiana laugh out loud. "But she does have servants and friends. Besides," she pointed out, "I am not there every night."

"Let me talk to the apothecary before the Crimson Cavalier goes sniffing around the Lucky Bell," said Emily.

"There's no reason not to do both," said Georgiana. "I'd like to talk to Harry. He may be able to tell me something useful."

"About Lord Wickerston?" Emily looked puzzled.

"No, but he has also had a spell in prison, and unlike James he didn't patiently serve out his time – he bought his way out. Of course he was sentenced to hang, so one can't really blame him."

"Lord!"

Georgiana grew thoughtful again. "I'll wait for James's return but I'd like to go to the Lucky Bell in any case. I'd like to find out if Lord or Lady Wickerston were ever stopped on the road."

"Is that important?"

"It could be, depending on when, and what was found."

"Arsenic?"

"Yes."

"You think Lady Wickerston could have been carrying it around."

"It is possible. We don't know how long it is since she decided to kill her husband."

"Would a highwayman steal it?" asked Emily.

"Possibly. It would depend on the highwayman, whether he knew what it was and thought he could profit from it." She paused. "It wouldn't interest me. I suppose it could be sold, but I'd be concerned about what it might be used for. There's little point in getting some money to help someone in need if the item sold kills someone else."

"No, I suppose not," said Emily.

"We mustn't forget, it appears Lady Wickerston did not succeed in her attempt to kill her husband. So we will need to find out if anyone else purchased arsenic."

"Which could have originally come from her ladyship?"

"Possibly."

Emily's forehead creased. "If it had been bought legally, surely it would be noticed if there was a high demand in a short time. Wouldn't an apothecary be concerned if he was selling a lot?"

Georgiana shrugged. "Certainly I would expect a responsible one to be concerned. Although…" She trailed off as a thought came into her head.

Emily waited. Georgiana seemed to be weighing her words. "I have heard that occasionally certain items can be obtained from a back room for… favoured clients."

Emily's eyes widened. "Just like that?"

"Apparently," said Georgiana. "The law, such as it is, can't be everywhere. I believe Bow Street's priorities tend to be loss of revenue and property."

"I see," said Emily.

Georgiana checked the clock again. James seemed to have been gone a long time, though she knew it would probably take him a while to speak to the guards and find Edward, in addition to the journey back and forth to Newgate.

Emily watched the direction of her eyes. "Now you know how it is waiting for the Crimson Cavalier to return," she said.

Georgiana smiled. "Yes, Emily. It is one reason I detest waiting."

Georgiana went downstairs to dinner and slowly ate her solitary meal, anxious for James's return. She had left instructions that he was to be brought to her immediately, and as she started nibbling a piece of fruit the door opened.

James looked tired. He wore an air of harassment much removed from his usual calm demeanour.

"James!" Georgiana rose from her place instantly and went immediately to him. She motioned him to a chair and herself went to the tray on the side table and poured a glass of wine which she handed to him.

"Thank you, miss." He took a grateful drink.

Georgiana sat down, her eyes on James. She waited until he seemed more settled. James took another mouthful of wine, then looked up at Georgiana. He shook his head.

"I'm sorry, Miss Georgiana. It didn't go as well as I'd hoped."

"What happened?" she asked. "Did you see my brother?"

James drew in a breath, then nodded. "Yes, miss, I saw him.

"Is he all right?"

"Well enough. A bit drawn." James seemed to be struggling for words. "I couldn't get him out, miss. I'm sorry, I did everything I could think of. Spoke to the guard, even the chief jailer. They wouldn't release him."

"And Edward?"

James pressed his lips together. "He sends you his compliments, miss."

"His compliments?"

James nodded. "Yes, Miss Georgiana. He asked about Mrs Grey, was concerned that she was all right, but that was all."

"I don't understand."

"No, nor I, miss. I hope it wasn't out of place but I stopped at your brother's house to let Mrs Grey know, to save her worrying further."

"No, of course it wasn't out of place, James, it was very thoughtful, thank you. How did my sister-in-law seem?"

"Concerned, though she was grateful I went to tell her."

"I'm sure she was. Thank you, James."

James shrugged. "I wish I could have given her better news, miss, or taken your brother home."

"You did what you could," said Georgiana.

"He was in a cell on his own, miss," James offered by way of consolation.

"I see."

Georgiana took a deep breath and decided this was not the moment for discretion. "Did he mention Lady Wickerston?"

James shook his head. "No, Miss Georgiana. He didn't tell me anything. I expect he thought it wasn't my place."

"Perhaps," said Georgiana thoughtfully. "So he said nothing at all about… the reason for his arrest?"

"No, miss. I'm sorry. It's not very helpful."

"Please don't worry, James. I appreciate you making the effort and it is good to know he has his own cell."

"Yes, miss," said James impassively.

"Yes," said Georgiana, recalling James's own spell in prison. "Thank you for your help, James. Now you must go downstairs and get some supper; I'm sure you are hungry."

"Yes, miss. Thank you, Miss Georgiana."

Georgiana remained in her place at the dining table for some minutes after James's departure, pondering what he had told her. Was Edward trying to protect Lady Wickerston? Surely he would know how shaken Amanda was over his imprisonment; why would he add to that by choosing to remain in Newgate?

Georgiana considered James's observation and had to agree Edward would think it inappropriate to give details to her footman.

The shadows grew long as Georgiana continued to sit deep in thought. The parlourmaid came to clear her dishes, and not many minutes later, Emily came in search of her. Georgiana smiled as she entered.

"James told me he'd spoken to you, miss," said Emily. "Are you all right?"

"Yes, Emily," said Georgiana. "Thank you. I was wondering about my sister-in-law, though. Perhaps I should go to her."

"You can't go on your own at this hour," said Emily.

"No, I suppose not," said Georgiana. "I should have insisted she stay here."

"She wanted to go home," said Emily. "She'll have the children to think about."

"Yes, you're right, and I'm sure that will help." Georgiana paused, "It seems Amanda is surprisingly strong-willed."

"Yes, miss."

"I will call on her tomorrow," said Georgiana. "Right now, I must change."

11

Emily rolled her eyes. "Miss Georgiana."

"I know, Emily, I know. Come, let us discuss it upstairs." She picked up a branch of candles as she spoke and led the way up to her bedchamber. Emily remained silent until the door was securely closed behind them.

"I know what you're going to say, Emily."

"Do you, miss?" Emily's tone was disapproving.

Georgiana was already lifting the lid of the heavy wooden chest at the foot of her bed. Shirt and breeches were in her hand when a resigned Emily came to help.

"You'll get yourself hanged yet," muttered the maid, taking the clothes from her.

"Not tonight," said Georgiana in prosaic tones. She stood up and closed the chest. "In any case, it might be useful. If there are any passing travellers they might be willing to contribute to a needful cause." She went to her night table. The bits of jewellery she had taken from Sir Thomas Drysdale's niece lay there. "I'll see what Harry can offer for these. That young woman Sir Thomas dismissed from his household a few months ago might be glad of some help."

"The one with the child?" said Emily.

"Yes."

Emily was shaking her head. "Wasn't she another of the gentleman's 'nieces'?"

"I believe so," said Georgiana, engaged in buttoning her coat. She sat down on the bed as Emily approached with her boots.

"Be careful, won't you, miss?"

Georgiana looked at her maid in some surprise. Emily

always worried about her going out on the road but on this occasion she seemed to be more concerned than usual.

"Of course. You needn't fear, Emily. I don't intend to get myself arrested."

"Nor did your brother, I'm sure," said Emily, standing. "Nor mine."

Her cousin's absence from the house made Georgiana feel a little easier as she slipped quietly down the back stairs and out the door; it would be hard to manufacture a satisfactory explanation if she were to encounter Selina on one of her forays as the Cavalier. Saddling Princess in the dark always had an element of awkwardness about it but practice had accustomed Georgiana to the business. As long as everything was left in the same place she managed tolerably well, and she wore gloves to ensure her hands remained smooth and unmarked as befitted a lady.

The night was mercifully clear, and Georgiana led Princess slowly from the back of the house, keeping to shadowed areas to conceal them wherever she could. Only when she was sure she was out of sight and earshot of the houses did she mount; and even then she reined Princess in and continued to move slowly.

With an opportunity to reflect, Georgiana realised how worried she was about Edward's predicament. He was no weakling, but even in a private cell she could not imagine he would fare well. And if the worst were to happen, Amanda would be devastated.

Georgiana frowned. What reason did the authorities have for arresting Edward? Had he been seen in Lady Wickerston's company? Even if this were the case, Georgiana doubted it would be enough to take him to Newgate. Her blood ran cold at the thought of him in possession of the poison, or worse, purchasing it. Would he be so foolish?

111

The road was quiet and the slow clip-clop of Princess's hooves echoed loudly in Georgiana's ears through the silence of the night. There were no passing carriages as she continued on to the Lucky Bell, meeting point of highwaymen and footpads, whose proprietor, Cedric, had a gift for being selectively deaf, dumb and blind.

As usual the tavern was crowded, but Georgiana caught sight of her quarry at a small table across the room, deep in conversation with someone she did not recognise. Harry Smith raised his hand as he saw her. Still masked, she threaded her way across the room, receiving barely a glance from the other patrons. More than one was also masked, mainly around the eyes, which allowed for easier drinking. Georgiana found the unconventional atmosphere refreshing.

"Hello, lad," said Harry as she approached. He made no shift to stand, something else which quietly amused Georgiana. There was no reason he should, of course, since he believed her to be a young man.

"Harry." Georgiana gave his companion a brief nod of acknowledgement, receiving a gruff grunt in return as his head disappeared into his tankard.

"Have a seat, lad," said Harry, pulling out the chair next to him one-handed without rising. "Drink?"

Georgiana shook her head. Harry's companion rose, taking Harry's tankard and his own to the bar for replenishment. Georgiana took advantage of the moment and put her few trinkets on the table.

"Not bad," said Harry. "Bit gaudy but worth a bob or two."

Georgiana was pondering the incongruity of Harry's impeccable taste and eye for quality jewellery in one of such rough appearance when he suddenly looked up and grinned at her.

"Weren't that cove with all the nieces, was it?"

Georgiana stared in wonderment.

"How did you know?"

"Held him up once or twice myself. So did Len here." He gestured towards his returning friend, laden with refreshment.

The thought which occurred to Georgiana seemed to strike her companions simultaneously. "Paste?" she said, looking from one to the other.

Harry gave a crack of laughter.

"Not quality," said Len. "Never quality." He dived once more into his tankard. "Never got more than a couple of bob for anything I took from him."

"Not pieces he'd give to his loving wife," said Harry.

Georgiana shook her head, her own laughter suppressed for fear it would disclose her femininity.

"A waste of time, then?" she said.

"No, no," said Harry. "Still a couple of bob." He glanced towards Len. "Worth stopping the old cove just for the fun of it, eh, Len?"

"Oh, aye," said Len. "Different niece every time. Mayhap worth asking one day what he'd give for us not to send a note to his wife."

Harry shook his head. "Welcome to it, Len. Blackmail's not my game." He turned his attention back to Georgiana. "Want me to see what I can get for the gewgaws?"

Georgiana nodded, pushing the tawdry bits across the table to him. Even 'a couple of bob' would be useful to someone in need. The fact that she was able to live quite comfortably herself did not grant her the right to turn down whatever small amounts the Crimson Cavalier could obtain, when it could make a difference to someone struggling to survive on meagre means.

"Thank you, Harry." Georgiana pushed a coin across, nodding towards her compatriots' tankards.

113

"Much obliged, lad," said Len, scooping up the coin and the two tankards, now empty again. "One for yourself?"

Georgiana shook her head.

"The lad don't drink," said Harry. "Keeps a cool head." He turned back to Georgiana. "Little takings for you this time."

"It was the same night as that fire," said Georgiana.

"Ah," said Harry. "Bad for business, that."

"Yes," said Georgiana, interested to hear Harry's interpretation of the event. "I hear the house owner was killed. Had you ever come across him while you were working?"

"Once, if he's the bloke I'm thinking of. Nice wife, at least I suppose she was his wife – she was no fancy woman. He was drunk, threw some coins out the window, swore a bit." Harry shook his head. "In front of a lady like that."

Georgiana was amused at his disapproval. She suspected Harry had a straitlaced streak under the highwayman's exterior. There were times she wondered how he came to this occupation but it was not, of course, the accepted thing to ask.

"Told his wife to hand over her trinkets," Harry continued. "Quite rough tone he used. I didn't have the heart. She seemed more scared of him than of me. I thanked him, a bit snooty-like, and sent them on their way. Felt right sorry for the poor lady."

"I see," said Georgiana. "Did you at least get a decent haul of coins?"

Harry shrugged. "A few. Mostly scattered about the road, they were, couldn't find them all. Thought I might as well leave them for the next one working the High Toby and welcome." He turned to the returning Len. "You come across that cove killed in the fire?"

"What? The drunken nob?" said Len, setting down the two tankards with a slosh. "Stopped him once or twice. Never had anything worth much. Surprising, his lady looked a decent sort, nervous though."

Georgiana was not sure whether or not this was helpful. She felt sure the two highwaymen were telling the truth. She could not really imagine Harry wanting any involvement in dealing poisons, and though she was not acquainted with his friend, he struck her as a traditional highwayman, interested in the tangibles of money and jewellery.

Tossing another coin on the table, adjuring them to get themselves another drink, Georgiana rose to depart. As she turned, the two highwaymen's thanks in her ears, she was astonished to see Sir Thomas Drysdale's 'niece' walk through the door. A confident, perky girl, it was clear she had numerous acquaintances in the Lucky Bell. Georgiana's astonishment grew as she bounced straight over to where Harry and Len sat. She gave Georgiana a smile and a bright, "How'd ya do?" before her eyes alighted on the trinkets still on the table.

"'Ere, that's mine," she said.

"Your uncle give them to you?" asked Len.

Harry's hand was quicker than the girl's. "Now then, the lad got them fair and square."

The girl looked at Georgiana. "I suppose so," she said. "Do I get a share?"

"We'll see," said Georgiana.

The girl's face took on an aspect of surprise and dawning respect. "Much obliged. Nice job, by the way, though the old cove did complain the rest of the way. Wore me ear out."

"Sorry about that," said Georgiana.

"I hope he saw you safe to your door," said Len.

"Don't you be cheeky." The girl turned back to Georgiana. "I'm Polly. You'll be the Crimson Cavalier."

Georgiana nodded.

"Pleased to meet you. Not staying for a drink?"

"No. Business."

"Oh, well, maybe another time." Polly flounced down in the chair Georgiana had vacated and sent Len off to fetch her some refreshment. He obeyed, grumbling.

Harry shook his head, laughter in his voice. "It's always the same. The girls clap their daylights on the Crimson Cavalier and lose interest in the rest of us."

The irony of this was not lost on Georgiana, especially since her mask was firmly in place. Polly gave Harry's arm a playful slap.

"Don't you be cheeky either."

Georgiana judged it time to make her escape, which she did without further delay, giving her companions a wave as she went.

Heading into the open air to untether Princess, Georgiana was far from certain she had learned anything which could be of help in discovering Lord Wickerston's killer, interesting though the exchange may have been. She found herself wondering whether Polly had latched on to Sir Thomas as a possibly generous 'nob' who could show her a good time or whether she had gone to him deliberately, perhaps at the instigation of Len or Harry, to fleece him in return for finding only trashy items of jewellery on holding him up. This did not strike Georgiana as Harry's style. Polly's apparent interest in the Crimson Cavalier suggested she could be persuaded to tell the story but Georgiana's curiosity did not extend far enough to offer the price the girl might expect.

Riding Princess slowly back towards the road and home, Georgiana's reverie did not leave her oblivious to her surroundings, and within a few minutes, the slow clip-clop and rattle of horses drawing a carriage could be heard along the road. She pulled Princess back into the cover, waiting.

If there was an opportunity, she might as well take it. She already had embarrassingly little to offer the girl Sir Thomas Drysdale had turned out.

The elegant carriage progressed along the road at an even pace, and rumbled to a sudden, incongruously awkward halt when Georgiana pulled Princess out in front of the carriage.

She was startled to find she recognised the feminine voice which cried, "Oh, my!"

12

Georgiana's eyes looked straight into those of an equally startled Lady Wickerston. It was hard to tell which of them was the more surprised. For a brief moment, Georgiana wondered whether she had been identified, but she realised her ladyship was simply reacting in the normal way of stylish females held up by highwaymen. Suppressing the questions in her head, Georgiana got down to business.

"Your jewels, please, ma'am."

"I have very little," faltered her ladyship. "You see, I am in mourning." Her hand clutched at her wedding ring.

Georgiana's eyes followed. Could she? Dare she? Was it too heartless, a step too far? Her mind went to Edward in Newgate and the situation over Lady Wickerston's marriage.

"If you please, ma'am."

Lady Wickerston gave a small forlorn sigh, or was it one of resignation? Slipping off the ring, she placed it in the Crimson Cavalier's black-gloved hand. The masked figure gave a nod of thanks before riding off.

Why had she done it? Georgiana wasn't even sure herself. A part of her felt heartless, guilt-ridden. What was she even going to do with the thing? She didn't feel right passing it on to Harry as just another item of booty. Her thoughts returned to Edward; perhaps she could sell the ring on and use the proceeds to make his incarceration more tolerable? He would certainly disapprove of her actions in any event.

Coupled with this was the question of how much – or how little – Lady Wickerston's wedding ring had meant to her. Not only had she been unfaithful to her husband; she had even admitted that she tried to kill him. And given the difficulties her ladyship had experienced in her marriage, did she truly mourn her husband?

These thoughts were still in Georgiana's head sometime after her arrival home. Now clad in her nightgown, she sat at her dressing table, chin resting on hands, staring at the gold band which sat in front of her. She was aware of Emily's murmurs of disapproval as she put away the Crimson Cavalier's clothes.

"I know, Emily."

"Whatever are you going to do with it, miss?"

"I don't know. Perhaps I was hoping for some sort of clue," Georgiana said, picking the ring up to study it.

"A clue?" Emily stood behind her mistress, pausing in the act of folding the crimson scarf.

"Weak, I know," said Georgiana, peering inside the ring. "Nothing. No inscription." She turned it around in her fingers. "Not the finest gold but not poor quality."

"Is that what your friend Harry would say?"

Georgiana didn't answer but continued her inspection.

"I'm surprised she didn't lose it earlier if your friend held her up," commented Emily.

"I suspect that was down to Harry's chivalry," said Georgiana. "He said he felt sorry for her. Unless…" She paused, looking up thoughtfully as an idea occurred to her.

"Unless?"

Georgiana glanced towards her maid. "Unless he did take it, and she offered a reward for its return. I wonder…"

Emily looked horrified. "Oh, Miss Georgiana, you wouldn't?"

"Not money. Information." Georgiana stood up. "Perhaps her ladyship would be willing to offer a little more in exchange for the ring's return."

"Lord, miss, you'll end up in Newgate yourself yet," said Emily.

Georgiana shook her head. "I am more careful than you imagine, Emily," she said. "At present, the only time I plan to spend in Newgate is when I go to visit Edward. I know James went there so that I would have no need, but at this moment I see no other course open to me."

"I don't think it occurred to James that you would consider going yourself, nor to Mr Lakesby neither."

"To tell you the truth, I hadn't," said Georgiana, "but I should have. Edward is a very private man, very conscious of his dignity. Of course he wouldn't wish to discuss his situation with James and as for Mr Lakesby... Well, Edward doesn't like Mr Lakesby. He would probably refuse to see him, and would certainly hate to be beholden to him."

"Mr Grey won't be happy if you visit Newgate."

"Didn't you visit James when he was there?" asked Georgiana.

"That was different."

"I thought it might be," said Georgiana. "Why?"

"Well, for one thing, I had to tell him about our mother."

"Yes, of course," said Georgiana, remembering the brief illness and sudden death of their parent. "Even so, Emily, I think I must go. Edward can be very stubborn..."

"He's not alone in that," Emily interrupted under her breath.

"And," continued Georgiana, "I may have a better chance of getting him to talk than James or Mr Lakesby."

"But if the jailer won't release him anyway..."

"Well, we'll see what can be done. Perhaps if I can persuade Edward to explain things to me, I will have a better chance of explaining them to the jailer."

"Will you at least take James with you?"

"Certainly, if he is willing to make another visit there."

Georgiana was awake before dawn the next morning, and

when Emily came in with her chocolate she found her mistress searching her wardrobe for some practical attire. Putting down the tray, Emily waved Georgiana away and took over this task. Georgiana poured her chocolate from the long spouted pot and stood sipping it as Emily briskly ran her hand through the range of Georgiana's clothing. She selected a simple walking dress and woollen cloak, holding both out for her mistress's approval. Georgiana nodded and set down her cup, determined to dress and depart on her errand as soon as possible.

When the suggestion was put to James, he agreed to accompany Georgiana without hesitation, though he did look a little concerned at the prospect of her paying a prison visit. "Begging your pardon, Miss Georgiana, but I can't imagine Mr Grey will be very happy about you setting foot in that place."

"I know, James, and it's not that I don't appreciate your going yesterday, but I can't think what else to do. Since he couldn't be persuaded to tell you what happened, I see no alternative but to go and ask him myself."

James shrugged. "Well, he wouldn't talk to me, would he, miss? It's not really my business."

"Perhaps not, but these are hardly normal circumstances. My sister-in-law is extremely worried."

"Yes, miss."

"By the way, James, do you know if Tom managed to deliver my note to Mr Lakesby?"

"I believe so, miss. He didn't mention otherwise, and I didn't get the impression there'd been anyone else at the prison asking about your brother."

Georgiana nodded her thanks. James spoke again.

"Miss Georgiana, if you don't mind me suggesting, you might find it helpful to put up the hood of your cloak."

121

Georgiana followed his advice as the barouche began to slow on approaching the prison. The coachman pulled up outside Newgate, and Georgiana became aware of the odour of humanity emanating from its walls. The combination of stale sweat and cheap gin at such an early hour made her glad she had left the house before breakfast and unsure whether she could face any on her return home.

Springing down from the carriage, James scattered the cluster of ragged beggars approaching with hands held out, their collective pleas for help almost musical. He turned back to the carriage, a hand outstretched to help Georgiana alight. After a fleeting hesitation, he put a hand to her elbow to steer her through the soggy debris which made the walk to the gate a potentially slippery affair. The coachman raised his whip as they began to walk, and drove the carriage towards the side wall of the prison.

On the other side of the gate, James led Georgiana first to a small room which seemed to serve as an office. There was a table with an incongruous arrangement of papers scattered over its surface, along with a tin plate containing a large piece of bread and irregularly broken block of yellow cheese, its edges cracked and dry. Georgiana glimpsed a grey mouse sniffing at the food. It jumped off the table and fled across the floor to a hole in the wall with a speed she had never previously witnessed, apparently unnoticed by the burly unshaven individual who stood behind the table, taking a deep draught from a tankard. As they approached he lowered it and wiped his arm across his mouth.

"Oh, it's you again, is it?" he said on seeing James. He glanced towards Georgiana without interest, then blinked.

"This is Miss Grey," said James in a dignified tone. "Mr Edward Grey's sister. She would like to see Mr Grey."

"Oh, right. This way, then, miss." He fumbled with a ring of keys jangling at his waist.

Georgiana drew in a breath as the jailer walked past and instinctively fanned a hand in front of her face, making James smile. The stone corridor was cooler but its scent was no sweeter. It grew stronger as they passed a locked door from which emerged a cacophony of wails, groans and screeches. The jailer thumped the door as he passed, shouting something unintelligible to the occupants. The gesture sent a few more mice scuttling, and Georgiana caught sight of a rat running for cover in a gap between the stones.

Georgiana and James continued to follow the jailer along the musty corridor, their individual steps echoing differently on the stone floor. They arrived at a row of heavy doors. There was no sound from the rooms behind them: none of the noise and liveliness which characterised the one they had already passed.

The jailer stopped before one of the silent doors, and his fat greasy fingers fumbled through the large ring he carried as he selected a key. He bowed low to Georgiana and stepped back as the door opened. James dropped a couple of coins in his hand and nodded dismissal, then stood back to allow Georgiana to enter.

Edward stared in astonishment as his sister entered the sparse room. He rose slowly, his eyes fixed on the door.

"Georgiana!"

"Oh, Edward."

Edward looked past her, to where James was standing just outside the door. "Cooper, how could you?" he reproved.

"Don't blame James," said Georgiana. "I wanted to visit you, he was kind enough to accompany me."

"Well, I suppose I should be grateful for that, but he'd have done better to try to persuade you not to come at all."

Georgiana raised her eyebrows.

"I'm sorry, Cooper. I am grateful to you for escorting my sister." Edward bent down and kissed her on the cheek. "I am pleased to see you, Georgiana, but I wish you had not come to this place."

"Yes, well never mind that. How are you?" Georgiana studied his face; the skin was greyish and drawn, and dark circles surrounded his eyes.

"I'm well enough," he said. "How is Amanda?"

"Extremely worried. She has gone home."

"What? She's there on her own?"

"She was concerned about the children. I could hardly keep her with me by force," said Georgiana.

Edward sighed. "No, I suppose you couldn't. But what of you? I expect you too are still in your own home, by yourself?"

"Oh, for heaven's sake, Edward," said Georgiana in exasperation. "You are in prison. My living arrangements are hardly a matter of priority." She sat down on the hard-backed chair at the writing table and looked around the room. "Why, Edward?"

"What do you mean?" Edward sank down on the edge of the thin, narrow mattress. His fastidious gaze grew grim as it flickered over the bed and around the small room.

He glanced towards the cell door, and Georgiana followed the direction of his gaze. James had retreated to a discreet distance, and was out of earshot. She lowered her voice nonetheless.

"Edward, you must tell me. Why would the authorities think you had killed Lord Wickerston?"

Edward rose to his feet. "You shouldn't be here, Georgiana."

"Yes, yes, we've established that. But neither should you."

Edward looked at her. Georgiana held his gaze steadily.

His eyes dropped first, and he sighed and sank back down on to the bed.

"Now, will you tell me what happened?" Georgiana asked gently. When he did not speak, she continued, "Lady Wickerston has told me she killed her husband."

Edward had been sitting with his head lowered, his eyes focused on the ground. He looked up at this.

"What?"

Georgiana nodded. "Yes. She came to visit me."

"I don't understand."

"Neither did I," said Georgiana in a prosaic tone. "She said she couldn't live with what she'd done. I am not sure why she felt a need to tell me, though." She paused, considering how best to phrase her next sentence. "Amanda came in while she was there."

Edward groaned and dropped his head in his hands, shaking his head.

"Quite," said Georgiana.

"Amanda must hate me."

"No," said Georgiana. "In fact, she is very worried about you."

Edward looked up again. "She is?"

Georgiana rolled her eyes. "I have already told you so."

Edward appeared dumbfounded. Wonder dawned on his face.

"I don't deserve such concern."

"Yes, well, never mind that now. Why are you here, Edward? Are you protecting Lady Wickerston?"

"She didn't kill him," said Edward. "She couldn't have. It's not in her nature."

"I don't know about that," said Georgiana, "but I do know Lady Wickerston wasn't responsible for the death of her husband."

Edward looked closely at his sister. Scepticism and a hint of wariness showed through his harrowed expression.

"Oh?"

"It's quite true," came a voice speaking pleasantly from the doorway.

Brother and sister turned in unified surprise to see Mr Lakesby framed on the threshold. He strolled in, smiling affably and looking from one to the other.

"Your servant, Grey. Ah, Miss Grey, I am much obliged for the message you sent with… your page, wasn't it?"

Georgiana thought she detected an edge to his voice, as though he were not pleased to see her here. Very likely he wasn't but she could not worry about that now.

She inclined her head. "Good morning, Mr Lakesby."

Edward was less welcoming. He rose stiffly from his make-shift seat on the narrow bed and stood rigid. "What are you doing here, Lakesby?"

"Visiting you, my dear fellow," Lakesby drawled. His eyes took in the details of the cell. "Not quite to your usual taste, Grey."

Edward's face darkened. "If you've just come to amuse yourself, you can get out," he said savagely.

"On the contrary, Grey, I came to offer my help."

"Did you indeed?" said Edward with awful sarcasm. "Well, Lakesby, I am very much obliged, but it's not necessary. Might I suggest you take your offer of help and…"

"Edward!"

Having heard a selection of colourful language in the Lucky Bell, Georgiana was less concerned about the words Edward had been about to use than the fact that he had so far forgotten himself that he was ready to give vent to it in front of her. Her interruption seemed to recall him. He glanced towards her and begged pardon. Facing Lakesby, Edward drew in a breath

126

and spoke with more dignity.

"As I said, Lakesby, I am obliged to you for the offer but there is no need. This matter is not your concern."

"True," said Lakesby, flicking his eyes towards the scratched table, apparently debating whether or not to lay down his gloves. He decided not. "If you choose to go to the gallows over your *mesalliance*, that is quite your own affair."

Edward stiffened further. "Pray do not concern yourself. There is no likelihood of that."

Lakesby continued as if he had not spoken, "However, it does seem a trifle unkind to make a widow of your wife and orphans of your children. As I'm sure your sister has already told you, your wife is very distressed by this business. I am not well acquainted with Mrs Grey, but I do hold her in high esteem. She paid me the compliment of requesting my help. While I am not normally of a philanthropic nature, I feel honour bound to make some attempt to justify your wife's faith in me."

Edward seethed throughout this speech. When Lakesby fell silent he seemed unable to speak. Georgiana looked from one man to the other.

"Why don't you sit down, Edward?" She gave a quick glance towards the cell door.

"You need not worry about your footman, Miss Grey. He has gone to speak to the guard."

Her eyes flickering back to the door, Georgiana nodded then returned her attention to her brother. He remained standing but looked calmer.

"What happened, Edward?" Georgiana asked.

Edward looked at her in open astonishment.

"I don't know what you mean, Georgiana. This is all a foolish mistake."

Georgiana frowned. She did not speak immediately, but

spent a few moments trying to fathom Edward's attitude. She was disinclined to take as light a view of the matter as he appeared to. She looked pointedly around the cell, then back at Edward, one eyebrow raised.

"A mistake?"

"Certainly," Edward said. "I believe the authorities imagine that since I was acquainted with Lord and Lady Wickerston –"

"A particular friend?" Lakesby interrupted.

Edward ignored him and continued, "They thought it possible I might know something about the accident."

Georgiana could not believe her ears. Did Edward really think Lord Wickerston's death was an accident?

"I would hardly expect you to be locked up if that were the case," said Georgiana. "However, Lord Wickerston's death was not an accident. He was murdered."

"Of course it was an accident," said Edward. "Murdered, indeed! He died in the fire. It was a shocking accident and quite dreadful, but it could not have been anything more. I beg you will cease any talk of murder, Georgiana. It can only cause trouble and will be extremely distressing for Lady Wickerston. I do not intend to fuel such distasteful speculation by adding to it. The truth will be discovered soon enough."

Both of Edward's visitors stared at him. Could he could really be so naïve, or did he harbour an excessive faith in the justice system, bordering on overconfidence?

It was Lakesby who spoke.

"Grey, if you are trying to protect Lady Wickerston, it is not necessary. Her ladyship was not responsible for the death of her husband."

Georgiana looked intently at Lakesby. "How do you know?" she inquired.

Lakesby glanced towards Georgiana then back to Edward. "My understanding is that her ladyship could not have had the opportunity."

"What do you mean?" Georgiana was puzzled. She had not been able to speak with Lakesby since James had told her about the position of the wine glass on the floor of Lord Wickerston's study. It seemed unlikely that James would discuss it with anyone else – especially Lakesby.

Lakesby's hesitation was fleeting. "Lady Wickerston was not at home on the afternoon of the day her husband died." He paused. "Is that not correct, Grey?"

Edward made no answer.

Georgiana looked from one to the other, seeking an answer.

"Edward? How can you know this? Where was she?" she demanded.

Lakesby's eyes were fixed on Edward. "She went to Brooks's in search of your brother. Isn't that true, Grey?"

"What?" Georgiana's eyes widened.

Edward said nothing.

"Surely they would not let her in," Georgiana said.

"They did not," Lakesby responded, his eyes still on Edward. "I believe your brother escorted her away. Unfortunately, the mere fact of her arrival at the front door was enough to raise comment."

Georgiana looked towards Edward, who still sat silent.

"I don't believe this," she said. "Did Lady Wickerston tell you that she had killed her husband?"

"No, of course not," Edward snapped.

"There's no 'of course' about it, Edward," said Georgiana. "After all, she did tell me –"

"That she'd killed her husband?" asked Lakesby in astonishment.

Georgiana nodded.

"Unbelievable." Lakesby shook his head. "Is that why she called on you yesterday?"

"Yes," said Georgiana. She continued to recount the incident, attempting to forestall questions from Edward about how Lakesby could know who was calling on her. "Lady Wickerston told me she had poisoned a glass of her husband's wine with arsenic."

"There was no wine glass within reach of Wickerston when we found him," said Lakesby.

"Yes, James has already told me that," said Georgiana. "He also mentioned that wine had been spilt on the hearthrug, and that it appeared to be the entire contents of the glass."

Lakesby nodded. "Yes, I can agree with that. The wine stain was all in the one spot, not splashed or trailed across the floor as one would expect if he had drunk some of it and dropped it."

"Yes. If he had dropped the glass, it would hardly have rolled so far away from his chair," said Georgiana thoughtfully. She looked up at Lakesby. "What about the fire? Had it caused any damage which could have been misleading?"

Lakesby shook his head. "The fire hadn't reached that room by then. That was why your footman and I thought we might be able to save him."

Georgiana looked at her brother.

"What happened that afternoon, Edward? Where did you take Lady Wickerston?"

Edward looked haughtily at her.

"Pray don't tell me this is not a fit subject for discussion with me," said Georgiana. "You are in prison, accused of murder. This is no time for social niceties. You could hang."

"Really, Georgiana, this is quite distasteful. Where is James? It is time he escorted you home." Edward looked towards the cell door.

"Distasteful?" Georgiana could hardly believe her ears.

"I will be glad to escort your sister home when she is ready," said Lakesby. "However, I suggest you do her the courtesy of treating her as the intelligent lady she is, not some feather-brained, missish creature just out of the schoolroom. I can understand that you do not wish her to linger in this environment, but I must assume she has come here in an endeavour to help. I would advise you to cease wasting time with pompous outbursts which accomplish nothing."

Edward's face developed a puce tinge. He looked ready to call Lakesby out. Georgiana stared at him in open astonishment for a moment before rousing herself to prevent the two men coming to blows. She saw James near the doorway and rose to her feet.

"Thank you, Mr Lakesby. However, I am sure there is no need for you and my brother to argue." Georgiana tactfully forbore to mention the enmity she knew to already exist between them. Her eyes met James's, and she was relieved to see him nod and withdraw, though she knew he would remain within earshot in case she needed him. Her gaze returned to Lakesby and Edward.

"Mr Lakesby, there is another chair here. Why don't you sit down?" Her eyes quelled any objection Edward might have contemplated.

Lakesby glanced at her; he hesitated briefly since she made no shift to sit down herself, then he shrugged and followed her suggestion.

"Now," Georgiana continued, "this is a difficult situation. Edward, as Mr Lakesby has said, we are both here to try and help you. It is perfectly true that I can think of more pleasant places to spend a morning, as I'm sure Mr Lakesby can; and James, I know, has no desire whatever to be here."

"No," said Edward in a subdued tone.

"However, you are not helping yourself," she said.

Edward's manner and expression remained stiff.

"Are you trying to protect Lady Wickerston?" Georgiana persevered.

"Lady Wickerston did not kill her husband," Edward stated with dignity. "You may also accept my word that I did not. That will become clear when the matter is fully investigated."

"What about Amanda?" said Georgiana. "Do you think it's fair to let her worry while you remain here?"

"I think you should go."

Edward's tone was quiet but Georgiana knew her brother well, and perceived the thread of stubbornness underlying his words. She knew he would brook no argument. She looked at Lakesby in exasperation. He jerked his head towards the door. Georgiana smiled and gave a small nod.

"Very well, Edward," she said as she rose, drawing on her gloves. "But please give some thought to what I have said. It's not just yourself you have to think about; you have a family to consider. And I don't mean only your wife and children."

Edward looked up at this. Georgiana smiled. "I think I should miss your nagging if you were to hang. Goodbye." She bent and kissed his cheek before turning to leave.

"Georgiana."

Georgiana paused on the threshold.

"Thank you," said Edward stiffly. "I do appreciate your concern. But I think it would be better if you did not come here again. Goodbye."

13

James had fetched the guard who locked the cell, and the jangling of his keys echoed through the dank stone corridor. No one spoke as they made their way slowly towards the front gate; the only sounds were the guard's choking cough and the rusty metallic rattle of the keys against his jerkin as he walked.

It was James who broke the silence. "Beg pardon, miss, but since Mr Lakesby is here, I wondered if it would be convenient for him to escort you home. I have some business of my own which will detain me here for a little while."

"Here?" said Georgiana. A flicker in James's eyes warned her not to pursue it. "Yes, of course, if Mr Lakesby has no objection." She looked at him inquiringly.

"Not at all," said Lakesby. "I came on horseback, so perhaps you would you be good enough to bring my mount back for me, Cooper? He's tethered near your carriage. I left your coachman chasing those wretched urchins away from him."

James nodded and took his leave. Georgiana raised her eyebrows, surprised at Lakesby's willingness to entrust his precious horseflesh to someone else's servant. As she and Lakesby walked out of the prison, she caught sight of her footman in the doorway of the guard's room, accepting a glass of dark liquid.

Emerging into the morning air, Lakesby wordlessly offered Georgiana an arm, which she accepted willingly to help her negotiate the slippery cobbles. Unidentifiable refuse clung to the street, making the business of walking something of a challenge. Picking her way through the debris, Georgiana's eye was caught by a familiar face, its owner pushed into the back of a plain wooden cart, shafts held by a tired looking horse.

"A friend of yours?" came Lakesby's voice.

Georgiana looked towards him. "I beg your pardon?"

"The road to Tyburn." Lakesby was dry, unemotional.

Georgiana did not answer, looking back towards the cart. The individual she recognised from the Lucky Bell was bound securely, hands tied in front, a resigned expression on his face. She recalled her highwayman friend Harry Smith once telling her the nubbing-cheat was there for everyone in the end. It could easily be Harry on that cart, or even herself.

Georgiana was acutely aware of the incongruity of the situation when she arrived at her own carriage and her smartly dressed coachman sprang down to open the door for her. Georgiana thought he was glad to leave, though his manner betrayed no opinion on the subject. Lakesby handed her up, and immediately stepped in behind her. She thanked him but received no response. It was not until the wheels had begun to roll that he spoke.

"I had not expected to see you there." His tone was wooden, conveying neither opinion nor emotion. Georgiana sensed rather than heard the disapproval in his voice.

"It had not originally been my intention," said Georgiana, "but I gather Edward was somewhat reticent when James visited him."

"Yes."

Georgiana stole a sideways glance at him. "And you, Mr Lakesby? I had thought my note would save you the inconvenience of visiting Newgate."

"It occurred to me that your brother might not be very forthcoming with your footman."

"I see. You believed you might be more successful?" she inquired.

The look he cast her was pure ice.

"As you saw."

They travelled in silence for some minutes. Lakesby sighed. "What do you propose to tell your sister-in-law?"

"I don't know. I can't think what to do for the best." Georgiana smiled humourlessly. "I suppose I should go to stay with her."

"Would that curtail your activities?" Lakesby asked, the barest hint of a grin curving his mouth.

Georgiana ignored the comment.

"I don't know what Edward is thinking. He doesn't even seem at all concerned about Amanda and the children."

"No." Lakesby was thoughtful. "There is another possibility, which may not have occurred to you." He spoke slowly.

Georgiana looked towards him, her face questioning.

Lakesby drew in a breath. His voice was low. "Edward may be guilty."

Georgiana's eyes widened. The exclamation which sprang to her lips was held in check only by the presence of the coachman.

"You're not serious?"

"I have no wish to offend," said Lakesby.

"Edward?"

"I grant you it is out of character. But surely we cannot ignore the possibility."

Georgiana stared ahead of her. Her immediate instinct was to refute the suggestion, astonished that it could even occur to Lakesby, amazed that he had voiced it. Yet there were many aspects of Edward's behaviour which had taken her by surprise of late. She sat in silence, mulling over Lakesby's words.

"I beg your pardon," he said, breaking the charged silence. "I realise it is not something you will wish to hear and is obviously quite improper of me to raise the subject."

"Yes," said Georgiana, hardly taking in his attempt at retraction. "That is… I don't know. What if…?"

She bit her lip, and their eyes met. The notion hung in the silence between them.

"Tell me about Lady Wickerston's visit," he said suddenly.

"It was quite brief. My sister-in-law was preparing to return home, and came upon us in the drawing room."

"I see."

Georgiana nodded. "Yes. Lady Wickerston seemed quite distressed. She said she needed to confide in someone about what had happened. I gather it was preying on her mind."

"Understandable."

"Yes. She told me she and her husband had had – difficulties."

Lakesby nodded.

"Apparently, things were growing quite bad for her," said Georgiana.

"I can believe that," said Lakesby. "Did she tell you very much?"

Georgiana shook her head. "No, nothing in detail, though, of course, that would hardly be proper. She did say he was cruel and that she was afraid. I gather it was growing unbearable."

"It must have been."

Georgiana sat silent, thoughtful as she considered Lady Wickerston's situation. "She must have been very desperate, to take such action." Georgiana's voice was quiet, almost distant. She looked up suddenly. When she spoke again, her tone was brisker. "Emily is going to visit the apothecary."

"Is she unwell?" Lakesby looked puzzled about the abrupt change of subject.

"I understand there's been some scratching in the cellar. We thought it might be worth purchasing something in case there are rats."

Lakesby looked even more confused.

"I understand she will have to sign the Poison Book," Georgiana continued. "Fortunately she is quite well educated; she reads and writes very well."

"I see." Enlightenment dawned on Lakesby's face. "I'm sure that must be very useful."

"Yes."

"Can you trust her?"

"Of course."

Lakesby's eyes narrowed, his expression thoughtful as he looked at Georgiana. She smiled, and made no attempt to elaborate on what she had already divulged.

"You think she will learn anything helpful?" Lakesby inquired.

"She may," responded Georgiana. "Lady Wickerston was very open in what she told me. Yet if she is not responsible, the end result was the same. I can only conclude that someone else obtained a quantity of the same substance. Or that Lady Wickerston had a generous supply, and it was used by someone else as well."

"With or without her knowledge?"

Georgiana looked sharply at him.

"It would have to be someone in a position of remarkable trust or intimacy," said Lakesby slowly. "A family member for instance. Or a lover." He cast a glance towards her to determine her reaction.

"She may have disposed of it carelessly," said Georgiana, "or entrusted its disposal to someone else."

"Yes," said Lakesby. "Someone who may have had a different notion of disposal."

They had by this time arrived outside Georgiana's front door. It was opened almost immediately as the carriage drew to a stop. Horton stood waiting. Lakesby sprang down as the carriage reached a standstill, and stretched up a hand to assist Georgiana.

"Have you breakfasted, Mr Lakesby?" she asked as she stepped down, recalling the impropriety of such an invitation as soon as the words left her lips.

The ghost of a smile flickered across Lakesby's face, his eyes moving fleetingly towards the waiting Horton then back to Georgiana.

"Yes, thank you, Miss Grey, but please don't let me detain you from your own."

"Oh, Georgiana!"

The voice which came from the direction of the front door was as familiar as it was unexpected. The mousy-haired figure of Georgiana's cousin, Miss Selina Knatchbull, came rushing down the stairs as swiftly as her dignity would allow. Georgiana was speechless with astonishment; she had understood that her cousin's return home would be delayed by her friend's continuing illness. She found herself submitting to an anxious embrace, then Selina stepped back, studying her intently.

"Oh, my poor dear Georgiana. How dreadful! How absolutely dreadful for you."

"What? Selina, what are you doing here?" said Georgiana. "I beg your pardon, I am glad to see you, of course, but I thought your friend was still quite unwell."

"Dear me, yes, yes, but when I heard what had happened, well, I just couldn't stay another minute. Good morning, Mr Lakesby."

"Good morning to you, Miss Knatchbull."

"You need not worry about Hetty," said Miss Knatchbull, holding up a hand. "I took the liberty of engaging a nurse. I knew you would wish it. My place is here, at your side."

The disclosure that she was apparently expected to pay for

a nurse to attend someone she had never laid eyes on did nothing to alleviate Georgiana's exasperation. She caught a hint of amusement in Lakesby's eyes. Ignoring it, she focused on Selina. "Yes, well, let's go inside. We can't talk out here."

"There's something else." Selina adopted a confidential tone. She cast a sideways glance in Lakesby's direction. "You have a visitor."

"What?" said Georgiana. "At this hour? Who is it?"

"Sir Anthony Dixon," whispered Selina. "He said he was acquainted with you. He seems very distressed, or of course I should never have presumed…"

"On reflection, Miss Grey, I would be glad to join you for some breakfast," said Lakesby, "assuming your kind invitation is still open?"

"Yes, of course," said Georgiana, relief outweighing her awareness of the solecism she was committing.

Selina looked horrified but said nothing. Georgiana walked up the stairs to the front door, followed by the scurrying, nervous figure of her cousin and the relaxed, cool one of Lakesby. Georgiana looked inquiringly at Horton.

"The breakfast parlour, miss," responded Horton. "I took the liberty of offering your visitor some coffee."

"Thank you, Horton. By the way, James has some other business to deal with and will be a little delayed."

"Very good, miss."

"Georgiana, do you think…?"

But Georgiana was not paying attention. She walked towards the breakfast parlour with an anxious Selina close in her wake. Lakesby casually wandered behind, wearing an expression of light amusement.

Sir Anthony stood as Georgiana entered the room, but the greeting on his lips seemed to die as he became aware that she was not alone. He looked taken aback and responded rather cursorily to Lakesby's salutation and Miss Knatchbull's fussing and offers of further refreshment. Georgiana stood silent until her cousin had completed her ministrations, then smiled and begged her unexpected guest to resume his seat. This he did with only the slightest hesitation, casting his eyes yet again towards the other occupants of the room. Waiting only until both Georgiana and Selina had seated themselves, Lakesby followed suit.

"I must beg pardon for intruding on you so early, Miss Grey," began Sir Anthony. "Perhaps you have other plans?" His glance fell again upon Lakesby.

"Not at all," said Georgiana.

"I was just escorting Miss Grey home from a call we had both made to the same acquaintance," said Lakesby.

"So early?" squeaked Selina.

"A friend who is in some difficulties," said Georgiana.

"Oh. Then perhaps I shouldn't…" Sir Anthony looked uneasy.

"Please do not concern yourself, Sir Anthony," said Georgiana. "What can I do for you?"

After another brief hesitation, Sir Anthony continued, "It's my sister. I believe she came to see you yesterday?"

Georgiana nodded. "Yes. Is everything all right?"

Sir Anthony shook his head. "No. That is…" He drew a deep breath. "There is no easy way to say this. My sister has tried to kill herself."

The company fell silent. All eyes were on Sir Anthony.

Selina rose to her feet. "Let me ring for some tea."

"Not now, Selina." Georgiana's eyes never left Sir Anthony's face.

"But, Georgiana, I'm sure Sir Anthony –"

"Not now."

Cowed, Miss Knatchbull returned to her seat.

"How is she?" asked Georgiana. "Please tell us what happened."

Sir Anthony ran a hand through his hair. "She swallowed something, a sleeping draught, laudanum, I'm not sure. In any case, she took too much of it. We were lucky to find her in time."

"Are you sure it was not an accident?" asked Lakesby gently.

Sir Anthony shook his head. "No. She – she wrote a note saying how sorry she was, and asking me to thank our aunt and her acquaintances for their kindness. I don't understand any of this." He looked at Georgiana. "I'm so sorry, I know this is an imposition, but I needed to speak to you. You saw my sister yesterday; did she say anything which might lead you to suppose she'd do... something like this?"

Georgiana hesitated. Her glance at Lakesby was fleeting and, she hoped, not noticeable. She studiously avoided his eye.

"No, Sir Anthony. She was very distressed over the circumstances of her husband's death, of course, but I never imagined she would attempt to take her own life. I trust she is in no danger now?"

"Thank you, no. She is resting. My aunt is distraught. She blames herself, thinks she didn't keep a close enough watch on Theresa."

"Oh, I'm sure that's not true," said Selina.

"No, of course, not," said Sir Anthony. "In fact, if anyone is to blame, it must be me. I should have been more vigilant. I know what a difficult time she has had."

"You could not have predicted something like this," said Lakesby. "No one could."

"Of course not," said Georgiana. "It is no one's fault."

"Perhaps not," said Sir Anthony doubtfully. "Although I knew of her situation. I should have done something."

The door opened and the parlourmaid entered, bearing a large tray of silver dishes, from which emanated the aromas of a substantial breakfast. She placed it on the sideboard and left the room, returning after a few moments with a pot of tea and another of coffee which she set down on the table.

The girl took silverware for two additional place settings from the tray, and looked at her mistress for confirmation that these were to be set on the table for her visitors. Georgiana nodded and dismissed the maid.

No one moved after the parlourmaid closed the door behind her. It seemed the aroma of eggs, ham, fresh bread and fruit preserve was insufficient to tempt anyone from their seat. Miss Knatchbull hunched in her chair with hands clasped, her tentative glance flickering between Georgiana and the teapot. Georgiana took the hint.

"May I offer you gentlemen some refreshment? Selina, would you be kind enough to pour?"

Selina obeyed with alacrity but before she had time to do more than set out the cups, Sir Anthony protested that he had already taken up too much of their time. Selina's solicitous nature would have none of it. She insisted a hot drink was just the thing he needed, and the polite argument which ensued came to an end with Selina serving coffee to the two gentlemen and passing a cup of tea to Georgiana. Each thanked her, and sipped their steaming beverages in pensive silence. Still no one showed interest in the food, which remained under its covers.

"Are you certain your sister will make no further attempts?" said Lakesby eventually.

"I am not certain of anything," said Sir Anthony. "I would not have believed... My aunt is sitting with her now. I think she is afraid to leave Theresa alone. Dr Masters has seen her; it is his view that she needs rest more than anything."

"As must you," chipped in Selina. "I'm sure this has all been a terrible strain."

"Oh, I am well enough," said Sir Anthony. "But thank you for your concern, Miss Knatchbull," he continued hastily, lest his dismissive tone sounded uncivil. "We were fortunate to find her before... She had gone to lie down. If Mr Morris hadn't called, we would not have disturbed her and might not have discovered her in time."

"I see," said Georgiana.

"I must go," said Sir Anthony. "I have trespassed on your time long enough." He rose. "Thank you for the coffee, and for your concern. I do appreciate your kindness. It is so difficult to know what to do for the best."

"Do please let us know if there's anything we can do to help," said Georgiana.

"Thank you," Sir Anthony responded.

"I'll bear you company, if you've no objection," said Lakesby, also standing. "I must beg your pardon, Miss Grey, but I have recalled a prior engagement. I have arranged to breakfast with my friend Alfred at Brooks's."

"Of course," said Georgiana.

After the gentlemen had departed, Georgiana remained seated for some moments, lost in thought. Selina perched on the edge of her own chair, looking uncertainly at Georgiana. Finally she spoke in a timid voice.

"Georgiana, if you don't mind, I'll just help myself to a little bread and butter, just to go with the tea, you know."

"What? Oh, yes, of course, Selina, please do."

"And perhaps just the tiniest portion of this excellent ham, since Cook has gone to the trouble."

"Yes," said Georgiana, still abstracted.

"It's so difficult to know what is proper under such trying circumstances," said Selina.

"I don't think there are any rules of propriety regarding a suicide attempt," said Georgiana, rising and making her own way across the room to inspect the breakfast fare. "And there really isn't anything we can do at present. I'm sure Lady Wickerston's brother will tell us if we can help."

"Yes, I imagine so," said Selina, looking shocked at her cousin's use of the word suicide. "But there are moral rules about… such things. The Church frowns upon it."

"True but we need not concern ourselves with that," said Georgiana, to her cousin's horror. "I don't propose to tell the bishop and I don't imagine Mr Lakesby or Lady Wickerston's family will. I suggest you don't mention it either."

"Oh, no, no, no, I should not dream… It is not my place…"

"By the way," said Georgiana, having made her selection of ham, eggs, devilled kidneys and bread, "what did bring you home so early, Selina? You were not quite clear on the subject."

Selina looked shocked. "Why, my dear Georgiana, the news about Edward."

"What news about Edward?" asked Georgiana cautiously.

"Why, that he was in prison, of course."

Georgiana was surprised to learn that this news had reached Selina's ears.

"Did Amanda write to you?" If this had been the case, the letter must have gone by express post.

"No, Georgiana. It was in the newspaper."

14

Further questioning over the breakfast table elicited from Selina the information that a small item had appeared in the newspaper delivered early that morning to her friend's house. It reported that a death which had been thought an accident now appeared to have happened in suspicious circumstances. A certain Mr G--- had found himself in trouble with the law and had been placed under lock and key pending a trial.

Georgiana groaned. Her experience of the process of law did not lead her to hope that matters would turn out well for her brother. And now, as if the circumstances in which they were all embroiled were not more than enough to deal with, there would be a scandal, something Edward abhorred above all things.

After they had breakfasted, Selina went to her room to unpack. Georgiana remained seated at the table, trying to make sense of what she had learned this morning. The maid came in to clear away the dishes and, if she was surprised to see her mistress still sitting there, she was well enough trained to conceal it when Georgiana signalled her assent to continue.

"Here you are, Georgiana." Selina fluttered back into the room. The newspaper was clutched in her hand, clearly folded over to the page of interest.

Georgiana stifled a groan as Selina handed her the paper, pointing at the offending item with her forefinger. Georgiana's eyes flickered briefly to the maid, who was still clearing the table. She seemed fully occupied by her task and gave no sign of interest, but Georgiana suspected Selina's excitement would have pricked the girl's curiosity. She accepted the newspaper with a sigh, and read with Selina standing behind her, peering over her shoulder.

Lord Wickerston was not mentioned by name anywhere but the allusion to the fire made it clear that it was his death to which the article referred. Georgiana was a great deal more disturbed to note that Mr G--- was described as a former magistrate. No one of Edward's acquaintance reading this could imagine it to be anyone else.

"Thank you, Selina," said Georgiana, maintaining an even tone, but not without a struggle. "Why don't you go and finish your unpacking?"

Selina's disappointment was plain; clearly she had hoped to discuss the article with her cousin. However, since Georgiana refused to be drawn, there was nothing for her to do but follow her cousin's suggestion. She murmured her assent and left the newspaper with Georgiana.

Georgiana wondered what evidence the authorities must have if it was considered sufficient to bring Edward to trial. Surely he could not have confessed to a crime he did not commit? The position in which this would put Amanda and their children was quite unthinkable. While they would certainly not be left to starve, they could hardly remain untouched by the scandal. If Edward were to hang, it was certain they would become social outcasts. Georgiana was less concerned for herself; she could weather the storm. But Amanda's social position formed the very bedrock of her life, and she was astonished that Edward seemed not to have considered this.

His silence was not helping. Niggling at the back of her mind was Lakesby's suggestion that Edward could be guilty.

Georgiana's instinctive reaction to this was to reject it out of hand. Edward was not a killer. Yet what was he doing, sitting in Newgate, and as far as she could see, making little

146

push to defend himself? Could Lady Wickerston mean so much to him – or did he genuinely believe her husband's death to have been an accident, and that he would make matters worst by suggesting otherwise?

Edward had once, when pressed, explained the complexities of his liaison to Georgiana, assuring her he was happy in his marriage to Amanda. He had certainly seemed broken when she left the house a few days ago. Perhaps he was afraid she would not return, and felt he had little to lose once she had gone.

As Georgiana sat turning over her thoughts, Emily returned from her visit to the apothecary. She stood before Georgiana, still wearing her cloak, a small brown parcel clutched in her hands, clearly bursting with news. Georgiana immediately suggested they repair to her bedchamber. No words passed between them as they walked up the stairs. As soon as the bedroom door was closed behind them, Emily handed Georgiana the little parcel.

"This is it?" Georgiana turned it over wonderingly in her hands.

Emily nodded. Georgiana sat down to unwrap the packaging, signalling Emily to follow suit. Still wearing her cloak, Emily took the chair by Georgiana's dressing table, eyes focused on her mistress. Georgiana untied the string and unwrapped the brown paper. Inside it she found a more delicate, yet serviceable sheet of white paper, folded over on itself. She opened this carefully and sat looking down at the small quantity of white powder it contained.

"Such a small amount," said Georgiana, "to do so much damage." She looked up at Emily. "Did you manage to learn anything?"

"Oh, yes, miss," said Emily, shrugging off her cloak and laying it across her lap. "Mr Scott said it wouldn't kill the…

um... rats all at once. You need to do it a bit at a time."

"Really?" said Georgiana.

Emily nodded. "Said it needs to build up, inside the body." She shuddered.

"I see. Did you manage to find out who bought it? Was it Lady Wickerston's maid, as we thought?"

"Oh, yes, miss. She put her name in the Poison Book. There's something else, though. It seems Lord Wickerston also bought some arsenic."

"What?"

Emily nodded again. "Oh, yes, miss. Mr Scott got quite chatty about it. Of course, I had to promise not to breathe a word."

"Of course. Tell me what he said."

"Well, it seems there's some people, gentlemen in particular, take small amounts of it occasionally, mixed in a drink or something. Makes them feel good."

"That sounds very dangerous," said Georgiana. "Would it not make them ill, at the very least?"

"Well, it could do, probably would, in fact," said Emily. "I think it would depend on how much they took."

"So your apothecary friend thinks that's what Lord Wickerston was doing?"

Emily grimaced at the word 'friend' but continued. "Yes, miss. In fact, when Lady Wickerston's maid went to buy some, he thought it was for his lordship."

Georgiana thought about this. Lord Wickerston's consistently odd and moody behaviour had generally been attributed to drink, but from what Emily now told her, it seemed this was only part of the story. She wondered if his lordship's wife had known of his habit.

"Thank you, Emily. Did you have to promise Mr Scott anything except your secrecy?"

"Nothing I can't handle, Miss Georgiana."

Georgiana had to be content with that.

"Very well. However, something else has happened. I received a visit from Lady Wickerston's brother, Sir Anthony Dixon, this morning. It seems Lady Wickerston has tried to take her own life."

Emily's jaw dropped. "Is she all right?"

"Yes. She is resting. Her brother thinks she took something."

Emily's eyes went to the open packet on Georgiana's lap.

"That was my thought," said Georgiana. "Dr Masters has seen her, I understand. Mr Lakesby mentioned that he had a breakfast engagement with his friend, Mr Alfred Masters."

"Oh."

Neither young woman made any other comment on this but digested its implications for a moment or two.

"If I might ask, miss, how is Mr Grey faring?"

"Well enough in himself, I think," said Georgiana, "though he won't tell me anything. He doesn't seem inclined to make any attempt to defend himself. He said it's a mistake, his lordship's death was an accident and he thinks the investigation will establish this."

"So it wasn't just that he wouldn't talk to James?"

Georgiana shook her head. "No. He was reluctant to discuss it with me as well. It is not a fit subject for a lady and so forth."

Emily nodded her understanding.

"He told me not to go there again," said Georgiana.

"But you're going to."

"Well…"

Emily shook her head in resignation as she rose to her feet, her cloak over her arm. "He could refuse to see you."

"I suppose he could," mused Georgiana. "He does not know

about Lady Wickerston's attempt to kill herself. I wonder if it would be proper to tell him?"

"Did you tell him her ladyship said she'd killed her husband?"

"Yes," said Georgiana. "He said she didn't."

"But we knew that, from what James told us."

"Yes, and I told Edward as much," said Georgiana. "In fact, Mr Lakesby paid a visit while I was there and said the same thing."

"Mr Lakesby? Didn't he receive your note?" asked Emily, surprised.

"Yes, but apparently he thought Edward might not be inclined to say much to James so he decided to visit anyway." She paused, smiling a little as she spoke again. "I don't think he was very pleased to see me there."

"No, I don't imagine he was," said Emily. "James wasn't happy with it himself."

"Well, I survived the experience." Now standing, Georgiana looked down at the little package of white powder in her hand. "I must lock this safely away. We don't want anything else to happen." She refolded the paper and tied up the packet securely, then placed it in the drawer of her night table, next to the Crimson Cavalier's pistol. "I suppose it is possible Lord Wickerston's death was an accident," she said thoughtfully as she locked the drawer. "If he was in the habit of taking doses of arsenic himself anyway, he could have misjudged the amount. Or since it appears to take a while to have an effect, he may have simply taken it for long enough. Perhaps he took the final dose – the one that killed him."

"Perhaps," said Emily. "Whatever happened, though, I don't understand why your brother's been arrested. His name wasn't in the Poison Book."

"Well, not in that apothecary's, at least," said Georgiana,

half to herself.

"Oh, Miss Georgiana, you don't think…?"

"No, no, of course not," said Georgiana hastily. "But something must have happened to cause the authorities to put him in Newgate."

"They were looking for somebody to lay the blame on," said Emily dryly.

She was clearly remembering her own brother's trial and imprisonment. Georgiana forebore to point out that the law regarded men of Edward's standing rather differently from a mere servant. Instead she said, "By the way, James remained at Newgate this morning. He said he had some business and would be back a bit later."

"Oh. All right. Thank you for telling me, miss," said Emily.

Georgiana glanced towards the clock. "I can't imagine he would be very much longer."

"No, I suppose not," responded Emily.

"My cousin has arrived home," said Georgiana.

"Yes, miss. I saw her coat in the hall."

"It seems she saw an item about Edward's arrest in the newspaper and thought she should be here."

"So soon?"

"Yes, I know, I have been puzzling over that," said Georgiana. "It almost makes me wonder…" Her voice trailed off.

"What, miss?"

"Whether news of his arrest was given to the paper before it actually happened," said Georgiana.

"What? Who would do such a thing as that? Besides, if that were the case…" Emily's eyes widened in horror.

Georgiana nodded. "Either someone knew Edward would be arrested or arranged for it to happen." She took a deep breath and continued decisively, "Emily, I have another task for you. I recall Edward mentioning he was acquainted with a

Bow Street Runner. Would you mind talking to him? I'm afraid I don't know his name, but I hope he would have been the one to take Edward in; surely they would have shown him that much courtesy. Of course we cannot know if the authorities would have shown such sensitivity, but if we can discover this person's name there might be useful information to be obtained from him. I would suggest asking my sister-in-law, but this is hardly the right moment, and it is likely Edward wouldn't have told her anyway."

"Not to worry, miss, I'll call in at Bow Street. I'm sure I can think of some tale."

The mention of Amanda set Georgiana thinking.

"I should really call on my sister-in-law, to see how she is."

"Will you take Miss Knatchbull?"

Georgiana sighed. "She is unpacking, but I suppose I should give her the choice. She has come back with the intention of being useful, so it would be awkward to exclude her."

In the event, Georgiana was not called upon to make a decision at this juncture. Emily had barely closed the bed-chamber door behind them when the parlourmaid appeared in the upstairs corridor to tell Georgiana she had a visitor. She assumed it was Amanda, and was surprised to see Mr Richard Morris's card on the small silver tray the maid held out to her.

"Good heavens! Where is he?" Georgiana asked.

"In the drawing room, miss," said the parlourmaid.

"Very well. I suppose I should take my cousin with me. Would you ask her to come downstairs, please?" Georgiana asked the maid.

"Yes, miss." The parlourmaid walked a little way down the corridor and tapped on the door of Miss Knatchbull's room.

"Emily, I suggest you go down to the kitchen and get yourself some refreshment before you set out on your next errand."

"Yes. Thank you, miss."

Georgiana made her way to the drawing room and found Mr Morris standing with his back to the door, looking out of the window. His posture was straight, his tan coat fitted smoothly around his back and shoulders and his right hand idly swung a quizzing glass from its ribbon. He turned as the door opened and gave Georgiana a pleasant, slightly crooked smile.

"Good morning, Miss Grey. I'm sorry to intrude."

"There is no intrusion, Mr Morris. Please, won't you sit down? Ah, Selina." Georgiana smiled as her cousin appeared in the doorway. "Come in. May I present Mr Morris? He was visiting Lady Wickerston when I paid her a call after the death of her husband. Mr Morris, this is my cousin, Miss Knatchbull."

Selina dropped a little curtsey, then tripped forward, her right hand stretched out courteously.

"How do you do, Mr Morris?"

"I am very pleased to meet you, Miss Knatchbull." Morris took Selina's outstretched hand in one of his and briefly raised it to his lips.

Selina appeared a little flustered by the gesture, and clasped the hand in her other as she made her way to a chair.

"I hope all is well with you, Miss Grey," Mr Morris said, seating himself at Georgiana's invitation. He seemed hesitant as he formulated his next sentence. "I was under the impression your sister-in-law was visiting you. Perhaps I was misinformed?"

"Not at all. My sister-in-law was staying with me while my cousin was away nursing a sick friend. However, now Selina is back, Amanda has returned home." Georgiana looked attentively towards him. "Did you wish to see her particularly?"

"No, nothing in particular, though I had hoped to pay my respects. I trust she is well?"

"Yes, indeed," said Georgiana with a smile, "though anxious to get home to her children. I believe she was missing them quite dreadfully."

"Yes, of course," he said. "I can believe her to be a fond parent."

"I expect my cousin and I will call on her today if you have some message you would like us to give her," said Georgiana.

"Thank you. That is very kind," Morris replied. "I should be glad to have my warm regards conveyed to her. You must miss her now she has returned to her home."

"I have certainly been glad of my sister-in-law's company in my cousin's absence, but I am sure she is pleased to be back in her own house. And of course I am grateful for my cousin's return."

"Yes, I am sure you must be," said Morris with a smile towards Selina. "I can see you would value Miss Knatchbull's company."

"Oh, no, good heavens, not at all," protested Selina, blushing. "Stuff and nonsense, I'm sure, indeed, Georgiana has been so kind to me, I don't know what I should have done…" Selina floundered, flustered at the ease with which the compliment came from Mr Morris's lips.

"How is your brother?" said Morris. "I have not seen him since the day of the fire. We met in Brooks's."

Miss Knatchbull looked uncertain. Georgiana remained composed. She wondered if Mr Morris had been at Brooks's more recently. She smiled. "He is well, thank you."

"I had thought that his close friendship with the Wickerstons, and his wife's, too, of course, would make this a rather difficult time for them," Morris said.

Georgiana continued to smile pleasantly at her guest. "How

kind of you to think of that," said Georgiana. "Don't you think so, Selina?"

"Yes," said Selina in a small voice.

"Not at all," said Morris. "The whole business has been quite horrible."

"It must be difficult for all of Lord and Lady Wickerston's friends," said Georgiana, "and for their family, too, of course."

"Of course," said Morris. "Have you been acquainted with the Wickerstons long?"

"A few months," said Georgiana. "And you?"

"A year or two," he responded. "Lord Wickerston's death in the fire was quite horrific. I hope he did fall asleep as his family believe. One does not like to imagine the suffering he may have endured otherwise."

"Indeed, I was very shocked when I learned of it," said Selina earnestly.

"Yes," said Morris, his eyes on her. "I understand Mrs Grey helped to take care of Lady Wickerston when she received the news of her husband's death."

Georgiana inclined her head.

"That was extraordinarily kind of her," said Morris.

"It was kind of her, certainly," said Georgiana. "I have always known Amanda to be a kind creature. However, I'm sure anyone would have done the same in the circumstances."

"Some people, perhaps," said Morris. "Sadly, however, such occurrences are often fodder for the curious. There are those who spare little thought for those who have been affected."

"Oh, if ever there is a kindness to be done, Amanda will be the one to do it," said Selina.

"I do not doubt it," said Morris.

"Are you well acquainted with Amanda?" asked Selina eagerly.

"A little," said Morris. "I have not seen her for some time.

However, I always held her in high regard. A most gracious, thoughtful lady."

"Perhaps you would like to accompany us when we call upon her?" said Selina.

"Thank you," said Morris. "I should like it of all things."

15

There were few circumstances which made Georgiana uncomfortable. Yet sitting in the barouche with Selina and Mr Morris, en route to call upon an unsuspecting Amanda, Georgiana had to own that this was one of them.

The last thing Georgiana had expected was that Morris would accept Selina's invitation. When he did, she was too surprised to protest, and to override it would have been most uncivil. Obviously, Selina could not have been aware of any history between Mr Morris and Amanda. Nevertheless, it had seemed unlike her to take it upon herself to invite a gentleman to accompany them on a call. Georgiana could only assume Mr Morris had made a very favourable impression on her cousin.

After the initial polite conversation upon settling into the carriage, they travelled in silence for a few minutes. Selina sat with hands folded in her lap, offering an occasional smile to her companions, with intermittent glances towards the road, looking contented and comfortable.

Georgiana felt Mr Morris's gaze upon her. As she met his glance, he smiled.

"Tell me, Miss Grey, have you seen anything of Lady Wickerston since I had the pleasure of meeting you at her aunt's house?"

"Yes, as a matter of fact, she called on me yesterday."

Morris looked solemn. "How did she seem?"

"She was rather distressed," said Georgiana briefly.

"Yes, of course," said Mr Morris. "I believe her husband's death has proved very difficult for her." He shook his head. "Perhaps more difficult than she expected."

"I'm sure no one knows how they will react in such circumstances until they are called upon to do so," said Georgiana.

"No," said Morris, his deep tone drawing out the word. "Yet I understand…" He paused, moistening his lips as he considered how to continue. "I understand she – she took it very badly indeed."

"In that case, it is for her friends to help her through this difficult period," said Georgiana.

"Of course," he responded. "I only wish one knew what to do for the best. It is difficult to know how one can help."

Georgiana looked closely at Morris. As the carriage at that moment drew up to Amanda and Edward's front door, there was no opportunity for further conversation.

The butler had no hesitation in welcoming both Georgiana and Selina into the house but on Selina's announcing that they had brought an acquaintance to pay his respects, his dignified tone stated that he believed Mrs Grey to be occupied and he would ascertain whether she was able to receive visitors.

"Oh, dear," said Selina, tripping along the corridor, "I do hope there is nothing wrong."

"No, Miss Knatchbull, but if I could beg you to wait but a moment or two, I will ask."

"Selina, I really think we should wait here," said Georgiana, coming to the rescue of the exasperated butler. "In fact, perhaps it would be more convenient if we were to come back another time."

"I certainly do not wish to impose if Mrs Grey is busy," said Mr Morris.

"Good heavens, what an idea!" said Selina. "Why, dear Amanda is always so welcoming, I cannot imagine…"

A door opened towards the far end of the hall and Amanda

emerged. It appeared she was about to issue some instruction to her butler but the words trailed off as she saw her visitors. Coming out of the room behind her was Mr Lakesby.

"Georgiana, Selina, how very pleasant to see you." Amanda's face paled as she saw who had accompanied them. "Oh, Mr Morris, isn't it?"

Morris smiled. "Yes. How do you do, Mrs Grey? I must beg your pardon for the intrusion. I was anxious to pay my respects and I'm afraid I took something of a liberty when your sister-in law and cousin mentioned they would be calling on you."

"No. That is, do not concern yourself. You do not intrude. Not at all. Are you acquainted with Mr Lakesby?" Amanda turned to present her other guest.

Selina had been looking at Lakesby since he followed Amanda into the hallway. Her eyes were wide and round with shock, her lips pursed into a small and silent 'O'. Georgiana suppressed a smile. She was almost as surprised as Selina to see him there, but she was certain of her ability to school her own features.

Morris smiled and nodded at the other man. "Of course. How are you, Lakesby?"

"Well enough," said Lakesby briefly, his own eyes fixed on the newcomers. "Good day to you, Miss Grey, Miss Knatchbull."

"Good day, Mr Lakesby," said Georgiana. She thought she knew the reason for his visit and while she would have been quick to pooh-pooh any suggestion that Amanda was in any way betraying her husband in his absence, she wondered what Edward's reaction would be to the knowledge that Lakesby had been in his home.

Amanda turned back towards the drawing room.

"Please, do go in," she said. "I'll arrange for some tea."

"Oh, pray, do not go to any trouble," said Selina, apparently uneasy all of a sudden.

"It is no trouble, Selina. I am very pleased to see you," said Amanda. "When did you return?"

"This morning," said Selina, in a strangled tone.

"And your friend, is she recovered?" Amanda asked.

"Well, no, not quite… I mean to say… that is…" Selina floundered, looking helplessly at Georgiana.

"I am very pleased to have Selina home," said Georgiana with a smile. "She was anxious to see you, Amanda, but I must apologise if we are interrupting. Are you leaving, Mr Lakesby?"

"Oh. Yes," said Amanda, "Mr Lakesby was just about to go…" Her gaze flickered back and forth between Lakesby and Georgiana.

"I should be glad to stay a few minutes to pay my respects to Miss Grey and Miss Knatchbull," said Lakesby. "That is if you've no objection, ma'am?"

"No, of course not," said Amanda.

Despite the note of awkward tension in Amanda's voice, Georgiana thought she could sense a hint of relief. She noticed a small muscle tensing at the side of Lakesby's jaw. The small, ill-assorted party moved into the drawing room while Amanda gave instructions for refreshments. The gentlemen remained standing until she had entered the room and settled herself in a chair, having recovered her composure.

Ironically, it was Selina who broke the tension. "How are the children, my dear Amanda?"

"Very well, thank you, Selina." Amanda smiled. "They have gone to the park with their nanny. We thought some fresh air and exercise would be beneficial. They will be sorry to have missed you." She was clasping and unclasping her hands in her lap. She gave a quick glance in Lakesby's direction; Georgiana sensed that she felt a need to explain his presence.

"Not to worry," said Georgiana. "We will see them another time."

"Is your husband well, Mrs Grey?" asked Morris.

"Yes. Thank you, sir, it is most kind of you to ask. He has some business to deal with, and is away from home at present. Mr Lakesby was kind enough to bring me a message from him, through some mutual friends."

Amanda's head was high as she spoke, her voice clear and unwavering. Georgiana was filled with admiration for the confidence with which her sister-in-law offered this explanation. She was facing an awkward situation with every appearance of composure and control.

"Have you just returned, Lakesby?" inquired Morris.

"Yes," Lakesby responded. He made no attempt to elaborate.

"Of course, everyone is talking about Lord Wickerston's sad death," said Selina, shaking her head. "Such a tragedy. His poor wife."

"Yes, indeed," said Morris. "He turned back to Lakesby. "I understand you tried to rescue him from the flames?"

"I cannot take all the credit," said Lakesby. "Miss Grey's footman played a part. Indeed, it was he who managed to break through Lord Wickerston's locked study door. However, in view of his lordship's unhappy demise, I hardly think I can take any pride in my efforts."

"It was a very brave thing you did," said Miss Knatchbull, "you and James, of course. It was no one's fault things ended so tragically."

"No, indeed," Morris agreed.

Amanda sat with her head bowed slightly, her eyes on her hands clasped in her lap. The arrival of a parlourmaid bearing a tray of refreshments suspended any further talk for a few moments, while Amanda served. Georgiana noticed that Selina looked nervous; her eyes darted about the company as if she was unsure what to expect. Georgiana herself was slightly mystified, having been under the impression Lakesby had intended to spend much of the morning with Dr Masters's brother. Perhaps his friend had been unavailable, and Lakesby had wanted to inform Amanda about her husband's situation as soon as possible. Georgiana was aware of the tension in his eyes when he looked at her. His glance flickered occasionally towards Morris, and she sensed disapproval.

Morris's voice was slow, his demeanour pensive. "I have heard it said that his lordship's death might not have been an accident."

"Oh, dear," said Selina.

"What a dreadful notion. Where could you have heard such a thing?" asked Amanda.

Georgiana observed the expressions of each occupant of the room in turn. Lakesby's was thunderous. Morris remained thoughtful. Selina seemed acutely uncomfortable, but ironically it was she who asked the question. "You think the fire was started deliberately?"

"I really don't know," said Morris. His glance at Amanda was almost apologetic. "There is talk, I'm afraid. You know how people like to speculate on any unusual event. I'm sure it was an accident. Perhaps Lord Wickerston threw something into the fireplace."

"That seems an unlikely cause of such a devastating fire," said Lakesby in a cold voice.

"I am sure you are right," said Morris. "An accidental fire is tragedy enough. It would be overwhelming to Lord Wickerston's family for it to be anything more." He turned to face Amanda. "I understand you were a great comfort to her ladyship on the night her husband died."

It was Amanda's turn to look uncomfortable.

"Indeed, it was of no consequence. I'm sure anyone would

have been glad to help in the circumstances."

"Did Lady Wickerston tell you how... kind my sister-in-law was, Mr Morris?" asked Georgiana.

"Her brother, Sir Anthony Dixon," he replied.

"I see." Georgiana felt Lakesby's eyes on her.

"He was very grateful," said Morris.

"No doubt," said Lakesby curtly. "Why shouldn't he be?"

"Of course," said Morris. "I'm sure he would appreciate any kindness to his sister."

The company fell silent, apparently at a loss what to say next. Amanda was flushed. Only Morris seemed unconcerned by the awkwardness of the situation, directing a small smile at the ladies. Georgiana turned the conversation back to the suggestion at which Morris himself had hinted.

"Have you reason to suppose the fire at the Wickerstons was started deliberately, Mr Morris?"

"Oh, no, not reason as such," said Morris quickly. "I apologise. I had no wish to distress anyone."

"Oh, come," said Lakesby. "You must harbour some suspicion, or you would not have thought to mention it."

"Talk, nothing more," said Morris. "Merely gossip among the curious. I'm sorry. I should not have said anything." He paused. No one responded. "I don't imagine it is a secret that Lord and Lady Wickerston had a difficult relationship."

"It seems to have become less of a secret since Lord Wickerston's death," observed Lakesby wryly. "Surely you do not mean to suggest that some well-meaning friend set fire to the Wickerstons' house to release her ladyship from a difficult marriage?"

"Not at all," said Morris. "That would be a trifle far-fetched."

"Certainly a somewhat extreme solution," said Lakesby.

"I had heard that the Crimson Cavalier had held up some-one on the road not far from the Wickerston house that very

163

evening," said Morris in a tentative tone.

"Good heavens, has that dreadful robber not been caught yet?" said Selina.

"Hardly a *dreadful* robber, Miss Knatchbull," said Lakesby, "not in view of his level of success." He turned back to Morris. "Surely you don't think the Crimson Cavalier set fire to the house? Whatever for?"

"I agree it seems unlikely on first thought," said Morris. "However, if he had taken to housebreaking and had been trying to escape… or if he had taken refuge from pursuit in the Wickerstons' house…"

"Was there a pursuit?" said Georgiana.

"I don't know," said Morris. "Quite often that is the case, is it not?"

"True enough," said Lakesby. "However, I believe on that particular night most able-bodied men were occupied in battling the fire. In any case," he continued, "if the Crimson Cavalier had taken refuge in the house, destroying it would hardly aid his escape."

"Quite true," said Morris. "However, it could have been an accident. A candle knocked over or some such thing."

"I'm sure it was just a dreadful accident," said Amanda. "Indeed, it seems in very poor taste to suggest otherwise."

"I'm sure you would wish to see any guilty party brought to justice, Mrs Grey?" said Morris. "If it was deliberate, of course."

"Certainly, if that were indeed the case," said Amanda, with her head high. "I simply think it is unfair to leap to conclusions. It would be difficult for Lady Wickerston and – and – anyone else involved."

"You are quite right, of course, Mrs Grey," said Lakesby in soothing tones.

"None of this is helpful," said Amanda with some asperity.

"You are right, Amanda," said Georgiana. "It is hardly fair

to make assumptions based on nothing but gossip and hearsay."

"No, of course not," said Morris penitently. "I do not mean to accuse anyone. I'm so sorry if you mistake my meaning." He paused, looking thoughtful. "All the same, I'm afraid a certain amount of gossip is unavoidable."

Georgiana knew this was true. Once compassion for Lady Wickerston had been exhausted, talk would be inevitable. She wondered whether her own misgivings about Lord Wickerston's death were already contributing to conjecture. While she knew Lakesby would not break her confidence, if he had begun to ask questions, particularly of his indiscreet friend, someone would get wind of it. However, Mr Morris's curiosity struck her as more than mere casual speculation. His concern appeared genuine, but it seemed as though he was deliberately seeking out information or aiming to stir up trouble. Georgiana could not help but wonder about his motives.

"I believe the Wickerstons may have quarrelled," said Morris.

"Hardly a remarkable occurrence," said Lakesby dryly.

"Under normal circumstances, no, but when her husband is found dead several hours later…"

"Stop," said Amanda. Her voice was quiet yet had an angry edge, and her hands were clenched in her lap. "Please stop now. This is my home. I have already said I do not like the turn this conversation is taking, and I would like it to end immediately. I must ask you all to respect my wishes."

Everyone looked at Amanda in surprise. The gentlemen hastily begged pardon. Georgiana was surprised to see Lakesby's gaze fixed on Morris. While there was no open hostility or dislike in his expression, there was a shadow which Georgiana interpreted as displeasure. Perhaps it was merely indignation on Amanda's behalf, she told herself.

The whole situation was clearly difficult for her sister-in-law. Naturally she wanted nothing more than to maintain discretion regarding Edward's imprisonment; and it was clear that she found speculation over the nature of Wickerston's death distressing.

But the discussion was proving more than usually interesting. Georgiana cast about her mind for a means of continuing it without causing Amanda further distress. She eyed her cousin's pale, nervous figure. "Selina, it occurs to me that as you have not seen the children for a while, you might like to wait for their return."

"Oh, yes. That would be delightful."

The anxious lines around Selina's eyes began to soften, and Georgiana turned to Amanda.

"I'm afraid I have a number of matters in need of my attention. Will you forgive me if I run away?"

"Of course."

"Mr Morris, perhaps I could trouble you to escort me home?" Georgiana asked sweetly.

"Of course," he responded with a smile. "It would be my pleasure."

Ignoring Lakesby's compressed lips, Georgiana turned back to Amanda. "I shall send the carriage back for Selina in about an hour. Unless you'd prefer to send a message when you are ready, Selina?"

"No, no, there's no need for that. Send the carriage whenever is convenient for you, Georgiana," said Selina, her tone betraying her bemusement at this new turn of events.

Georgiana rose, drawing on her gloves. The gentlemen followed her lead; Lakesby was not impervious to hints. Amanda rang for the footman and asked for Georgiana's carriage to be brought round.

Out on the footpath, Georgiana turned to Lakesby with a

smile and held out a hand of farewell. He accepted politely, though without warmth, offering no more than a curt nod. With a brief gesture of farewell to Morris, he turned on his heel and strode away down the road.

"Shall we, Miss Grey?" Morris held out a hand and assisted her into the carriage, the door of which was held open by a waiting groom.

As she settled in her seat, Georgiana reflected that she would have to endure an outpouring of anxiety from Selina on her cousin's return. She suspected Emily would not approve of her actions either, but at present she had not the leisure to worry about the feelings of either of her self-appointed guardians.

"Are you quite comfortable, Miss Grey?" Morris asked, looking at her with an attentive and attractive smile as he took his own seat.

"Yes, thank you, Mr Morris." Georgiana eyed him speculatively. "You seem very concerned about how Lord Wickerston died."

"I am sorry to have distressed your sister-in-law," he said. "It was not my intention. I am just a little... uneasy... about the business."

"You believe he was deliberately killed?"

Morris hesitated, choosing his words carefully. "I think it is a possibility, especially in view of –" He broke off abruptly, his expression stricken.

"In view of what?" inquired Georgiana.

"Miss Grey, I am so sorry, I have said too much. This is too distressing for you."

"I am not at all distressed," Georgiana assured him. "Pray continue. In view of what?"

Morris hesitated. The words seemed almost wrung out of him. "In view of Lady Wickerston's attempt to do away with herself."

16

Georgiana stared, finding herself incapable of speech for a moment or two.

She swallowed hard to release the constriction in her throat. "I beg your pardon, Mr Morris?"

"Oh, dear," Morris said. "I'm so sorry, Miss Grey. I should not have blurted that out to you in such a brutal fashion."

"No. That is…" Georgiana paused for a moment and drew a deep breath. When she spoke again, her voice carried more conviction. "It is I who must beg your pardon, Mr Morris. I may have misled you. I knew about the… incident you mention. Sir Anthony Dixon was kind enough to call and inform me."

"Oh, I see." Morris looked nonplussed.

Georgiana recalled that Sir Anthony had said Mr Morris had called on Lady Wickerston, and it was when her maid went to find her that her attempt to take her life had been discovered. However, she was not certain Sir Anthony would have discussed the incident in detail with a casual acquaintance.

It did occur to Georgiana that at such a time of crisis, discretion might well have been the last thing on Sir Anthony's mind. The fact that he had told Miss Knatchbull and Mr Lakesby, as well as herself, also suggested that he might have discussed it with other people.

Georgiana smiled at Morris. "I can see you are a good friend to Lady Wickerston."

"I hope so," he said, his tone doubtful.

"It is all rather disturbing," said Georgiana. "I'm surprised to find anyone speaking about it." She paused. "Sir Anthony paid me a visit this morning. He was very distressed, of course. I had seen Lady Wickerston only yesterday, and I rather assumed the… incident had happened shortly before he called."

"It was yesterday evening," Morris replied. "I had gone to visit her ladyship, to try to offer some comfort. I was given to understand she had taken to her bed; the hour was rather late, after all. It came as a great shock…"

"Yes, of course," said Georgiana. She paused, attempting to frame her next observation with a degree of diplomacy. "I beg your pardon, Mr Morris, but I am a little unclear how Lady Wickerston's… unfortunate act is connected with your theory that Lord Wickerston may have been killed deliberately. Do you believe the same theory had occurred to Lady Wickerston?"

Mr Morris looked intently at her. "No, Miss Grey. I thought – your pardon again, this will sound most irregular, but I rather feared her ladyship might have killed her husband."

"I see," Georgiana said slowly, betraying no emotion. "What prompted that idea, Mr Morris?"

Morris looked ahead. "It is no secret that Lord Wickerston was difficult. I believe he was growing increasingly so: temperamental, one might say, or even volatile. Between his drinking and… other things, his wife cannot have found him an easy man to live with."

"No, I'm sure that's true," said Georgiana. "But to burn down her own house in an attempt to kill her husband seems a little extreme."

"I imagine one would not always look at things logically in such a situation," he said, his rich deep voice reflective.

"Lady Wickerston must have been very unhappy," Georgiana said.

"I believe so."

"But surely…" Georgiana tilted her head slightly and looked speculatively at Morris.

"What is it, Miss Grey?"

"Only that Lady Wickerston was at Lady Bertram's when the alarm was raised over the fire. She was invited to dinner party, and had been there for some hours. I was invited myself, but I left early because I was… unwell."

"I was aware of Lady Wickerston's whereabouts at the time of the fire."

"Yet you still believe she killed her husband."

"I would not say I believe it. That would hardly be fair." Morris hesitated. "I should not say this, particularly to you, of all people."

"Say what?" inquired Georgiana innocently. "And why particularly to me?"

Morris's hesitation was accompanied by a sombre look. "I beg your pardon," he said. "It is just that there has been some… talk."

"Talk?"

"Yes. Regarding… regarding your brother's… er… friendship… with Lady Wickerston."

"I see."

Suddenly Morris seemed embarrassed and awkward. "It is a somewhat… delicate situation."

"I think I understand, Mr Morris," said Georgiana gently.

Morris's embarrassment seemed to increase, yet Georgiana thought she perceived relief in his expression.

"Lady Wickerston sought your brother out on the day of her husband's death, at Brooks's," he continued.

"I had heard it mentioned," said Georgiana.

"Everyone was… well, shocked, of course, that a lady should arrive, seeking out…"

"A gentleman who was not her husband," Georgiana

prompted.

"Well, any gentleman," said Morris. "I'm sure I need hardly tell you, Miss Grey, it is a trifle unusual."

"I can see how it would be regarded," said Georgiana.

"The older gentleman in particular were rather… And your brother was certainly startled. I understood her ladyship was extremely upset when she arrived. Her voice could be heard in the smoking room."

"My goodness," said Georgiana.

"Oh, no one heard what she said," Morris told her hastily. "We had no wish to eavesdrop, of course. It was… the tone of her ladyship's voice. She was angry, frightened, and to be quite frank, hysterical."

Georgiana sat silent, her eyes facing front, absorbing what he had said.

"I gather she had quarrelled with her husband," Morris continued. "Your brother spoke to her on the front steps of the club. He was rather embarrassed, I'm afraid."

"Yes." Edward would be mortified at becoming entangled in such a breach of etiquette.

"However, he seemed quite determined to calm her down. I think she might have been talking wildly, threatening some drastic action. He sent for his carriage and took her away. I had assumed he took her home, but in view of what happened later, that now seems unlikely."

"Yes."

The carriage halted outside Georgiana's own door, curtailing further conversation for the moment. However, as he bowed low over her hand once he had helped her to alight, Mr Morris asked if he might have the pleasure of calling upon her. She assented, and when he had taken his leave, she walked slowly up the steps, attempting to make sense of the wealth of information she had acquired in the course of a most eventful morning.

Two questions stood out. Who else, in addition to Lady Wickerston, had been in possession of arsenic? And where had Edward taken her ladyship when they left Brooks's?

Georgiana was greeted with the news that James had returned from Newgate. She asked for Emily to be sent to her room.

She felt uncharacteristically tired. She glanced at the clock. It was only the middle of the day, yet it had already seemed an interminably long one. Smiling to herself, she reflected it was likely that as few young ladies started their days with early morning prison visits as ended them with holding up carriages.

This led her to consider what her next steps should be. She sat down at the chair before her dressing table, gently tapping her gloves against her legs.

It was thus that Emily found her when she answered her mistress's summons. Georgiana bade her sit down and recounted the morning's events.

This brought a frown to Emily's face. "Well, I'm very sorry for her ladyship," she said in a matter of fact voice. "It's a shocking thing to happen."

"Yes," said Georgiana. "I was wondering whether I ought to pay her a visit."

"Do you think it would serve a useful purpose?"

"I don't know," said Georgiana. "However, it occurred to me that she would not have known that her attempt to kill her husband did not succeed."

"But someone else's did."

"Yes. I'm not sure whether that makes the situation better or worse."

Both women fell silent for a moment, contemplating their shared knowledge. Emily was first to speak.

"Beg your pardon, miss, but I spoke to James when he returned from Newgate this morning."

"Did he have anything interesting to say?"

Emily's brow furrowed. "I'm not sure, miss. It didn't sound like he learned much. Your brother hadn't had any other visitors. I think James was wishful to go back and talk to him again after you left but…"

"Edward refused to see him," Georgiana finished.

"I believe so. I'm sorry, miss."

Georgiana sighed. "That is so like Edward. It is all very frustrating. How can anyone help him if he will do nothing to help himself?"

"There is one thing, miss. James made an arrangement with the jailer. If anyone else should visit your brother, he'll let James know."

"Thank you, Emily. Do pass on my thanks to James. That could be useful."

"I hope so, miss."

Georgiana looked thoughtful. "I was wondering what I ought to say if I call on Lady Wickerston. It's a little difficult to mention her attempt at killing herself, or her husband."

"True," said Emily. "A condolence call?"

"I have already done that. I suppose I could just say I wanted to see how she did and discover whether there is anything I could do."

Emily nodded. "That sounds charitable."

"I suppose so," said Georgiana doubtfully. "It seems rather weak to me."

"I'm sure it will be all right, Miss Georgiana. After all, her brother did visit you this morning. And her ladyship was here herself yesterday. I'm sure they would be glad to see you."

Georgiana glanced towards Emily through narrowed eyes, wondering if she had imagined the slight edge to her maid's tone when she mentioned Sir Anthony Dixon. She decided to ignore it, and asked Emily to lay out a suitable change of dress, so that she could set forth straight after luncheon. She asked Emily to accompany her; her cousin's presence at so delicate an errand was inadvisable. Emily was glad to concur – but less pleased when Georgiana added that the Crimson Cavalier would be visiting the Lucky Bell that evening.

Miss Knatchbull's return provided Georgiana with a companion for luncheon, but conversation was slow, since Selina knew little of the morning's events. She reported that she had told Amanda about Lady Wickerston's attempt to kill herself. "For, you know, Georgiana, dear Amanda may be trusted not to spread the news abroad. She was very much shocked, of course and sorry to hear that Lady Wickerston has taken her husband's death so badly."

It came as no surprise to Georgiana that Amanda had been less than forthcoming about Edward's situation, or about the reason for Mr Lakesby's visit. Selina was obviously disappointed that her cousin-in-law had maintained such discretion. "I dropped a hint, of course, but I could scarcely tell her outright that I read of Edward's arrest in the newspaper. That would have been in very poor taste, would it not?"

Georgiana suppressed a smile and refrained from reminding Selina that she had volunteered this information within moments of arriving home. Instead she rose from the table and expressed her intention of taking some fresh air. She made haste to assure Selina that she had already asked Emily to accompany her, since she knew her cousin would wish to finish her unpacking, and rest from the exigencies of her journey. Selina seemed relieved to hear this and expressed effusive gratitude for Georgiana's thoughtfulness before retiring to her room.

Emily was awaiting her mistress in her bedchamber. Georgiana's wardrobe was laid out on the bed, and it did not take not many minutes to change into the simple walking dress. Emily held out her bonnet and pelisse, and they were ready to go.

Georgiana chose to walk to Lady Wickerston's to allow time to talk privately with Emily. She relayed to her maid the conversation with her cousin over luncheon; she had been disappointed by the lack of information Selina brought back, but not entirely surprised. She resolved to find an opportunity to call on Amanda alone, in order to discover if she had heard anything from Edward. For the moment, she gave her attention to what she could accomplish herself.

As they walked, she and Emily conferred on the best approach to take during the visit to Lady Wickerston. Georgiana thought it likely her ladyship would be resting and not at home to callers. She dared not assume Lady Wickerston had taken her brother into her confidence, and however one looked at it, there was no easy way to ask whether the late Lord Wickerston had made a practice of taking arsenic for pleasure.

As Georgiana rang the bell, Emily stood several paces behind her mistress, hands clasped, capped head bowed, expression demure. They were kept waiting only a moment while the butler went to ascertain whether the family was receiving visitors. Sir Anthony Dixon himself came out to welcome them, face suffused with pleasure and hands out-stretched. As he led Georgiana through to the drawing room, Emily was ushered to the kitchen to be given some refreshment there.

Lady Wickerston was seated in an armchair, a shawl about her shoulders and a colourful knitted blanket covering her legs. Her normally pale complexion seemed to have lost a shade and there were dark shadows below her eyes. She managed a wan smile for her visitor.

"Good afternoon, Lady Wickerston, Mrs Hobbs." Georgiana nodded to her ladyship's aunt.

"Let me ring for some refreshment," said Mrs Hobbs, rising from the chair where she had been occupied with some knitting.

"Oh, no, please do not trouble," said Georgiana. "It is not yet an hour since I ate luncheon. I merely called to see how her ladyship was faring, and whether there was anything I could do."

"That is very kind of you," Lady Wickerston rasped in a hoarse voice. "Really, there is nothing…" Her voice trailed off.

Georgiana thought she saw a tear fall from Lady Wickerston's eye.

"I am so sorry," said Lady Wickerston. "I do not wish to seem ungrateful. You have been so very kind, much more than I deserve –"

"Theresa…" began Sir Anthony.

"No, please, Anthony, it is quite true. You have no idea…"

"I think you are being much too hard on yourself, Lady Wickerston," said Georgiana. "You've had an extraordinarily difficult time of late."

"But that is no excuse for the way I behaved, for what I did –"

"Indeed, you reproach yourself too much," said Georgiana quickly, noticing the alarm in Mrs Hobbs's expression. She wondered to what extent her ladyship had confided in her relatives. "You are not to blame for your husband's death," she said, choosing her words carefully, and hoping that Mrs Hobbs and Sir Anthony would assume she referred only to the distress of bereavement in the most general terms.

Lady Wickerston met Georgiana's eyes, her own expression

bewildered as she tried to read the silent message there. Sir Anthony Dixon was watching his sister closely and with evident concern.

"Theresa, you must cease blaming yourself," he said. "There was nothing you could have done. Heavens, you weren't even there."

"Indeed, it is quite dreadful," said their aunt. "But perhaps he didn't feel anything, if he was – um – well – taking a nap."

"That is quite possible," said Georgiana. "My footman mentioned that there was a glass knocked over and its contents spilt on the hearthrug. That is just the kind of thing that might happen if one fell asleep and accidentally knocked against a table."

"Oh." Lady Wickerston looked at Georgiana blankly. Her head was still, her eyes uncertain as she took in this information. "Yes. I see. Thank you, Miss Grey."

Both aunt and brother were watching her ladyship with some apprehension. It was Mrs Hobbs who spoke first.

"My dear, I think perhaps you should lie down. You are overwrought."

"No. No, indeed, I am much better. Truly. In fact, I should like to go out for some air." Lady Wickerston's gaze seemed more alert as it returned to Georgiana's face. "Miss Grey, would you be good enough to accompany me?"

17

There was silence for a moment as the eyes of everyone in the room fell upon Lady Wickerston. Mrs Hobbs looked flustered, and a little horrified. Sir Anthony seemed solicitous, and fearful that his sister had taken leave of her senses. Georgiana, for her part, was mystified and, she had to confess, intrigued. This was an ideal opportunity to further her quest for information about the death of Lord Wickerston, and not one she was about to refuse. Fearing that it would be in poor taste to accept with too much alacrity, she decided upon an expression of concern and a desire to fall in with her ladyship's wishes.

"Theresa, I really don't think…" began Sir Anthony.

"I am feeling quite well," Lady Wickerston insisted. "I have been indoors for far too long. A short drive is the very thing I need." She looked steadily at Georgiana, waiting for an answer.

"Well, if you are certain you feel up to it, Lady Wickerston," Georgiana said, "I have no objection to bearing you company. However, my maid is in your kitchen."

"That is not a problem. We will advise of her of the change of plan. I'm sure my aunt's footman could escort her home, if necessary. Anthony, will you take care of it, please and send for the carriage for Miss Grey and myself?"

Her brother hesitated, then with a shrug reached for the bell pull. "I will join you," he said.

"There is no need," her ladyship said. "We shall have the coachman and a groom, and I am sure Miss Grey and I are sufficient chaperones for each other. Do you not think so, Miss Grey?"

"Yes, if you are content with the arrangement," said Georgiana.

This air of decisiveness in one who had so recently appeared weak and incapable took everyone by surprise; it was clear her relatives thought she was in danger of some sort of brain fever. However, no one seemed disposed to argue with her. Within a few minutes both ladies were being assisted into Mrs Hobbs's rather old-fashioned coach by Sir Anthony, with admonitions to wrap themselves up warmly and not travel too far. Lady Wickerston raised a gloved hand in a farewell wave to her brother, then sank back against the cushions.

"Where would you like to go?" said Georgiana, with an encouraging smile. "Perhaps a short ride around the park?"

"No," said Lady Wickerston. "I beg your pardon, but no, thank you. Forgive my little subterfuge, Miss Grey. I have a most particular destination in mind, and I did not know any other way it might be accomplished. I should like to call on your brother."

Georgiana was stunned. It was a moment before she could formulate a sentence. "I – I beg your pardon, Lady Wickerston, but I'm afraid my brother is away from home at the moment, on some personal business."

"He is in Newgate Prison, as you well know, Miss Grey, under arrest for the murder of my husband."

It seemed futile to argue. "May I ask how your ladyship comes to be so well informed?" Georgiana inquired.

"Your brother is a gentleman," said Lady Wickerston. "When I told him... what ... what I had done," she said, "he was, well, very concerned, even alarmed." A small, sad smile appeared on her face. "I quarrelled with my husband. He had been drinking, of course, but on this occasion matters were even worse than usual. I cannot tell you how upset I was. That is when I..." Her voice trailed off, and her face took on an air of distant melancholy.

"Pray continue," Georgiana prompted.

Lady Wickerston roused herself. "I'm so sorry." She pressed her lips together, moistening them before she continued. "I knew there was something in the house, some powder to kill rats in the cellar. I sent my maid to find it, and then... Oh, I wasn't thinking clearly, I know. It was foolish and wicked but I was desperate. I put the powder in his glass with some wine."

"I see."

Her ladyship continued after a brief pause. "I didn't know what to do. I found myself out in the street, walking, quite without aim or intention. I felt I needed help, so I went to Brooks's."

"Seeking my brother?" Georgiana asked.

Her ladyship nodded. "He had always been so kind, such a good friend to me. I know it was not at all the thing to do, but under the circumstances... I fear I embarrassed him, and he was very shocked, of course. However, he still wanted to help. I had not even realised I still held the packet of poison in my hand."

This gave Georgiana pause for thought. "My brother noticed it?"

"Yes. He took it from me and said he would dispose of it."

"Do you know what he did with it?" Georgiana asked.

"No. I don't know."

"I'm sorry if this is impertinent, Lady Wickerston, but that wasn't what you took yourself?"

"I – had some still in my reticule. I had forgotten, I had divided it into separate small packets."

"I see."

Her ladyship fell silent for a moment then looked up at Georgiana. "You mentioned the glass on the hearthrug. You said the contents had been spilled?"

Georgiana nodded. "That is what my footman told me he saw when he went in search of your husband." She paused. "Mr Lakesby also said this."

"I see." Her ladyship slowly digested this information. "So my husband didn't drink it." She looked up. "Then it was the fire?"

Georgiana didn't answer. She looked out of the window at the increasingly dark and murky streets, peopled by a rabble of ragged urchins and beggars. She asked a question of her own.

"Where did you and my brother go?"

"I don't know."

"I beg your pardon?" Georgiana looked at her in disbelief.

"I know how it sounds," said her ladyship, "but truly, I was so dazed I took no heed of my surroundings." She paused, her nose wrinkled and her brow furrowed in thought. "Edward – Mr Grey – sent for his carriage, and we went for a drive. I'm not sure how long we were out. He was very concerned about calming me down."

"Of course."

"Eventually he took me to my aunt's home. He didn't think I should return to Marpley Manor. I didn't see him again until the dinner at Lady Bertram's. I naturally assumed that he had gone home himself after leaving me in my aunt's care."

Georgiana was not fully convinced, but she did not pursue the matter, sensing that this was all Lady Wickerston was prepared to say.

The walls of Newgate Prison met her eyes for the second time that day.

"It occurs to me that my brother may refuse to see us," said Georgiana.

Lady Wickerston looked at her in surprise. "Why should he?"

181

It was Georgiana's turn to be surprised. Was this woman's acquaintance with Edward so shallow?

"I'm sure you must know, my brother has very high notions of propriety," said Georgiana. "He would not approve of any lady visiting a prison."

"No, of course not, but under the circumstances –" Her ladyship paused, looking thoughtful. "It's reassuring that he should be so concerned for my reputation. My husband never was."

"I see." Georgiana could understand that Edward would make a favourable impression compared with Lord Wickerston, although she herself found him quite stifling.

Georgiana's thoughts wandered as her eyes went to the pathetic creatures crowding around the bars of the tiny, low prison window and crying out as their carriage passed through the gate. She thought how fortunate Edward was to have a cell of his own. It also struck her as ironic that she felt more apprehensive on this visit than on her first. Nevertheless, her curiosity was aroused. She had been as startled as Lady Wickerston's family at her ladyship's sudden recovery and brisk manner. She had certainly been surprised at Lady Wickerston's desire to visit Newgate, and quite astonished that she had been chosen as companion for the excursion. She was moved to wonder whether her ladyship had some other motive for the visit, as yet undisclosed.

"Forgive me, Lady Wickerston, but have you heard from my brother since he was imprisoned?"

Lady Wickerston shook her head sadly. "No. I have been very concerned."

Watching her closely, Georgiana asked the question which had been plaguing her since her own visit to Edward. "Has he agreed to take the blame for your husband's death in order to protect you?"

Lady Wickerston's blue eyes widened in horror. What little colour remained in her face drained away.

"Good heavens, I had not thought of that. No, indeed, no! He could not have. He must not!"

The carriage was drawing to a halt so there was no opportunity for more. However, Georgiana was not entirely satisfied. It was difficult to reconcile the fragility of the creature so distraught she had attempted to kill herself with the decisive woman now breaching convention by entering Newgate to visit a prisoner held for murder.

Her ladyship's groom concealed any disapproval he might have felt about this errand as he accompanied the two ladies to the jailer's room. The portly individual seemed surprised to find yet more members of the gentry visiting his establishment. Georgiana thought she saw a glimmer of recognition in his eyes as they landed on her, but he gave no outward sign, and shuffled off down the dank stone corridor which led to Edward's cell. The groom respectfully bowed the ladies ahead of him and Georgiana found her glance flickering around the dark floor as she heard the scurrying mice.

The heavy wooden door opened ponderously to reveal Edward seated at the table. His expression was more shocked than any Georgiana had ever seen. He stood slowly, transfixed, the focus of his eyes not moving from the doorway.

Lady Wickerston preceded her into the cell and Georgiana suddenly realised she had been invited solely to play the role of chaperone. She was acutely conscious of the awkwardness of the situation, and felt as if she was the intruder and had no business here. Yet she would not willingly have missed the scene about to unfold.

"Ther... Lady Wickerston. Georgiana. What have – ? Why are you here?"

Georgiana stood in silence a few paces behind Lady

Wickerston. Her ladyship's eyes roved over the scant furnishings of the room before coming to rest on Edward's face.

"I'm sorry to intrude, Edward," Lady Wickerston said, as though disturbing Edward at his correspondence. "But under the circumstances, I thought…" She stopped, closed her eyes, took a deep breath and seemed to pull herself together. "I must beg your pardon. I know I should not – *we* should not be here." She gestured towards Georgiana. The groom, as James had done, remained in the corridor. "I asked your sister to accompany me."

"You should not have come." Edward's voice had a strangled quality. When his eyes moved from Lady Wickerston to Georgiana, there was a reproachful look.

Georgiana shrugged, making no attempt to speak. Lady Wickerston continued, "I do not understand what has happened? Why are you here?"

Edward stiffened. "Please, your ladyship, it is best that you go."

"I shall not go." Lady Wickerston stamped her foot. "Tell me. My husband is dead. Why are you accused of his murder?"

Edward remained silent. Georgiana recognised the familiar stubborn streak. Lady Wickerston looked from Edward to Georgiana.

"I have told your sister – what… what I did."

Georgiana had thought Edward could not look more horrified than when the jailer opened the cell door. She was mistaken.

"You – you… I beg your pardon, but –" His face grew even more grey as he struggled for words. He turned to Georgiana. "It is not what you think."

Georgiana spoke quietly. "What is it that I think, Edward?"

He seemed unable to tell her. His glance travelled uneasily

between the two women. Georgiana sensed he was wondering whether Lady Wickerston had mentioned the nature of their relationship. All that was needed was for Amanda to join them and his nightmare would be complete.

Lady Wickerston addressed Edward earnestly. "Your sister told me the glass of wine was spilt, the one I had given him. He had not drunk it."

"What?" Edward's look grew bemused.

"It was spilt. Her footman saw it when he and Mr Lakesby brought my husband out of the house. Is that not so, Miss Grey?"

"It is true James mentioned it. So did Mr Lakesby," said Georgiana.

Edward looked too puzzled to raise his usual objection to the mention of Lakesby.

"So you see," Lady Wickerston insisted, "it was the fire that killed him."

"I don't understand," said Edward, confused. "Please, it is best that you don't interfere. Once the authorities have investigated, they will realise their mistake and I shall be released."

"No," said her ladyship.

Edward looked at both his visitors. His glance lingered slightly longer on Georgiana.

"It appears his lordship was poisoned," he said. "The doctor who examined him found this to be the case. He was quite certain."

It was her ladyship's turn to look horrified. "No. That cannot be. Not if the glass was spilt."

Georgiana offered no comment on the doctor's opinion. She had no wish to explain what she was not supposed to know.

"So someone else poisoned him?" asked Lady Wickerston,

her voice falling to a whisper.

Edward nodded slowly, still looking confused. "That seems to be the conclusion."

"Is that why you were arrested, Edward?" asked Georgiana calmly.

"Georgiana," he began.

A flash in her eyes warned him this was not the time to suggest this was not a fit subject for discussion.

"Why were you so determined to persuade me Lord Wickerston was not murdered?" Georgiana asked.

"As I said, I don't think speculation on the subject is helpful."

Georgiana looked exasperated.

"Please, Georgiana," Edward continued, "there is no evidence that his lordship was poisoned deliberately. I see no need to make accusations for which I have no proof."

"What about your own position?"

Edward hesitated, then looked around the sparse cell as though suddenly aware that its shabbiness did not offer a suitable place to welcome visitors. Placing his coat on the faded wooden chair, he offered the seat to Lady Wickerston. As she sat down, Edward looked doubtfully at the narrow bench which served as his bed, then at his sister. He took out his handkerchief to spread it on the threadbare blanket for her. Georgiana shook her head. She had spent enough time among thieves to know that such furnishings, even in a private cell such as Edward's, could be home to unwelcome visitors.

Edward looked from one lady to the other. His audience watched him expectantly.

"I understand someone approached the Watch and mentioned I had… escorted her ladyship to her aunt's home on the day of the fire."

Georgiana rolled her eyes. Even now, Edward felt it necessary to observe the proprieties.

"Georgiana, I'm sure you recall that I am acquainted with a Bow Street Runner."

"Yes," Georgiana nodded. Edward had mentioned this to her some months earlier, when he had been asked by magistrates in the area to assist in finding the murderer of a local citizen.

"He came to see me at my home," said Edward. "He told me there was some doubt that Lord Wickerston's death was an accident. He thought that since I had seen her ladyship on that day, I might have seen or heard of something. I think he was hoping I could clear up one or two questions he had."

It sounded very mild. Georgiana wondered if Edward was deliberately seeking to make the matter appear less serious.

"That is a far cry from imprisonment," said Georgiana. "Did something else happen?"

"No," he said baldly.

Georgiana was unconvinced. Had it not been for the presence of Lady Wickerston, she would have been inclined to argue. Unfortunately, she knew it was probably her ladyship's presence which would make Edward maintain his silence. She raised an eyebrow.

"I'm afraid they did not consider I had been very helpful," Edward said.

"Oh?"

"No."

"And thought you might be more so within prison walls?" queried Georgiana.

"Perhaps."

"I see."

Lady Wickerston watched the verbal sparring between brother and sister with a puzzled but anxious expression. Georgiana waited a moment, giving Edward a quizzical look.

"Georgiana, there is no evidence I killed his lordship and I can only assure you I did not. The authorities can hardly send me for trial on the basis of gossip."

"Which you do not wish to encourage," said Georgiana.

"It is unfortunate that I am not able to help," said Edward, "but I do not know anything about Lord Wickerston's death."

"Apart from Lady Wickerston's attempt to kill him."

Edward looked angry. Her ladyship bowed her head sorrowfully. Georgiana grew frustrated by the waste of time.

"This is not achieving anything," said Georgiana.

"We must tell the truth," said Lady Wickerston. "It is true I tried... tried to kill my husband. You know how desperate I was. But it is of no matter. He did not drink what I gave him so I did not kill him."

"I don't think it will be as simple as that," said Georgiana. "Whether or not your husband ultimately died by your hand, he is dead and you made an attempt to bring that about."

"But..." Lady Wickerston looked pleadingly at both Georgiana and Edward.

"I'm afraid Georgiana is correct," said Edward. "The authorities will not look kindly on an attempt to kill."

"I should not say anything?" said Lady Wickerston, sounding forlorn.

"I do think you ought to tell the truth," said Georgiana before Edward could get a chance to speak. "It may go ill for you if you do not." She turned towards her brother. "You would also be wise to tell the truth, Edward."

"I beg your pardon?" While Edward did not sound indignant, there was an air of mild angry surprise in his tone. He seemed to struggle with his words for a moment or two, as though weighing the impropriety of an argument with his sister before a third party. "I have told the truth," he said with quiet dignity. "You should go. It was very kind of you to visit. I thank you."

"Edward." Georgiana was not so easily deterred. Her tone was insistent; to hear Edward thanking them for the visit, as though they were paying a morning call, tried her patience too far. "This is not a game. Do you have any idea of the seriousness of your situation?"

"I am perfectly aware of my situation, Georgiana," said Edward haughtily. "Now I think it best you that leave. I have already asked that you do not visit me here. I am very disappointed that you …"

"Disobeyed instructions?" queried Georgiana with a raised eyebrow.

"Please don't be angry with your sister, Edward," said Lady Wickerston gently. "It was my fault. I said I needed some air and asked her to accompany me. I did not mention where I wanted to go until we were in the carriage."

"Nevertheless…" Edward began.

"Oh, nevertheless fiddlesticks," said Georgiana impatiently. "Edward, what did you do with the remainder of the poison?"

"I beg your pardon?"

Georgiana wanted to hit him. "The arsenic. Lady Wickerston said she was still carrying the packet when she went to see you and that you took it from her. What did you do with it?"

Edward wrestled with his thoughts for a moment before deciding to speak. "I gave it to Lord Wickerston."

18

The ensuing silence seemed to go on for a very long time, but could not have been more than a minute or two. The light coming through the bars of the tiny cell diminished as the shadows lengthened.

"You, you… gave it to my husband?" Lady Wickerston's voice was barely above a whisper, and the colour drained from her face leaving a corpse-like pallor.

Georgiana's mind was moving in a direction which she suspected to be very different from her ladyship's. She thought her own dawning horror was the greater.

"Edward, when you say you gave it Lord Wickerston, what exactly do you mean?"

"I would have thought it fairly evident, Georgiana."

Her ladyship's head was in her hands. She seemed on the verge of tears.

Georgiana's eyes were steadily focused on her brother. Her words were careful and deliberate.

"When you say you gave it to Lord Wickerston, do you mean you put it into his hand, or something else entirely?"

Lady Wickerston's hands fell from her face. She looked up at Edward, eyes widened, as she took in the import of Georgiana's words.

"No," her ladyship whispered.

Neither Edward nor Georgiana paid her any heed. They continued to look at each other.

"Please go, Georgiana," said Edward eventually.

She did not move.

"You're saying you killed Lord Wickerston?" Georgiana asked quietly.

"I think it is better if I say nothing. Please go."

"No, you could not have," said Lady Wickerston, standing. "It is not possible."

"Please go."

Georgiana's mind, having passed beyond the initial shock of Edward's words, was moving ahead,

"How could you have done it?" she asked. "There was only one glass, which James saw on the floor, out of his lordship's reach. Surely you did not just throw it there?"

"It was already spilt. I simply refilled it."

"And replaced it on the floor where you found it when his lordship had finished drinking?" Georgiana asked.

Edward shrugged.

"Who let you into the house? Someone must have seen you."

"Good heavens, Georgiana, do you take me for a simpleton?"

"This is not a game, Edward," said Georgiana.

"I am aware," he snapped. "Nor are you a Bow Street Runner, Georgiana. It is not necessary for you to question me."

"True," Georgiana said calmly, "but I would like an explanation for Amanda when she questions me."

Edward flushed slightly. "Please go."

"Very well," said Georgiana. "Come, Lady Wickerston, it is growing late." She turned back to her brother. "Consider this, Edward. You could face the gallows. I daresay you regard this as a noble and unselfish course of action, but it is not. You have responsibilities, a wife and children. Do you think it's fair to make a widow and orphans of them, not to mention the scandal they would be forced to bear?"

Edward said nothing.

"Very well," said Georgiana. "Goodbye, Edward."

The two ladies left the cell. The hovering jailer was waiting to lock the door; as they reached the end of the corridor, about to venture back to the outside world, he addressed Georgiana.

"Beg pardon, miss," he said respectfully, "can I have a word?"

Georgiana glanced at him in some surprise, then towards Lady Wickerston. Deeming it to be something of a private matter, she smiled apologetically at her ladyship while she moved down the corridor a few steps with the jailer.

"Sorry to trouble you, miss." His accent was rough but his tone remained respectful. He had even removed his hat, which he clutched in his hands in front of him.

"What is it?" Georgiana asked.

"Your man Cooper asked me to let him know if the gentleman had any more visitors. He gave me to understand it was yourself what was wanting to know, like, so I thought it would be all right to tell you, being as you're here."

"Yes. Please continue," said Georgiana. "Someone has been to visit my brother?"

The jailer nodded. "Yes, miss. The other gent."

"Other gent?" asked Georgiana blankly.

"The one who came this morning, when you was here."

"I see."

Lakesby.

She plunged her hand into her reticule and produced a coin which she dropped into the man's grubby hand.

The jailer thanked her solemnly, then led her to the outer door where Lady Wickerston and the groom waited, and awkwardly bowed them out.

"Is everything all right?" asked Lady Wickerston.

"Yes. Thank you," said Georgiana. She offered no further information and the two ladies stepped into the waiting carriage.

The journey home was quiet, with neither lady disposed for conversation. The carriage called first at Georgiana's home. Georgiana thanked Lady Wickerston before stepping down. Her ladyship merely nodded, seeming incapable of speech. Concerned, Georgiana hesitated.

"Would you like me to accompany you home?" she asked gently.

Lady Wickerston suddenly seemed to become aware of her surroundings. Her head jerked towards Georgiana. She blinked for a moment, attempting to focus, then smiled bleakly.

"No. No, thank you, Miss Grey. It is extremely kind of you but there is no need."

"You're certain?"

"Yes, indeed." Her ladyship's smile grew warmer. "Thank you very much. I appreciate your kindness. I – I know this cannot have been easy for you."

With that she signalled her coachman to depart, leaving Georgiana to watch its progress along the street.

Georgiana walked slowly up the front steps, thinking over the events of the day. She was exhausted and her brain was teeming. The door was opened almost immediately by James. He offered no comment, but she sensed he had been watching for her. As he took Georgiana's cloak, Emily came down the stairs. The maid halted halfway, her eyes meeting those of her mistress. Georgiana thought both James and Emily seemed relieved to see her.

"Where is my cousin?" Georgiana asked in as casual a tone as she could manage.

"In her room, miss," said Emily.

Georgiana nodded thoughtfully.

"Dinner will be another half hour, miss," said James. He hesitated. "We – weren't sure what time to expect you back."

"Will you be wishing to change, Miss Georgiana?" asked Emily.

"No," said Georgiana. "At least – perhaps I should. I would like to freshen up. However, I need to speak to you both first. Ah, Tom."

The page had entered the hall carrying a plant. He paused. "Yes, miss?"

"I need to speak to James. Take his post at the front door for a few moments, would you please?"

"Me, miss?" said Tom, goggle-eyed.

"Yes, please."

James looked uneasy. "Miss Georgiana –"

Tom looked from one to the other.

"You sure, miss?"

Georgiana hid a smile. "Yes, Tom, perfectly sure. Please don't concern yourself, James, it will only be for a few minutes." She led the way to her small study.

James opened the door and allowed Georgiana and Emily to precede him into the room before closing it behind him. Georgiana walked to the fireplace and stood with her back to it, facing the two servants who stood side by side.

"How long have you been back, Emily?" Georgiana inquired.

"Well over an hour, Miss Georgiana. What happened to you? I was told you'd gone for a drive with Lady Wickerston. Sir Anthony sent me home with Mrs Hobbs's footman."

"Oh, yes?" said James.

Emily threw him a look of disdain. "Surly bloke, he was." She turned back to Georgiana. "I didn't know what to think, I was that worried, miss. James and I were going to go out to look for you."

"Oh dear," said Georgiana remorsefully. "I'm so sorry. I had not intended to make you so anxious."

194

"Beg pardon, Miss Georgiana, but I had thought her lady-ship was unwell," said James.

"When I arrived at the house she was looking far from well," responded Georgiana. "However, she made a rather remarkable recovery." She paused. "It seemed to begin when I mentioned that you had seen Lord Wickerston's glass on the floor of his study, out of his reach."

Emily and James exchanged glances.

"But where did you go, miss?" asked Emily.

Georgiana drew a breath. "To Newgate."

Her maid and footman stared at her in stunned silence.

"Newgate?" Emily said at last.

"But, miss…" said James.

"I know," said Georgiana. "It was Lady Wickerston's idea. However, she did not tell me of our destination until we were in the carriage."

"Oh," said Emily.

Georgiana wondered whether she had been over-optimistic in telling James that Tom would only need to cover his post for a few minutes. As briefly as she could, she told them what had occurred, including Edward's assertion that he had given the poison to Lord Wickerston. Both seemed shocked at the implication that Edward could have killed his lordship.

"Did Mr Grey tell you he had poisoned his lordship?" Emily asked.

"Not directly. It was implied." Georgiana turned to James. "There is something else. The jailer mentioned that he had agreed to tell you if Edward had any more visitors."

James nodded. "Yes, miss. Emily said she'd mentioned it to you. I hope I wasn't out of place."

"No, of course not, James. I'm very grateful for your help. However, the jailer mentioned that Mr Lakesby had been back."

The two servants exchanged glances, neither thinking it their place to comment.

Georgiana heard Miss Knatchbull's voice in the hall. She groaned and sank into a nearby chair, covering her eyes with a hand. After a moment or two, she raised her head, took a deep breath and rose to her feet.

"Come along, Emily. I'll need your help to change before dinner."

"Yes, miss."

"James."

"Yes, miss?"

"Would you be so kind as to let Horton and Mrs Daniels know I shall be ready in a few minutes?"

"Yes, miss."

As James opened the door, he again exchanged glances with Emily. Georgiana sailed out into the hall and greeted her cousin. She explained cheerfully that she had been detained, offering no details, and that she just required a few minutes to change. She ascended the stairs with Emily in her wake, leaving a bemused Selina staring up after them.

True to her word, it was not many minutes before Georgiana left her bedchamber. Dinner was an unremarkable affair. The food was excellent as usual, and Miss Knatchbull prattled inconsequentially throughout the meal. The day had already been eventful and it was not yet over; Georgiana was somewhat relieved to have to make no more than polite, automatic responses; she could briefly rest her mind and consider what was to happen next. If Selina cast her an odd glance or two, at least she was not required to give an account of her doings.

Selina was still tired from her journey; there was no need to linger at the table, and it was easy to retire early.

Emily was waiting in Georgiana's bedchamber, her expression disapproving. The Crimson Cavalier's wardrobe was laid out upon the bed.

"Are you sure about this, Miss Georgiana?" asked Emily.

"I am," said Georgiana. "I'm certain someone in the Lucky Bell would have an idea of where arsenic could be obtained."

"But if your brother had the arsenic..." Emily began uncertainly.

"He had what remained of the arsenic Lady Wickerston was carrying," said Georgiana firmly.

"Was it enough to kill his lordship?"

Georgiana sighed. "I don't know." She sank down on the bed, breeches on, white shirt partially buttoned. She stretched out a leg for Emily to help her put on her boots. "I can't believe Edward went to Marpley Manor intending to kill Lord Wickerston, if indeed he went there at all. However, since he refuses to say anything more, it is difficult to know what to think."

Emily nodded. Her expression was sympathetic.

"Perhaps I am not approaching this in the right way," said Georgiana, now booted and standing.

"What do you mean, miss?" asked Emily, handing her a cravat.

Georgiana draped the cravat around her neck and arranged it simply, looking critically at her reflection in the mirror. "Who else would have had reason to kill Lord Wickerston?" she said.

Emily frowned. "Surely only his wife had something to gain by being rid of him? Although –" She paused. Her frown grew deeper.

"Go on," said Georgiana.

"Perhaps someone wants your brother out of the way."

Georgiana looked thoughtful. "Safely locked up in Newgate," she said slowly. "I had not thought of that." Like Emily, she frowned. "I don't know, Emily. How could anyone know Edward would be arrested or that he would maintain this stupid silence?"

"Your brother is known to be very proper. I'm sure anyone that knows him would know he would always be gentleman-like."

"True," said Georgiana in a reflective tone. "But who could have known the circumstances, much less that Lady Wickerston would arrive at Brooks's with the remains of a packet of arsenic?"

"No, you're right there, miss," nodded Emily, looking gloomy. "Did she ever threaten to kill her husband?"

"I don't know," admitted Georgiana.

"Perhaps her brother would."

"Perhaps," said Georgiana. "In the meantime, I shall go to the Lucky Bell and see if anyone has been trying to obtain poison."

"It doesn't seem likely anyone acquainted with his lordship would be in the Lucky Bell," said Emily.

"No, but they may have sent someone to make inquiries about how such a substance could be obtained."

Seeing her mistress's mind was made up, Emily nodded doubtfully and handed her the three-cornered hat decorated with the crimson scarf. Georgiana opened the bedroom door slowly and put her face to the gap to check the corridor before venturing out. All was quiet, and she moved stealthily, hat in hand, her steps lit only by the candle she carried, which could easily be quenched if she came upon a wakeful servant. Good fortune smiled on her, however, and she went along the corridor and down the back stairs without encountering a soul.

She left the candle on the kitchen window ledge as agreed with Emily, and slipped out to the stables. Quietly entering Princess's stall, she lifted the saddle from its hook on the wall, and placed it easily on the horse's back, her practised fingers fastening it quickly into place as she murmured reassurance to the animal. Then she moved up to Princess's head and held out a carrot. When the horse had eaten it, she wrapped the reins around her hand and silently opened the door to lead her out. She did not mount immediately, but walked Princess around the back of the house, keeping to the shadows.

Once out of the yard, Georgiana cast her eyes around the square, ears alert for late night revellers or a more than usually conscientious Watch. All was quiet, however, and she mounted, walking Princess in the direction of Hounslow Heath, making no attempt to urge her to a trot until she was safely clear of the residential quarter.

With only the moon to light her way Georgiana kept to the deserted road, her experienced ears cocked for the sounds of carriage wheels. It was not her intention to stop anyone tonight and she was relieved to find no evidence of travellers along the road. However, she wanted to be prepared if anyone should come along, and she had no intention of being caught unawares. Facing the gallows at her brother's side did not form part of her plans.

Georgiana felt the cool, fresh breeze on her cheeks as she bent to stroke Princess's neck. She turned the animal into the wood, carefully picking her way through the darkness. They eventually emerged from the trees into a clearing, populated with tethered horses. The hum of chatter and merriment came through the air. The Lucky Bell was a little further away. It was an odd location for a tavern, isolated from the main roads, but since its main clientele consisted of lawbreakers, they probably preferred it that way. Georgiana occasionally wondered if the tavern had been deliberately established with that end in view.

She dismounted and tethered Princess with the other

horses, stroked her neck and offered another carrot, which was eagerly accepted. Georgiana began to walk towards the sound and the glimmer of light, mask tied in place, the scarf around her hat rippling in the breeze.

The quiet, gentle airiness of the dark outdoors was a significant contrast to the scene Georgiana encountered on opening the door of the tavern. Brightness, warmth and a crowd of chattering bodies greeted her; one or two individuals even waved in recognition, an irony since she remained masked. Making her way across the room, she cast her eyes about for Harry. She saw him at a small table near the taproom door, playing cards with two others of rough appearance and indeterminate age. They all hailed her jovially when she approached, and invited her to join their game. Shaking her head Georgiana declined, and her quip that she had no wish to be robbed caused hilarity and some good-humoured bickering. As Harry stood, collecting his own coins and tossing off what remained in the glass in front of him, his companions bade the Crimson Cavalier a cheerful goodbye and cordially adjured her not to keep their companion's money from the table for too long. Georgiana raised a hand in farewell as she followed Harry towards a small parlour they sometimes used to negotiate over the Crimson Cavalier's acquisitions.

Finding the room occupied, Harry ruthlessly ejected the amorous young couple who had neglected to lock the door, telling the dark, curly-haired girl dragging her dress around her shoulders to be about her business and fetch them a bottle. Georgiana did not know whether to blush or laugh until Harry's boot made well aimed contact with the grey-breeched backside of the surly youth as he left the room.

As he closed the door Harry muttered about the problems of a cove finding a bit of quiet to do business for the bridle-lay.

Georgiana was not certain of Harry's age, she guessed he could be in his forties or fifties and could almost imagine him, cleaned and shaven, in a drawing room among the *haut ton*, complaining about how things were not the same as when he had been young.

"No respect, these young ones," he was saying, "nor that saucy maid."

"I thought you liked her, Harry," said Georgiana mischievously.

"A comely enough wench but business is business," he said, dropping a few small coins on the table. "For what you got from Polly's friend. Not as much as usual, I'm afraid but –"

"Not quality pieces. Never mind. Thank you anyway. Harry, I'm trying to find out something."

Harry narrowed his eyes. Georgiana untied her purse from her belt and dropped it next to the coins. She knew this was a world in which one could not expect to receive anything without payment. Harry rubbed his stubbled chin and sat down. He waved her to the chair opposite.

"Oh, put your money away, lad. We're old friends, you and I. What is it you're wanting to know?"

Georgiana felt as if she needed to take a deep breath but her voice, when she spoke, was calm and matter of fact.

"Where could a person obtain arsenic?"

19

Harry's eyes narrowed still further. His fist clenched where it rested on the table.

"What's this? I hadn't taken you for a killer, boy."

"I'm not," said Georgiana. She did not know why, but she was anxious to retain the highwayman's respect.

Harry rubbed his chin. "Go on," he said.

"You remember that fire a few days ago?" Georgiana said.

"Aye."

Georgiana nodded. "The owner of the house was killed..."

Understanding dawned on Harry's face. "It wasn't the fire?"

Georgiana shook her head.

Harry frowned. "That's dark, that is. A fire's nasty but poisoning the cove, that's dark." He looked up at Georgiana. "How did you hear of it?"

"A friend of a friend," she said simply.

"Oh." Harry looked like he wanted to know more but did not pursue it. "Dead cove a friend of yours?" he asked instead.

"Hardly," Georgiana laughed. "But a friend of mine might be in trouble for it."

Harry sought no further explanation. "There's ways of getting hold of these things," he said. "I've heard of a woman, does a bit of... medical work. Not needed to visit her myself but I've heard of a few who've seen her."

Georgiana nodded. This was not something of which she had personal experience but she had an idea the term 'medical work' could cover a variety of things, from removal of bullets from those who wouldn't want to draw attention to themselves to assistance for young women who found themselves in a delicate situation.

"I see," said Georgiana. "Do you know if she's been… helpful?"

"Believe so," he said shortly. "Folk go back to her anyway."

Georgiana was thoughtful. "Could I approach her?" she asked at last.

Harry shook his head. "Not on your own. Best go with someone she already knows. Tends not to trust people, old Meg."

Georgiana nodded her understanding of the situation. She knew such individuals were wary of the authorities and that it would be all too easy for a Runner or informant to infiltrate their practice and have them seized.

"Do you know of someone who could take me to her?" Georgiana asked. "Or speak to her for me?"

"Best not visit her just yet. Odd woman from what I've heard, odd customers as well, I shouldn't wonder." He sat looking thoughtful for a moment or two. "I'll ask about. What you wanting to know?"

"Whether anyone was looking for arsenic."

"Oh-ho," said Harry, "so that's how it was." His brows furrowed in concentration. "I've heard there's one or two of the nobs go to Meg for the stuff."

"What?" Georgiana could not believe her ears.

Harry nodded. "Oh, aye. Take it sometimes for – well, a bit of a thrill, like. Don't want to go to their own sawbones or apothecary."

"No," said Georgiana.

"Think the dead fellow might have been one," he said thoughtfully. "Odd cove from what I've heard. He came in here occasionally."

"Really?" Georgiana was surprised at this.

Harry nodded, frowning at the memory. "Oh, aye. Not sure how he found the place but he seemed to take a liking to it, not that anyone took to him. Surly cove, drank a lot, on his own. There was talk he beat his wife. Well, the lads don't hold with that, no more do I. A bit of honest thievery on the High Toby's one thing, but beating women…" Harry trailed off and banged his fist down on the table, his expression angry. "A couple of the lads wanted to teach him a lesson but I told them I thought it best not – cause more trouble than the cove was worth."

"Probably," said Georgiana. She looked closely at Harry. "Was it in here that he heard about – the medical lady?"

Harry gave a crack of laughter. "Heard old Meg called many things but not that, certainly never a lady. Witch more than not." He grew serious again. "Suppose the cove may have heard of her here, may have known about her already. Never seemed to talk to anyone from what I saw, and no one talked to him. I'll ask anyway."

"Thank you, Harry."

As Georgiana turned to depart, there was a knock on the door and the girl Harry had sent out entered with a tray holding a bottle and two glasses.

"You took your time," Harry complained. "Never mind, I'll have it at the table." He looked at Georgiana and saw her attention arrested by a scene in the corner of the main bar room. Harry's eyes followed the direction hers had taken, and he gave a snort of laughter. "Aye, we don't often get the quality in here," he said.

"Do you know who he is?"

Harry looked closely at Georgiana. He shook his head slowly. "Not sure. Don't think he's a Runner or a nark. They usually try to fit in and look like one of us." He laughed again. "They always fail. The coves from the scandal sheets do better, at least buy a drink now and then."

Georgiana gave a smile under her mask. She valued Harry's unwitting compliment: he had included her in his 'one of us'. However, her eyes remained fixed on the scene in the corner.

"Looks like they've got some business," Harry commented.

"Yes," said Georgiana. She knew better than to probe but wanted very much to know why Richard Morris was in the Lucky Bell.

Harry lost interest in the business dealings of the two men in the corner, and gave Georgiana a brief farewell salute as he went back to his card table, clutching the bottle. Georgiana knew that to betray too much curiosity in the activities of anyone in the Lucky Bell could invite more than she would welcome into her own. With a final, fleeting glance towards Morris, who was now standing, she made her way to the door, glad to be out in the fresh air and quiet, with leisure to think about what she had seen and heard.

Georgiana walked steadily to where Princess was tethered. The visit had been more fruitful than she had expected, but left her wanting to know more. As she walked, she mulled over an idea which had occurred to her as she left the tavern. She wasn't certain she could carry it off. A number of horses stood in the stable yard, and all was quiet save for their breathing and an occasional low snort. Georgiana untied Princess, her mind on her plan as she stroked the animal and took hold of the bridle to mount.

Georgiana turned the mare and walked her gently out of the stable yard back towards the main road. She deliberately kept the animal's progress slow, silent but for the gentle clip-clop of hooves as they made their way through the night air. There was a full moon, a mixed blessing for Georgiana; while it would enable her to see, it could also assist any possible pursuers. She gave an occasional glance over her shoulder, ears alert. Her vigilance was rewarded when, before many minutes had passed, the faint sound of a horse's canter grew steadily louder.

Georgiana slowed Princess, reining her in to the side of the road. The steps she heard told her the horseman was a lone one, and she moved Princess out of sight behind the cover of some trees, so she could watch the new arrival without being seen.

The horseman was not many minutes behind Georgiana. Her mask was still in place and she put a hand to her belt. As the solitary figure ventured on to the road, he found himself facing the levelled pistol of the Crimson Cavalier.

Richard Morris looked her directly in the eye. For a moment, Georgiana thought he would offer more of a challenge than the indignation she was accustomed to.

"The Crimson Cavalier." Morris bowed. "I am honoured. Your name runs the breadth of the land. I believe the phrase is 'Stand and deliver.'" The situation appeared to amuse him.

"Down," commanded Georgiana, gesturing towards the ground with her pistol.

Morris hesitated, shrugged and obeyed.

"You have me at your mercy," he said "Do you intend to murder me?"

Georgiana ignored the question but kept her pistol firmly on him as she herself dismounted.

Morris handed over his purse in a lethargic, almost bored manner.

"Is that the business done?"

"Your watch and fob, please, and I should be grateful for that ring."

Morris obeyed, still looking vaguely amused, as though he regarded the incident nothing more than a tedious inconvenience.

"May I go now?"

Still not satisfied, Georgiana persevered.

"Your pockets, please."

Morris grew angry.

"Sir, you go too far."

Georgiana raised the pistol a fraction, in an effort to be more persuasive.

"Do I, sir? Your pockets, if you please."

Morris's expression hardened. Georgiana moved her thumb in readiness to cock the pistol. When Morris still made no move, she stepped forward and plunged her free hand into the right hand pocket of his coat. Her victim was too stunned to prevent her. She repeated the process with his other pocket.

"What the devil?" was all Morris could manage to expostulate.

"Perhaps it is now I go too far," Georgiana said, dropping her collection into her black velvet bag. "Thank you. You may go."

Morris stood for a moment, seething but powerless to retaliate. He snatched the reins of his horse and threw himself up into the saddle with very bad grace, glaring down at the Crimson Cavalier, who touched the edge of her hat with the barrel of her pistol in a gesture of salute. Morris pulled viciously at the reins, making his horse squeal as he turned it around. Georgiana stood patiently, watching as he rode away and making no shift to mount her own horse until he was out of sight.

As the sound of Morris's horse receded, Georgiana mounted Princess. She listened for a few more moments, until the silence left her as certain as she could be that no one was lying in wait to trap her. She started to walk Princess along the road, still alert for signs that she might not be alone. She gradually brought the animal to a canter; a galloping horse would attract attention and very likely suspicion at this time of night, and Georgiana had no wish to deplete Princess's energy unless it became absolutely necessary.

In the event, fortune smiled on her. There was no pursuit and no sign of her disgruntled victim. She managed to make the journey without incident from the woods, past the few cottages into the more heavily populated area.

Since Princess had progressed at a relatively comfortable pace, it did not take Georgiana long to rub the animal down and settle her in her stall. The house was quiet, and though the candle she had left in the kitchen window had burned low, there was still enough to light her passage up the back stairs to her bedchamber. She tossed her hat on the bed and drew off her gloves, sitting down on the top of the coverlet to empty out the black velvet bag.

She pushed aside Morris's watch, fob, ring and coins; for the moment her interest lay with the contents of his pockets. For the most part it was fairly ordinary: snuff box, handkerchief, a scrap of paper with some writing on it. Her hand quickly rifled through these items until she found what she was looking for.

She lifted a small packet of folded paper between thumb and forefinger, pushed the other items to one side and placed it on the bed. She unfolded the edges carefully, until it lay it open beside her. Georgiana looked intently at it, quite unaware that the door to her dressing room was opening quietly.

Emily found her mistress staring down at a very small pile of white powder.

20

"Lor', Miss Georgiana, is that what I think it is?"

Georgiana looked up. "I believe so, Emily."

"Did you get it in the Lucky Bell?"

"In a manner of speaking, I suppose. I took it from Richard Morris on the road after I left."

Emily looked confused. Georgiana gestured for her to sit and relayed what she had seen. The maid looked more confused than ever.

"You think he bought it in the Lucky Bell?" asked Emily. "But why would he want it now? You think he's one of those gentlemen Harry mentioned who take it sometimes for their pleasure?"

"It's possible, Emily. Although I must admit, I would not have thought it of him, when one compares him with someone such as Lord Wickerston."

"Yes," said Emily thoughtfully. "But why else would he want it now, miss?" she asked. "Lord Wickerston's already dead, so even if Mr Morris did kill him he wouldn't need more, not unless he's planning to kill someone else. He can hardly make a habit of it."

"One wouldn't have thought so," said Georgiana slowly. "Although –"

"What, miss?"

"Lady Wickerston did try to kill herself," said Georgiana. "If Edward took away what arsenic she had, she must have obtained more from somewhere."

"If it was arsenic she took," said Emily.

"True," said Georgiana. "I don't know what else there would have been in the house. Laudanum perhaps."

"We don't know whether she used all the arsenic they said was bought for the rats," said Emily.

Georgiana looked closely at her. "Lady Wickerston's servants weren't disposed to talk?" she asked the maid.

Emily shook her head. "Not much, I'm afraid, miss. The maid seemed a bit chatty, but the butler and the housekeeper —"

"Reminded her of the importance of discretion," said Georgiana. "Of course." She sat thinking for another moment or two. "I wonder if there's another way. Perhaps James…"

"Could take her for an ice, or a cup of tea?" finished Emily with a smile. "I'll ask him, miss."

"This does seem very unfair on him if he's not interested in the girl," said Georgiana. "Tell him I shall pay the expenses and ensure it is worth his while."

"Yes, miss."

Too exhausted to check the remains of the evening's proceeds, Georgiana scooped everything up and locked it in the drawer of her night table along with her pistol. Emily put away the Crimson's Cavalier's clothes, and Georgiana slipped gratefully under the coverlet, sinking into the warmth of the bed where Emily had thoughtfully placed a hot brick some time earlier.

Georgiana woke late the next morning. Emily told her she had thought it best not to disturb her. Selina had apparently been satisfied with the explanation that all the visiting of the previous day had exhausted Georgiana. This was not far from the truth, and Georgiana was more than a little relieved to find her cousin had not only breakfasted earlier but had gone out on some charity errand. Her solitude did not last long, however, and she was on her second cup of tea when James entered the dining room to tell her that her sister-in-law had called.

"Would you wish to see her, miss?" His tone and words were everything one would expect of an impeccable servant but Georgiana detected a hint of concern in his eyes.

"Yes, please, James. Show her in here if you please."

"Very good, miss."

Amanda hurried into the room. She looked anxious, and her gloves lay crumpled in her hands as though she had been nervously twisting them rather than wearing them. Georgiana immediately asked for a fresh pot of tea, but Amanda shook her head.

"Please sit down, Amanda," Georgiana said, as James closed the door behind him. She laid a hand on her sister-in-law's arm. "Are you all right?"

"Yes. That is... I... well, not entirely... Oh, I don't know, Georgiana."

"Has something happened?"

"It is this whole business. I don't know what to do for the best. The children know something is wrong and I don't know what to tell them. I feel so helpless."

Georgiana was silent for a moment, giving Amanda time to gather her thoughts.

"I understand," she said gently. "It's all right."

"It isn't," said Amanda. "It is far from all right. Mr Lakesby told me Edward wouldn't speak, wouldn't say what happened, why he had been taken."

Georgiana hesitated. Amanda seemed to read her expression.

"Please, Georgiana, I would rather know. Is he – is he trying to protect Lady Wickerston?"

"I don't know," said Georgiana truthfully.

Amanda sat silently for a moment. There was sadness in her eyes, and something else as well. Eventually she spoke.

"Georgiana, there is something I must explain. When you

visited yesterday, Mr Lakesby's presence…"

"Good heavens, Amanda, you have nothing to explain to me. I imagined Mr Lakesby was there to tell you what progress he had made over Edward's situation."

"Yes."

"Besides," continued Georgiana, "I know you too well to believe you to be engaging in anything improper."

"Still, how it must have looked…"

"Try not to let it worry you," recommended Georgiana. "Selina will not say anything."

"No, but I think she was very shocked."

"Possibly but she will realise soon enough that Mr Lakesby is trying to help."

"There is something else," said Amanda. "I – I was a little surprised to see Mr Morris with you when you visited yesterday."

"Yes, I'm sorry about that," said Georgiana. "I'm afraid Selina invited him to accompany us when he mentioned he was acquainted with you."

Amanda nodded. "I see. Normally it would not matter, but the circumstances are a little… peculiar."

"Yes, I know," said Georgiana. "Edward's imprisonment puts you in a difficult position. I am so sorry, I should have found some excuse."

"Oh, no, it is not that," said Amanda, "at least, well, I suppose it is part of it but not the main reason. You see…" She drew a breath. "The fact is, I knew Mr Morris before I married Edward. In fact, he made me an offer."

"I see."

"I declined," Amanda said hastily. "He was a pleasant enough acquaintance but I never felt able to, well…"

"I understand," said Georgiana. A finger of conscience was jabbing at her, telling her she should assure Amanda there

212

was no need to say more. However, curiosity prevented her.

"It must have been difficult seeing him again," Georgiana sympathised.

"Yes, it was, especially since it was so unexpected." Amanda smiled. "I'm afraid he did not take my refusal well. He grew angry. I had never seen him like that, it was frightening. I thought perhaps he would never forgive me but seeing him yesterday made me wonder –"

"If he had?"

"Possibly. It seemed to me he was more interested in you."

"Oh, I think that is unlikely," said Georgiana.

"Why? Georgiana, I know he is considered something of a prize on the matrimonial mart, but please, promise me you will be careful."

"Of course," said Georgiana, surprised. There was a twinkle in her eye. "I'm sure you know by now that I'm not going to rush into matrimony with the first man who makes me an offer."

"Or the second, or the third," concurred Amanda with a smile.

Before the conversation went any further, there was a tap on the door and James ventured in to tell Georgiana she had another visitor.

"Mr Lakesby has called, Miss Georgiana."

"Oh. Thank you, James. Show him in here, would you?" Georgiana glanced towards her sister-in-law.

Lakesby entered in brisk fashion, hesitating briefly when he realised Georgiana was seated at the table.

"I beg your pardon," he said. "Your footman did not mention you were still at breakfast."

"It is of no matter," said Georgiana. "I have finished, and as you see, my sister-in-law has called to visit. Won't you please come and join us, Mr Lakesby?"

Lakesby accepted the offer of a seat. "I'm sorry to intrude on your visit, Mrs Grey."

"That doesn't matter, truly." Amanda's eyes flickered towards the door, watching for it to close behind James. "Please tell me, Mr Lakesby, have you been able to learn anything?"

"A little," he said, "but not as much as I would like. I have been to Bow Street. I managed to talk to the Runner who questioned your husband."

"Yes?" Amanda said eagerly.

Lakesby hesitated; his eyes flicked briefly towards Georgiana before he addressed Amanda again.

"I'm sorry. The Runner is being quite discreet and your husband seems to be doing very little to help himself. He will not say anything in his defence."

"Why has he been sent to Newgate?" Amanda asked, beginning to sound desperate.

"I'm afraid," said Lakesby, "that the Runner mentioned he was found in possession of a small amount of arsenic and has not offered any explanation for it."

Amanda paled. However, when she spoke her voice gave no indication of discomposure.

"There could be any number of reasons for that," she said.

"Amanda, you are not going to say Edward obtained it for rats in your cellar, are you?" asked Georgiana.

Amanda looked directly at her. "Yes. Yes, of course, that would explain it. I must tell someone."

"Mrs Grey, I don't think it would help," said Lakesby gently. "I beg your pardon, I had hoped to spare you this – but he was seen in Lady Wickerston's company."

"Oh. I see."

Lakesby looked mortified to be the bearer of such news, and immediately sought to make amends. "I'm so sorry. Please forgive my clumsiness. Let me explain."

Amanda looked steadily at him, her eyes full of anxious inquiry. Lakesby glanced towards Georgiana again before addressing Amanda.

"Lady Wickerston went to Brooks's on the day of his lordship's death, looking for your husband. She was quite distraught. I'm afraid some talk is inevitable."

"Yes," said Amanda. "But why would she do such a thing? It must have been something exceptional for her to seek out a gentleman at his club."

Georgiana looked at her sister-in-law in growing admiration. There was no expression of shock, no prim horror that a lady could do such a thing, or even indignation that her own husband was the gentleman being sought. Her manner was very matter of fact.

"You're right, Mrs Grey, it was exceptional," said Lakesby. "Her ladyship had quarrelled with her husband, quite severely, I gather. My understanding is that she put something in his drink, with the intention of poisoning him."

"Oh, no," said Amanda. "How horrible. I had heard rumours, of course, about the difficulties between Lord and Lady Wickerston but I never dreamt…" She paused, looking at her companions in puzzlement. "If that is the case, why has Edward been imprisoned?" She looked from one to the other, the puzzlement gradually clearing. "The authorities don't know of her involvement? Edward is protecting her?"

"We don't know that to be the case, Amanda," said Georgiana.

"It is a little more complicated than that, Mrs Grey," said Lakesby. "It appears his lordship did not drink from the glass Lady Wickerston had left for him. However, he was poisoned."

"Lady Wickerston told me she still had the remaining arsenic in her hand when she visited Brooks's," said Georgiana.

"I expect Edward was afraid she would do something rash with it," said Amanda.

"I am sure you are right," said Georgiana.

"Unfortunately," said Lakesby, "he will say nothing on the matter. I visited him yesterday and he refused to tell me anything."

Georgiana suspected Lakesby's omission to mention her own visit was deliberate.

"I see," said Amanda, looking thoughtful. "Edward is not always very communicative, and I suppose if he thought he was breaking a confidence…"

"You need not skirt around the issue, Mrs Grey. I am aware your husband does not like me," said Lakesby dryly.

"Oh, dear, I'm so sorry, Mr Lakesby," said Amanda. "I had hoped that could be laid aside for the moment. I do appreciate your efforts to help him."

"That is of no matter," said Lakesby, "except that his unwillingness to speak to me prevents my making any progress."

"What about Lady Wickerston's attempt to kill herself?" asked Georgiana. "Was it arsenic she took?"

Lakesby nodded. "Dr Masters thinks so."

"All this arsenic does seem to have been very readily available," said Georgiana.

Lakesby shrugged. "Tell the apothecary one has a problem with rats, sign the Poison Book and it's a simple enough matter. Of course, there are – less conventional ways, if one is apt to need it on a regular basis and concerned about the pharmacist's suspicions.

"What?" said Amanda. "On a regular basis?"

It was Georgiana who spoke. "I've been told Lord Wickerston may have taken small doses himself occasionally."

Amanda looked perplexed, glancing from her sister-in-law to Lakesby in search of an explanation.

"Is it used as a medicine?" she asked.

"It can be," said Lakesby.

"Mr Morris mentioned the possibility to me," said Georgiana absently.

"Did he?" Lakesby turned his full attention on her.

Amanda's glance continued to flicker between the two. "He didn't say why?"

Georgiana thought it best not to be too specific. "Not really. He wasn't even quite certain," she said.

"In that case I'm astonished he should take the trouble to mention it at all," said Lakesby.

Amanda was frowning. "Perhaps it was an accident."

"Perhaps," said Lakesby.

"However one interprets it," said Georgiana, "there was arsenic available, which could have been a factor in Lord Wickerston's death or his wife's attempt to kill herself."

"But Lady Wickerston is staying with her aunt. She could not have known her house would burn down," pointed out Amanda.

"No," said Georgiana thoughtfully.

"Arsenic would certainly be an odd thing to take with her," observed Lakesby.

"That rather depends on her intentions," said Georgiana.

Her companions looked at her in puzzlement but Georgiana made no attempt to elaborate. Sounds in the hall suggested that her cousin had returned, and indeed, Selina's voice was heard a moment or two later. Georgiana heard her cousin inquire for her, and Selina entered the room a moment later.

"Oh, good heavens," said Selina, looking startled as she paused on the threshold. "Oh, I beg your pardon. I had not meant to intrude. Amanda, my dear, how are you?"

"Very well, thank you, Selina," said Amanda. "I'm so sorry but I really should go. Would you think it very rude of me?"

"Oh. Well, of course, I should never dream of such a thing," said Selina. "But please do not rush off on my account. It is so nice to see you, oh, and you too, Mr Lakesby, of course."

Lakesby gave a small bow and a smile of acknowledgement.

"Thank you, Selina, you are very kind," said Amanda. "I'm so sorry. Please don't imagine I am leaving because you have returned. I really must get back to the children."

"Oh, well, if you must go, you must," said Selina. There was just a hint of sullenness in her tone.

"May I have the honour of escorting you home, Mrs Grey?" said Lakesby.

Selina's eyes widened but Amanda seemed not to notice.

"Thank you, Mr Lakesby, that is very kind of you. I should be glad of your company." She turned to Georgiana. "Thank you so much. I can't tell you how much I appreciate…"

"Nonsense," said Georgiana, embracing her sister-in-law. "You know I am glad to do whatever I can." Georgiana turned to her other guest and held out a hand. "Goodbye, Mr Lakesby."

"Miss Grey," he said, shaking her hand. "Perhaps I could have the honour of taking you driving later?"

"Thank you, I should like that," said Georgiana.

Miss Knatchbull sat at the table, nibbling a biscuit. As the visitors departed, Georgiana sat down to join her, with a smile.

"Oh, Georgiana, I went to Mr Scott, the apothecary, for some corn plasters and I met Lady Wickerston's brother there."

21

Georgiana blinked. Her cousin's remark was quite innocuous, an innocent observation, yet she could not help seeing something sinister behind it.

"Oh?" she inquired.

"Yes, indeed," Selina prattled on. "Such a charming gentleman. He asked about you."

"Did he?" said Georgiana, pretending not to notice the curiosity in Selina's voice and expression. "I hope he is not ill?"

"Oh, no, I don't think so," said Selina. "He did not say so." She lowered her voice. "I did not like to ask but I rather thought he might have been getting something for his sister."

"Perhaps," said Georgiana absently. She had her own thoughts about what Sir Anthony might have been purchasing. She wondered whether she was growing obsessed with the subject of arsenic. After all, Lord Wickerston was already dead; what would be the point of obtaining poison after the murder? Unless there was to be another...

"That was an odd thing with Amanda and Mr Lakesby," said Selina.

"Odd?" said Georgiana.

"Well... yes," said Selina a little uncertainly.

"I see nothing odd in Mr Lakesby escorting Amanda home. He is nothing if not a gentleman."

"But with him visiting yesterday and Edward being... away."

Georgiana found Selina's speculation irritating. "You are suggesting that because Edward is not at home, Mr Lakesby is paying Amanda improper attentions and she is encouraging them?"

"Well, no, of course not… that is…"

"Really, Selina, that is the biggest piece of nonsense I have ever heard," said Georgiana with some asperity.

"I wasn't accusing Amanda of impropriety," said Selina, clearly stung. "But, well, it is just, it is just…"

Georgiana made no attempt to help. "Yes?" she inquired sweetly.

Selina looked uncomfortable. "Well, someone mentioned she was … staying with you, which I thought a little odd."

"Oh?"

Selina's colour rose further. "And since Edward is… where he is…" She floundered, looking helplessly at her cousin.

"She came to stay with me while you were away. That is all."

Selina did not respond, her expression nervous, as though fearful of saying the wrong thing. The silence was broken by the entrance of James.

"I beg your pardon, miss, but would it be convenient to clear the breakfast things away?" he asked.

"Oh, yes, of course," said Georgiana. She caught something in her footman's expression which suggested there was something more. She was about to look for some pretext to send Miss Knatchbull from the room when James spoke again.

"I beg your pardon, Miss Georgiana, but would it be quite convenient for me to take this afternoon off?" he said. "An acquaintance has asked to speak to me rather urgently."

"This afternoon?" said Selina. "Oh dear."

"Yes, James, quite convenient," said Georgiana, before Selina could continue.

"Thank you, miss."

Selina looked surprised but offered no comment; she simply gave a small shrug and shook her head. As she stood, she recalled something she had wanted to say to Georgiana.

"Sir Anthony mentioned he would like to call on us. I saw no objection; he seems a pleasant enough young man."

"Yes, very well," said Georgiana, reflecting that for a man whose family was in mourning, Sir Anthony spent a prodigious amount of time paying calls. She was also a little inclined to suspect his tendency to confide. Georgiana did not think it likely many family members would be so anxious to discuss such delicate matters with a new acquaintance.

"I suggested he come this afternoon."

"What? Today? Oh, Selina, really. That is not at all convenient. I am going for a drive with Mr Lakesby today."

"Well, I did not know that," said Selina defensively.

Georgiana sighed. That was true.

"Sir Anthony seems to have a great regard for you," Selina persevered.

"He barely knows me," said Georgiana. She looked at her cousin thoughtfully. "Did he say anything about his sister?" she inquired.

"Only that she was resting," Selina responded. "Such a dreadful business."

"Yes."

Selina hesitated briefly before continuing. "Have you heard anything more of Edward's… situation?"

"I have seen him," said Georgiana. "He is being very foolish, refusing to tell anything."

"See – seen him?" Selina looked ready to faint. "In – in Newgate?"

"Yes." The colour had left her cousin's face. "Oh, for goodness sake, Selina, these are hardly normal circumstances."

"No, but still, for a lady to visit a – a prison…" Her voice trailed away feebly before she summoned strength to ask, "Was it very dreadful?"

"Well, it wasn't pleasant. However, he does at least have a

cell to himself." Georgiana's tone was matter of fact. She frowned, her eye resting thoughtfully on her cousin as she considered whether such an unlikely source of information could be fruitful. "Selina, was there much detail in the newspaper account of Edward's arrest?"

"What? Oh, I really don't know, Georgiana, I was so shocked. It was very discreetly written but it was clear they were referring to Edward. I really could not believe he would do such a thing." She looked sharply at her cousin. "Good heavens, Georgiana, you saw it."

Georgiana did not have the heart to tell her she had barely glanced at the main points of the article before tossing it aside. "I did not really take it in. Please, Selina, it could be important."

"Oh, I see." Selina sat down, folding her hands as she frowned in an effort of concentration. "Well, as I recall, it mentioned the fire and that Lord Wickerston's death may not have been caused by it. Quite shocking."

"Yes."

Selina looked up, saw her cousin was waiting for more and nodded.

"Arsenic was mentioned and that a Mr G--- had been taken by the Runners and was in Newgate."

"Did it say he had confessed?"

"No, I don't think so. Good heavens, he hasn't, has he?" Selina looked horrified.

"Selina, please, can you remember any more?"

Selina screwed up her eyes and clasped her hands together more tightly.

"There was a Bow Street Runner mentioned, I think the one Edward said he was acquainted with. Yes, I'm certain of it. What was his name? Oh, yes, Rogers, William Rogers, I think. But Georgiana, I really do not understand. Why on earth should Edward do such a thing? Why should he even be involved?"

Clearly Selina imagined Edward to be a mere acquaintance of the Wickerstons. Georgiana could not shatter her cousin's naiveté. She simply told her that Lady Wickerston had had a difficult marriage, and that some of her friends had been concerned. Selina appeared to accept this explanation, and rose to her feet, announcing that she was going to her room.

As soon as she had left, Georgiana sent for Emily.

"Can you go to Bow Street? Immediately, if possible."

Emily looked surprised but nodded assent.

"Take a carriage. And Tom."

"As an escort? To Bow Street? Oh, he'd like that. No, I'll be quite all right, miss. What do you need?"

"I need you to speak to the Runner who arrested Edward. His name is William Rogers. See what you can find out about the case against Edward. I believe Mr Lakesby spoke to this man, but you may be able to do better."

"All right, miss."

"There is something else. My cousin saw information printed in a newspaper, very quickly after Edward's imprisonment – too quickly to have come from any official source. That tells me that either the murderer was arranging for Edward to take the blame, or –"

"Or the Bow Street Runner was seeking a little glory for himself," said Emily.

Georgiana nodded. "Exactly. You can take some of the money from my night table drawer. Is there anything else you need?"

"Don't think so, miss. Lady Wickerston's maid told me today's her afternoon out, so James said he'd call on her."

"Yes, he asked for the afternoon off. I thought it might be something like that." Georgiana paused. "I can't thank you both enough for your help."

Emily waved a hand dismissively. "'Tis nothing, miss. You've helped us enough."

"Come upstairs and help me get ready for my drive with Mr Lakesby. You can get the money you need at the same time."

Georgiana was ready and waiting for Mr Lakesby when he called. Her cousin was occupied with some household tasks and her maid and footman both absent. Although Mr Lakesby was the essence of politeness, Georgiana sensed a certain frostiness in his manner. He spoke little as they set off, giving his full attention to his horses as they negotiated the relatively quiet roads at a sedate pace.

Georgiana watched him from the corner of her eye for some moments, her head tilted sideways in amusement. Eventually she spoke.

"Have I done something to offend you, Mr Lakesby?"

"In what way could you have offended me, Miss Grey?"

"I cannot imagine. Perhaps you are just… preoccupied?"

"Not at all."

Georgiana fell silent and watched the road ahead. Lakesby made no attempt at conversation. After a moment or two, Georgiana spoke again.

"Are we going to Newgate, Mr Lakesby?"

Lakesby looked towards her in surprise. "Is that your wish?"

"Not particularly," she answered. "But I understand you made a second visit to my brother yesterday and I thought perhaps it had become a routine."

A muscle at the side of Lakesby's jaw tensed.

"How do you come to be aware of my second visit?"

"James asked the jailer to let him know when anyone else visited my brother."

224

"I see."

"Was your visit successful?"

"It was successful in that I gained entry, less so in that your brother still refused to speak to me."

"Oh, dear. I'm sorry you went to such trouble for nothing."

Lakesby seemed to thaw a little.

"Your sister-in-law seems to be bearing up very well."

"Yes." Georgiana paused. "Mr Lakesby, I must own, I visited Edward a second time myself yesterday."

"Oh?"

"It was Lady Wickerston's suggestion." Georgiana wondered why she felt the need to explain. "I called on her yesterday and…" Georgiana paused, trying to think how she could word her next sentence diplomatically. "She expressed a desire for some fresh air and asked me to accompany her."

"This she thought to find in Newgate Prison?" Lakesby asked in astonishment.

Georgiana shrugged. "Her condition seemed to improve when I mentioned that you and James had found the wine glass spilled, untouched by his lordship."

"Well, that's understandable. Though why the devil –"

"It was only when we were in the carriage that she mentioned where she wanted to go."

"I'm surprised your brother agreed to receive you," said Lakesby grimly.

"I don't think he had a great deal of choice in the matter," was Georgiana's tart response. "It's not as if he's at home in his study."

"I am aware," Lakesby snapped. "However, he is a fairly privileged prisoner, as these things go."

Georgiana knew this to be true. Those of less standing in the community were tossed in the large communal area, without privacy or furniture, likely sharing their accommodation with rats as well as other prisoners. She sighed. "Yes, I know. Did you learn anything?"

Lakesby smiled sardonically at the turn of conversation. "I have already told you your brother wouldn't speak to me."

"You may have discovered something another way."

"I may. Did you?"

Georgiana considered, eyeing him as she debated with herself. Finally, she shrugged. "A little, but if anything, it seems more confusing."

"Go on."

Georgiana hesitated. There was something irritating about Lakesby's assumption that she would share information when he was so reticent about doing so himself. However, she could not deny that he was trying to help her brother, even in the face of Edward's own lack of co-operation.

"Lady Wickerston was urging Edward to speak out," said Georgiana. "She seemed to think that the failure of her own attempt to kill her husband put a different complexion on the matter."

"In a way it does," said Lakesby slowly.

"Not enough to make her seem an innocent party," pointed out Georgiana. "She would not have the sympathy of the authorities, or society, for that matter."

"True enough. Was that your brother's view?"

"I think so," said Georgiana. "He did not say as much but he did point out to Lady Wickerston that the matter was not as simple as she thought."

"No."

Georgiana hesitated before speaking again. "There is something else," she said.

Lakesby looked inquiringly at her. Georgiana moistened her lips.

"The day of the fire... The day Lady Wickerston appeared

226

at Brooks's... Edward said that after he had taken her to her aunt's home, he went to see Lord Wickerston."

Lakesby groaned.

"I know," said Georgiana.

"Is that all?"

"I asked Edward what happened to the arsenic he took from Lady Wickerston, and he said he gave it to his lordship."

"By gave, did he mean he put it into his lordship's hands or...?"

Georgiana shook her head. "I don't know."

It was a moment before Lakesby spoke.

"It sounds almost as if your brother is trying to get himself hanged. Did you mention any of this to your sister-in-law?"

Georgiana shook her head. "I would rather not, unless it becomes unavoidable."

"It may," said Lakesby.

"He told you nothing at all?" Georgiana persevered.

"Only that it was none of my concern and he would thank me to keep out of his affairs."

"I see."

They sat silent for a moment or two, frustrated by the lack of progress. It was Lakesby who spoke first.

"By the way, I ran into Richard Morris this morning. He mentioned he had been held up by the Crimson Cavalier last night."

"Did he? How unfortunate for him," said Georgiana.

"He was seething," said Lakesby, "much more so than one would expect from the loss of a few coins and trinkets. I got the impression he had lost something particularly important."

"Did he say what?" asked Georgiana.

"No, but I should not like to be in the Crimson Cavalier's shoes if they should meet again. I suspect Morris could be a dangerous enemy."

"Perhaps," said Georgiana.

Lakesby glanced towards her. "I daresay you have not seen that side of him. Morris can be charming to those he chooses to please."

"He has been courteous," said Georgiana evenly.

"It was certainly *courteous* of him to escort you to your sister-in-law's house yesterday."

"My cousin invited him. May I ask, Mr Lakesby, if there is some… difficulty here?"

"Not at all," he responded coolly. "Your choice of friends is your own affair. I am just a little surprised at your priorities at present. I would have expected you to be more concerned with securing your brother's freedom from imprisonment."

"Indeed?" said Georgiana frostily. "Yet I gained the impression you disapproved of my visiting Edward."

"It is not my place to disapprove of your actions."

"True," she said. "I am just a little confused. Would you like me to stay at home, a martyr to my nerves, lying on the couch clutching a bottle of smelling salts, or would you prefer me to storm Newgate Prison singlehandedly and free Edward by force?"

"You are being foolish beyond permission."

"Am I?"

They continued in silence. Lakesby drew up the carriage outside Georgiana's front door and stepped down to offer her assistance. She thanked him but did not invite him inside for refreshment. Their goodbye was civil but not warm.

Georgiana's arrival home was greeted by an animated Selina, hands clasped and wreathed in smiles. She had apparently no sooner heard the front door than she had come to meet her cousin.

"Georgiana, my love, I am so glad you are returned. We have visitors."

"Have we?" said Georgiana with little interest.

"Yes, indeed. Come, your pelisse, my love. Oh, do make haste."

"For heaven's sake, Selina, do calm down and give me a chance to draw breath. Who on earth is waiting, the Archbishop of Canterbury?"

Selina chastised Georgiana for so irreverent a response.

"It is Sir Anthony Dixon and his sister."

22

Georgiana blinked.

"Have Emily and James returned?" she asked.

"What? Good heavens, Georgiana, I don't believe so. What does it matter? Do come along. Our guests are waiting."

"For one so recently widowed, Lady Wickerston seems to spend a prodigious amount of time visiting."

"Georgiana! For shame! Hush now, they will hear you."

"I notice you do not deny it. You are merely concerned that they might hear me say it."

"Georgiana!"

"I am sorry, Selina, but I really am not in the mood for visitors at present. What do they want?"

Selina looked horrified. "I believe they have just called to be civil. What is wrong with that?"

"Nothing, except that I would have expected her ladyship to be in seclusion, as befits a newly widowed lady. I have no doubt Lord Wickerston was a difficult husband, but one would expect her to make some show of grief."

"She is wearing black," said Selina.

"Ah, well, that makes a difference, of course," said Georgiana. Clearly this was a battle she would not win. "Come, let us go in."

She swept into the drawing room with a confident air and welcoming smile. Her cousin trundled behind, her manner that of a nervous rabbit, fearful in case their guests should have heard Georgiana's comments.

Neither Sir Anthony nor Lady Wickerston gave any indication that they had heard anything untoward. They greeted their newly arrived hostess with all the propriety one would expect; Sir Anthony stood to shake hands, and waited until both Georgiana and Selina were seated before resuming his own chair.

"My sister and I wanted to thank you for your kindness, Miss Grey," Sir Anthony said.

"Oh?"

"It was so kind of you to accompany my sister yesterday when she needed to go out for some air. She seems very much the better for it."

Georgiana glanced towards Lady Wickerston. She did not look better. Her face was pale and her manner subdued.

"How are you, Lady Wickerston?" asked Georgiana.

"Well enough, Miss Grey. Thank you for your concern."

Ironically, the black garb was becoming to her ladyship's golden hair and pale complexion. It gave her an air of fragility which could not help but secure compassion.

"It must be a comfort to have the support of your aunt and brother," said Georgiana.

"Oh, yes," said Lady Wickerston, "and friends have been so kind: you, and Mr Morris."

"Yes," said Georgiana. "I know Mr Morris has been very concerned about your situation."

"Really?"

Did Georgiana imagine the ice which crept into her ladyship's voice?

"Yes," said Georgiana. "He called yesterday and spoke of it, how distressed you were, how badly you'd been affected by your husband's death." She paused and looked closely at her ladyship. "He seems to be a very good friend to you."

Georgiana was sure it was not her imagination this time. Lady Wickerston stiffened; her lips compressed and her face developed severe lines that made her seem older.

"Anthony, we should be going. We have taken up enough of

Miss Grey's time."

"Oh, no, please," twittered Selina. "I have just ordered another pot of tea. I'm sure your ladyship would be glad of an opportunity to be comfortable."

"No, really, we must go," said Lady Wickerston.

Sir Anthony looked bemused but followed his sister's bidding. He offered a civil farewell to both Georgiana and Selina, while Lady Wickerston sailed into the hallway, calling for her pelisse. The carriage was summoned, and they were gone at a speed which left their hostesses, and to some extent Sir Anthony too, stunned.

"Good heavens, what can have happened?" said Selina. "Lady Wickerston seemed offended."

"Lady Wickerston seemed uncivil," said Georgiana, turning on her heel to return to the drawing room.

"Perhaps she heard what you said," Selina remarked, trotting along in her wake.

"Perhaps." But Georgiana was unconvinced.

The parlourmaid brought the tea Selina had requested and Georgiana paid little heed as her cousin began to fuss, concerned that it would go to waste. As the parlourmaid left the room, Emily appeared. She looked triumphant, but checked herself as she caught sight of Miss Knatchbull.

Georgiana met Emily's eye and glanced towards the stairs. As Emily nodded her understanding and left the room, Georgiana turned to her cousin.

"Selina, I must go and change."

"What? Oh, very well, Georgiana. But do make haste, your tea will be cold."

As Georgiana walked towards the stairs, she heard Selina muttering about everyone behaving oddly. However, her cousin's disapproval was the least of her worries at the moment; she quickly joined Emily in her bedchamber.

"Well?" said Georgiana as soon as the door was closed.

"The Runner's not been to the newspapers, miss. I'd stake my life on it."

"You're as certain as that?"

Emily nodded. "Quite reserved he was, miss, almost shy. Didn't seem to want to talk about Lord Wickerston's death at all, that is until…"

"Until?"

"Until he heard you were Mr Edward's sister. Got very helpful then."

"Really?"

Emily nodded. "He knows your brother, knew him when Mr Edward was a magistrate, worked with him over that business of Sir Robert Foster."

"I see."

"Anyway, it seems he's got a lot of respect for your brother, and doesn't believe he killed Lord Wickerston."

"Oh?"

"It seems when they found Lord Wickerston's death was not an accident, Mr Rogers spoke to Mr Edward because he knew he was acquainted with her ladyship. He thought your brother would want to help."

"That makes sense," Georgiana nodded.

"You'd expect so, miss – but your brother wouldn't say anything. And because he had the arsenic, Mr Rogers's superiors said he must be arrested."

"Oh, for goodness sake, what is the matter with Edward?" said Georgiana in exasperation. "He'll sign his own death warrant yet."

Emily made no reply, but after a few moments she added, "There is something else, miss."

Georgiana looked at her.

"Well, as I said, Miss Georgiana, Mr Rogers seems to

respect your brother, and wasn't satisfied with what had happened. He'd heard that Lord Wickerston was in possession of arsenic himself, so he spoke to his lordship's servants. Seems his lordship's valet used to get it for him. The thing is, well, he talked about it, had a drop in and his tongue got loosened up with his cronies. Anyone could have known about his lordship's habit."

Emily stopped to draw breath, but that clearly was not all she had to say. Georgiana waited for the maid to continue.

"Then after his lordship's death Mr Rogers received a note. It mentioned his... habit with the arsenic, and that he... well, he beat his wife."

Georgiana felt a tingle of excitement. Now they were making some progress. "Not from Lord Wickerston himself, I suppose?" she said.

"No, miss, nothing so simple. Mr Rogers thinks it was from one of the gentry. Nice writing it was, and that thick paper like you use yourself. And like they might have at those gentlemen's clubs. Brooks's, for instance."

Georgiana mulled this over. "Did the note actually say Edward was involved?"

"No, miss, but when I mentioned about the newspaper getting to know so soon, he seemed shocked. He wondered if they might have had a letter as well. He sent a boy to check. Promised to send me a message when he returned."

"That's very obliging of him."

"Yes, miss." Emily's lips twitched and she looked at the floor.

"Was there anything else from Lord Wickerston's valet?"

"Mr Rogers said he wasn't too respectful of his master, but he was paid well. He thought the arsenic habit a bit of a lark. Mind, he reckons his lordship died owing a lot of money, mostly to wine merchants. The valet's got a bit owed to him but he doesn't really expect to get it. He's started looking for another situation."

Lord Wickerston's creditors would want to be paid speedily, and from what Georgiana had heard, it was unlikely Lady Wickerston would be able to manage this. The burden of his lordship's debts would no doubt fall on her brother, unless she remarried very well – and even were that to happen, no wedding was likely to take place until the year of mourning was complete. Creditors might be willing to wait on that expectation, but they would want to be very certain that they would be paid eventually.

"The letter the Runner received: did he mention whether he showed it to Edward?"

Emily nodded. "Yes, miss. Said Mr Grey looked shocked. Wouldn't say anything about Lord Wickerston's habits."

That sounded like Edward. Georgiana would expect him to be discreet, even when Lord Wickerston was beyond being harmed. And he certainly wouldn't write to a newspaper, proclaiming his own arrest to the world.

"Did the Runner find any other arsenic?" Georgiana asked.

"If he did, he didn't mention it, miss."

"Presumably Lord Wickerston's valet gave it straight into his master's hand," said Georgiana thoughtfully. "He may have known where his lordship kept it, though."

"Would you like me to find out, miss?"

Georgiana smiled. "That could be helpful, Emily, thank you." Best she didn't ask how Emily proposed to go about this piece of investigation.

She glanced towards the clock. "What time are we likely to expect James home?"

"I'm not sure, miss. I don't think it will be late; he was only taking Lady Wickerston's maid out for some tea."

"Lady Wickerston paid a call here today herself," said

Georgiana, "and left suddenly, in rather a temper, if I'm not mistaken."

"Really?"

Georgiana described the unexpected visit and Lady Wickerston's sudden, frosty assertion that they had taken up enough of her time.

"That's odd," said Emily.

"Yes," said Georgiana. "My cousin thinks she may have overheard what I said in the hall and taken offence, but I'm not sure."

"Is that likely?"

"Possible, I suppose, but all I said was that she seemed to go visiting rather a lot for a newly bereaved lady."

"She may have taken the hint."

"She may," said Georgiana doubtfully, "but surely she would have done so immediately? She was perfectly civil initially, her manner only changed when I mentioned Mr Morris, and how concerned he had been about her." Georgiana met Emily's eyes steadily.

"Well, either she doesn't like Mr Morris speaking to you about her, or she doesn't want him as a friend."

"Yes." More food for thought.

Miss Knatchbull's voice on the stairs intruded on Georgiana's reflections and put an end to further discussion with Emily. Selina sounded irritable and impatient, so Georgiana went to the door.

"I thought you were going to change," said Selina.

Georgiana glanced down at the clothes she had been wearing when she'd returned to the house.

"Yes. I cannot decide on anything suitable."

Selina tutted and turned to walk down the stairs again. Georgiana caught sight of James, back at his usual post in the hall. She went back to her bedchamber, told Emily her brother had returned and quickly changed into a day dress, then went down to rejoin her cousin, first sending Emily to fetch James.

Selina had barely handed her a cup of tea from the now stewed pot, when the footman appeared. Selina complied with ill grace with Georgiana's request for a private word with her footman, flouncing from the room and remarking that she would be in her bedchamber if anyone required her company.

James remained impassive. Georgiana sat silent, hands folded in her lap, until the door slammed behind her cousin. She sighed.

"I'm sorry, miss."

Georgiana shook her head. "It is not your fault, James. I think my cousin has been displeased with me since Lady Wickerston left rather suddenly a short time ago. It is unimportant. Now, tell me, how was your afternoon?"

"Very informative, miss."

"Really?"

"Lady Wickerston's maid confirmed that there'd been a quarrel between Lord and Lady Wickerston, said her ladyship was fair hysterical, screaming at his lordship something awful. The servants were all trying to be discreet, pretending not to hear."

"I see." This confirmed what she had already been told about the quarrel and Lady Wickerston's state of mind, and extended her knowledge a little further. She looked at James speculatively. "Have you any idea what they were pretending not to hear?"

He grinned. "Well, it seems her ladyship was upset by her husband's drinking – said he was boorish."

"Well, that was certainly true," said Georgiana in matter of fact tone.

James looked solemn. "Seems her ladyship screamed at his

lordship to leave her alone, called him a brute. Katy, the maid, said one of the footmen got concerned and thought of forcing his way into the room, but her ladyship came out before he did anything."

"What happened then?" said Georgiana.

"Her ladyship seemed near to tears. She shut the door behind her and asked for her cloak, and went out almost immediately. The only thing is, miss, before she went, she said something about wishing her husband dead. She even said she'd like to kill him herself."

"You're sure of this?"

James nodded. "Yes, miss. Katy was quite shocked. It seems everyone within earshot was, though no one spoke out, of course."

"Of course."

"But then when his lordship died in the fire, well, it seems some of them thought the quarrel had been a bad omen. Katy found it quite frightening, and so did one or two others."

"I imagine they did," said Georgiana. "James, do you know where this quarrel took place?"

"In his lordship's study."

"The room where you and Mr Lakesby found Lord Wickerston?"

"Yes, miss."

"I see. Do you know if anyone ventured in there after Lady Wickerston left?"

"The servants thought it best to give him a wide berth. Apparently, Sir Anthony Dixon and Mr Morris both called while her ladyship was out. It seems Sir Anthony wasn't best pleased to find his sister away from home and left almost immediately, but Mr Morris said he'd pay his respects to his lordship. A servant showed him in and found his lordship – er – asleep."

"I see."

"I understand it wasn't unusual, miss. Mr Morris didn't stay long, said he would write a note and left."

Georgiana considered this.

"There is one other thing, Miss Georgiana. I understand Sir Anthony Dixon had also visited his sister the day before the fire. Apparently there'd been something of an argument then, seems he was angry over the treatment his sister was receiving from her husband."

"Did he see Lord Wickerston?" Georgiana asked.

"I'm not sure, miss, but he'd got quite heated with her ladyship and said it was time something was done about it. Katy said he was mad as fire when he left."

Georgiana was growing to regard Katy as a very observant young woman. However, she was not sure if this latest piece of news clarified the situation or muddied the waters further.

"I see. Thank you, James. I appreciate your help in this. Please let me know what your expenses were. I'll see you are reimbursed."

"Thank you, miss."

James departed from the room leaving Georgiana prey to a mixture of thoughts. She was still sitting there when Selina found her some minutes later.

"Good heavens, Georgiana, what are you doing, sitting here all on your own? That tea is cold now. Let me get you some fresh."

Georgiana glanced at the forgotten cup over which her cousin had taken such pains. Feeling slightly guilty, she picked it up and ventured a sip. Selina screwed up her face.

"Dear Georgiana, no, that must be quite horrid. I'll get you a fresh pot."

"No, please, don't trouble, Selina. I'm sorry, I've been a little preoccupied today."

Selina murmured that it was of no consequence and Georgiana thought she detected a hint of sheepishness, perhaps because of her own irritability. Georgiana smiled and patted the couch next to her invitingly.

"Tell me, how long were Lady Wickerston and Sir Anthony here before I arrived?"

"About half an hour," said Selina.

"Did they have anything of consequence to say?"

"What do you mean?" Selina looked puzzled.

Georgiana was not sure what she did mean. However, it seemed to her odd that a newly widowed lady and her brother should spend so much time paying calls for the express purpose of thanking people for their kindness, especially so early in the mourning period.

"Did they mention Edward?" Georgiana asked.

Selina looked shocked.

"His name is not banned, Selina," said Georgiana, a little exasperated.

"No, of course not, but…" Selina's voice trailed away. She gulped. "Did you – did you expect them to mention Edward?" she asked.

"I don't know, but in view of the circumstances it is quite possible," said Georgiana.

Selina looked horrified. "But – but it would be so improper of them to ask!"

Georgiana glanced towards her, a fleeting look of cynical scorn in her eyes.

"Well, since they didn't, it doesn't matter," said Georgiana. "What did they talk about?"

"Oh, I don't know. This and that," said Selina vaguely.

"Selina, you must have some idea."

"Really, Georgiana, it was nothing out of the common way,"

Selina said. She thought for a moment. "Lady Wickerston said she was finding it very odd without her husband, and mentioned that she would have to find somewhere new to live now that the house was burned down. I think something was said about Lord Wickerston's funeral but I can't recall."

"What?" said Georgiana. "It could be important."

"Important?" said Selina. "In what way?"

Georgiana closed her eyes and drew a breath, forcing herself to remain calm. When she opened them after a moment, Selina was watching her curiously.

"I am sorry, Selina. I have no wish to appear impatient. However, I am concerned about Edward's situation, and time is not his friend."

Selina's puzzlement grew. "Edward? Well, yes, of course I understand your concern, but what has poor Edward's plight to do with Lady Wickerston and Sir Anthony?"

"I am not sure," said Georgiana honestly. "However, there is something very odd about it all."

"Surely the authorities will sort out the matter," said Selina.

Georgiana could not help but be touched by her cousin's naïve innocence and simple faith. She herself had good reason to distrust official sources.

"I think there was some mention of the funeral being delayed," said Selina, "because of, well, the circumstances. Lady Wickerston is finding it very distressing."

Georgiana nodded. That made sense. The cause of Lord Wickerston's death was still a mystery; there would be some reluctance to allow his burial too soon.

"I don't suppose they mentioned whether anyone visited his lordship before he died?" she asked.

"Well, no, I can't say that they did. Though Sir Anthony seemed very concerned about, well, um..." Selina cleared her throat uneasily; clearly she was having difficulty in expressing her thoughts with the necessary discretion. "Sir Anthony seemed concerned about his sister's welfare and some... difficulties she had been experiencing. He grew quite indignant, in fact. I would not have expected it."

Sir Anthony. Could he have been angry enough to murder his brother-in-law? Lord Wickerston's death had certainly rescued his sister from a difficult marriage although debts and the fire created difficulties of their own.

It occurred to Georgiana that Lady Wickerston's visit to Brooks's had not been to seek out Edward; perhaps her intention was quite different. No one had mentioned her asking for Sir Anthony first, though.

She found herself wondering how he might have occupied himself that afternoon.

"Georgiana?"

Selina's tentative voice broke Georgiana from her reverie.

"What? Oh, I beg your pardon, Selina, I was miles away."

"So I see."

The door opened to admit a servant carrying a silver salver. Two small white handwritten envelopes rested on it. Georgiana recognised the handwriting on neither.

The first was a note from Sir Anthony Dixon, apologising for their sudden departure, explaining that his sister was overwrought and begging leave to call and apologise in person.

The second offered to rescue her brother from the hangman's rope.

23

Georgiana sat looking intently at the note. It was unsigned, a fact which inclined her to tear it up and give it no more thought. Yet something caused her to regard it as a matter of some importance, and Edward's situation was such that she could not afford to ignore any offers of help.

She studied the paper closely. It was of much poorer quality than Sir Anthony's, though the writing was neat, if not elegant. The wording did not contain any thieves' cant, but it was simple enough to make Georgiana wonder whether it could have come from a patron of the Lucky Bell. Yet how would they have known she was Edward's sister, or where to find her? One answer came to mind.

Before pursuing it, she sent for Emily, slipped the two notes into her hand and suggested that they might be of interest to the acquaintance she had just visited. She then turned to her cousin.

"Selina, do you know where Tom is?"

Selina shuddered. She had never quite become accustomed to regarding the boy as a member of the household, although she did now seem to be less nervous about the possibility of being robbed or murdered as she slept.

"That boy!" she said.

"Yes, that boy, Selina," said Georgiana patiently. "Do you know where he is?"

"The kitchen, I imagine," said Selina. "Really, Georgiana, I'm sure it costs you more to feed *that boy* than to pay him."

Georgiana reflected wryly that this was probably true; Tom had displayed a healthy appetite since joining her household, encouraged by Mrs Daniels's tendency to spoil him.

The scrawny former errand boy from the Lucky Bell had filled out considerably. She rang the bell and asked for him to be sent to her.

Selina needed no persuasion to allow her cousin a few minutes alone with him and was leaving the room just as he entered. Remembering what he had been taught, he stood back to let her pass through the doorway, then came forward to Georgiana, his eyes eager.

"You sent for me, miss?"

Georgiana looked closely at the boy, considering how best to broach the subject. "Thank you for coming so promptly, Tom. There is something I need to talk to you about. It's quite important."

"Oh?" A hint of apprehension appeared on the boy's face.

Georgiana wondered briefly whether she should invite him to sit, then decided against it.

"Are you happy here, Tom?"

"Yes, miss." The apprehension seemed to increase.

"Does that mean I can trust you?"

"Course, miss." Apprehension gave way to astonishment.

"I'm sure you remember when you joined the household, I asked you not to go back to that tavern?"

"Yes, miss." Tom looked uneasy again.

"Have you been back there?"

The boy did not answer immediately. His eyes were downcast and his feet shuffled nervously.

"Tom, answer me, please. Have you been back there?"

Tom looked up. "Only to let me mate Harry know where I was."

"I see. Just the one occasion?"

Tom was silent again.

"More than once, then?" Georgiana pursued.

"Only to see Harry, miss, so he'd know I'm all right."

244

"Does that mean you told him about my household?"

"Not really, miss."

"What does 'not really' mean?"

"Well, miss, I… that is…"

Georgiana turned to her main point of concern. "You see, Tom, I've received a note."

The boy looked at her in some puzzlement. "I don't understand, miss."

"It is not from anyone of my acquaintance. In fact, it is not signed."

"Then how do you know, miss?"

A look from Georgiana quelled him.

"I mean, miss," he said in a more subdued tone, "if it ain't signed, you don't know who it's from. Maybe they just forgot."

"Maybe," she conceded, "although that has never happened before. However, the writing paper is not a kind I recognise, nor is the hand in which it is written."

"I didn't write it, miss."

"I did not imagine you did," Georgiana said. Tom's grasp of reading and writing was tenuous, although she knew some of her staff were making efforts to educate him. "However, it did occur to me you might have mentioned something – to your friend Harry, for instance."

"No," Tom said hotly. "I told you before, Harry ain't no ken-cracker."

"That is not the issue," Georgiana responded. Tom's defence of his friend against an imagined accusation of housebreaking was a spirited one, and Georgiana had reasons of her own for believing him. She continued, "You may have heard my brother is in some difficulty. This letter offers to save him."

"Oh. Well, that's good, isn't it, miss?"

"Possibly," Georgiana replied. "But how could the person who wrote this letter know my brother's situation? I have certainly not broadcast it abroad, and nor has my sister-in-law."

Tom did not answer.

"It occurs to me you might have mentioned my brother's situation to someone of your acquaintance, who may have seen a chance to profit by it."

Tom paled. "Not me, miss. Never, miss."

The protestation convinced Georgiana of his guilt.

"Tom, I am not seeking to punish you. However, it is important you tell me the truth."

The boy hesitated.

"Please, Tom. My brother is in a great deal of trouble."

"Well, miss, I – I might have mentioned it to my friend Harry."

"I see."

"Yes, miss." Tom was looking at the ground again, shuffling his feet. Eventually he raised his eyes to her face. "I ain't been on the High Toby," he said, "or told anyone where this ken was."

"All right," said Georgiana. "You had better tell me about it."

Tom looked at his feet again. He seemed to be considering what to say next. "The thing is, miss, Harry was a good mate, an' it didn't seem right just to run off and not tell him where I was going. He's a good bloke."

"Very well. Tell me what happened."

"I only went to visit him, didn't mean no harm."

"Yes, Tom, but what happened?"

"Well, Harry was telling me about how he – er – how things were with him, and he mentioned that fire, you know, where the posh cove died. Harry said things were quiet on the road that night, not many folks about."

Georgiana saw no need to mention to Tom that Harry had

told her this much himself. "So trade was slow for him?"

Tom looked uneasy. He did not address this question but continued with what he was saying. "Harry said it was odd about the cove being dead, when the fire hadn't killed him. Said it was a rum go."

"How do you know the fire didn't kill him?"

"Some of the lads was talking about it, miss."

"Really?" Georgiana was surprised at this.

Tom nodded. "Some of them had seen him, surly cove. Thought his lady might have set the fire. One or two of the lads had seen her before, out on the High Toby. Thought she was having a bad time with the cove."

"I see," said Georgiana. "However, she wasn't there when the fire started."

"I know, miss, I heard that."

"Where did you hear it?" Clearly the Wickerstons had been the subject of gossip in many walks of life.

"Dunno, miss. Here or there," he said evasively.

"All right. Go on."

"Heard some talk the surly cove's death might not have been an accident. One of the lads said if that were right, the one what did it ought to have his hand shook." Tom looked down again, his face growing red with embarrassment as he forced out his next words. "I'm sorry, miss. I'd heard your brother had been taken and I… I…"

"You told your friends he had been sent to Newgate?"

Tom looked uncomfortable again. "Yes, miss."

"It made you feel important?"

Hanging his head, Tom nodded. "Yes, miss. I'm sorry, miss, really I am. I know I spoke out of turn but I didn't mean no harm."

"All right. Never mind that now. Is your friend Harry or one of these 'lads' in a position to help my brother?"

Tom thought. "I dunno, miss. P'raps Harry knows a guard there." His face brightened. "Or mebbe one of the lads could break him out."

Georgiana could well imagine Edward's reaction to such a prospect. He would be unable to show his face in society again, and Amanda and the children would certainly be shunned and forced to live in the shabby-genteel quarter.

"That wasn't quite what I had in mind," Georgiana said. "Perhaps I should talk to your friend Harry?"

"Well, miss…" Tom hesitated then looked directly at her. "The Lucky Bell's not really a place for a lady, miss."

"I can't ignore this, Tom. My brother's life is at stake."

"Well," Tom said doubtfully, "perhaps you could ask a gentleman to speak to Harry. Or…" He looked at her hopefully. "I could do it. If you tell me what you want to know."

"I suppose you could," she said. "However, I have to know I can trust you, Tom. If this is just an attempt by your friend Harry or one of 'the lads' to extort money from me and you choose to help them, it will go very ill for you."

"Oh, no, miss," said Tom earnestly. "I wouldn't do that, and nor would Harry. He knows you been good to me, miss, and he's a good bloke."

Georgiana hesitated.

"I won't let you down, miss, really I won't. You can trust me."

"Very well. You may go. Speak to your friends as soon as you can; ask if they have any knowledge of this note offering to help my brother. And let me know immediately if you learn anything. My brother is in a very serious situation."

"Yes, miss." Tom turned to leave the room, his manner focused and grave.

When Tom had gone, Georgiana sat awhile and considered what to do next. It occurred to her Amanda might be growing anxious for news and in need of some company. Georgiana was not sure whether she had anything reassuring to impart, but decided to make the effort.

Persuading her cousin that she should call on Amanda alone proved easier than she expected; Selina understood that Amanda was likely to be overwhelmed by the number of visits she was receiving. Breathing a sigh of relief, Georgiana went to change into an outdoor dress, took her bonnet and pelisse from Emily and gave her leave to use her discretion in making what inquiries she thought necessary.

The carriage was waiting outside for Georgiana, and the journey to her brother's house was accomplished in too short a time to allow her to decide what she could say to reassure Amanda. The butler welcomed her with all the warmth the dignity of his position would allow, and Georgiana sensed a degree of concern in his demeanour. He immediately showed her in to the room where Amanda was sitting.

As soon as Georgiana entered the room, she knew something was wrong. Amanda's face was tinged red, and she sat straight and tense. Georgiana followed her sister-in-law's gaze to the other side of the room. Mr Morris was standing near the fireplace, an arm laid nonchalantly along the mantelpiece. However, for all his relaxed air, Georgiana sensed that he was as much on edge as Amanda.

"Good afternoon," said Georgiana pleasantly. "And to you, Mr Morris. I hope I'm not intruding, Amanda."

"Georgiana! No, of course you are not. I am very pleased to see you."

Amanda rose and approached, hands outstretched. Georgiana sensed that Amanda was more than merely pleased to see her; she was relieved as well.

"Good afternoon to you, Miss Grey," Morris said.

"Please do join us, Georgiana," said Amanda, indicating a

chair. "Would you like some tea?" She turned to the butler, who had not quite closed the door behind him. "Please arrange for some tea for my sister-in-law and me, would you?"

"Yes, ma'am," said the butler.

It did not escape Georgiana's notice that Mr Morris was excluded. As she sat down, she looked from Amanda to him and back again with great interest. "How are you, Mr Morris?" she inquired.

"Very well, Miss Grey, very well." His eyes slid away from her and rested on Amanda. "But I am concerned about your sister-in-law. Do you not think she looks pale?"

"No, not particularly," said Georgiana, with a glance towards Amanda.

"I am perfectly well," said Amanda.

"I am sure you are well, my dear Mrs Grey," said Morris. "I am just concerned you may be over-tired."

"There is no need to be concerned."

Amanda's minimal responses to Mr Morris were out of character and disturbed Georgiana. It was clear she wanted her visitor out of the house and he did not seem disposed to move.

"Mr Morris, I heard you had an encounter with the Crimson Cavalier," said Georgiana.

Mr Morris's face hardened.

"I hope you did not lose a great deal?" Georgiana continued innocently.

"Money, a few trinkets. I must say, the fellow's got a nerve, holding up people on the public highway."

"I understand that this is the way of highwaymen," Georgiana observed dryly.

"It happens a great deal," said Amanda. "He is not the only one." Her tone was matter of fact, and quite lacking in sympathy for Morris's ordeal. It drew a curious look from Georgiana.

"If it happens again," said Morris, "I shall be forced to shoot."

Georgiana frequently heard threats against highwaymen. More often than not it was merely indignant and idle boasting, and a way of hiding the speaker's own cowardice for capitulating to the robber's demands. Morris's warning seemed different; the level, quiet tone he adopted was quite chilling.

"We have no wish to detain you, Mr Morris," said Amanda crisply.

"You are very thoughtful, Mrs Grey, but I have no pressing engagement."

"Nevertheless, there are matters I must discuss with my sister-in-law and I'm sure you would be shockingly bored."

Georgiana had never known Amanda so abrupt. She noticed the ghost of a smile playing about Morris's lips, and thought for a moment that he would refuse to move, but Amanda put the matter beyond question when a footman arrived with the tea.

She addressed the servant as he laid down the tray. "Mr Morris is leaving. Would you be so good as to show him out? We will take care of the tea ourselves."

"Yes, ma'am." The footman stood straight and looked towards Morris, waiting for him to take his leave.

The door closed behind him. Amanda remained in her chair, neither moving nor speaking for a few moments. Suddenly she burst into tears. Georgiana rose and went over to her, putting an arm about her shoulders. "Amanda, whatever has happened? What has Mr Morris done to distress you?"

"Oh, Georgiana, I'm so sorry, but he frightened me."

Amanda looked up. "He – he threatened Edward."

"How? What can he do?" Georgiana refrained from observing that Edward's position could be little worse.

"He said he would ensure Edward was hanged if I – if I –" She finished in a rush, "if I did not leave him and… Oh, Georgiana, Morris wants me to go away with him." Her last words were barely audible, uttered in a hoarse whisper as if she were ashamed at having to utter them.

"What?" Georgiana wanted to be certain she had heard correctly.

Amanda nodded, misery suffusing her face as she sniffed into a handkerchief.

Georgiana sat down in the chair next to Amanda's, absorbing this new development.

"I don't understand. How can he ensure Edward is hanged?"

Amanda was shaking her head. "I don't know. He said he has a friend among the justices, and he has – evidence. I don't understand. There can be no evidence. Edward did not kill Lord Wickerston. I will never believe it."

"What was this evidence?" Georgiana asked.

"He wouldn't say."

Georgiana was frowning, trying to relate her own experience of the justice system to what Amanda had told her.

"I would think it unlikely any honest justice would hang a gentleman without being certain the evidence was genuine. Admittedly, many are less particular about the lower classes but there would surely be a huge scandal attached to the wrongful execution of a gentleman."

"Execu…" Amanda burst into fresh tears.

"Come, try not to worry," said Georgiana, reaching over to pat her hand. "Tell me what else Mr Morris said."

"He said that Edward was concerned only about Lady Wickerston, and that even if he is released he would probably leave me for her now that her husband is dead. Oh, Georgiana, do you think that is true?"

"No," said Georgiana without hesitation. "Edward will do nothing of the sort."

"Well, I suppose the scandal…" said Amanda dubiously.

"It has nothing to do with the scandal," Georgiana laughed. "Amanda, Edward adores you. He would be quite lost without you. Trust me in this. I saw how he behaved when you came to stay with me."

"Mr Morris *flaunted* Edward's… association with Lady Wickerston to me," said Amanda tearfully.

"I don't deny Edward has behaved foolishly over Lady Wickerston – almost as foolishly as refusing to speak out now – but it is no more than that, I promise you. He would be quite devastated if you left him."

Amanda's tears had stopped. She stared miserably ahead of her. "Mr Morris did not even mention the children. It was as if they didn't exist. He just wants… me." The last word was not said boastfully but seemed wrung out of her, her mortification evident. She raised her handkerchief to her eyes and dried her tears.

"You have been making great efforts to help Edward, and I have done nothing at all," she said. "Tell me what you have discovered, then tell me what I can do. I shall be the better for it."

Georgiana poured Amanda a cup of tea. "From what I understand, Edward was arrested because he was seen with Lady Wickerston and he took away the arsenic she had in her possession. However, Emily and James have been making some inquiries among their own acquaintances. Lord Wickerston also had arsenic in his possession and I've learned

253

Mr Morris also had some, though I'm not certain if he had it before Lord Wickerston's death."

Amanda looked at her in wonderment.

"How have you all managed to learn this?"

"That's not important. I've also received a note offering to help which I suspect may have come from one of Tom's – er – old friends."

"Oh, dear, some highwayman. Oh, Georgiana, please be careful."

"Tom is going to see what he can find out for me. Don't worry, I have no intention of arranging a meeting with a highway robber on the road at dead of night."

Amanda rubbed her hand across her forehead. "What about Mr Lakesby?"

"Has he not spoken to you?" asked Georgiana.

"Not since you met him here. I wondered if he had learned anything new. I thought you might have seen him since then," Amanda said hopefully.

"He has had scant co-operation from Edward." Georgiana frowned. "Everyone agrees Lady Wickerston quarrelled violently with her husband and wished him dead. And apparently both Sir Anthony Dixon and Mr Morris visited the house that day after Lady Wickerston's departure." Georgiana paused and gave Amanda a cautious glance before continuing. "Edward told me he went to see Lord Wickerston after taking Lady Wickerston to her aunt's house."

"But no one saw him there?"

"I don't know. No one else has mentioned it," said Georgiana. Her brow wrinkled. "What concerns me is the speed with which the newspaper report of Edward's arrest appeared. It was as if someone knew in advance."

Amanda said nothing. She seemed at a loss. The butler entered and announced Mr Lakesby. Both ladies looked up and Lakesby checked briefly on the threshold at the sight of Georgiana. The pause was fleeting, however, and he continued smoothly into the room, greeting both ladies politely as Georgiana returned to the chair she had formerly occupied.

Despite her worries, Amanda did not miss the slight hesitation, and she glanced from Lakesby to Georgiana. "Please sit down, Mr Lakesby. May I offer you some tea or would you prefer something stronger?" Amanda glanced to a tray on the other side of the room. "Oh, dear, the decanter is empty."

"Please don't trouble, Mrs Grey. Tea will do very well. Thank you," said Lakesby with a smile.

The butler was still standing in the doorway. Amanda nodded to indicate another cup was needed, then turned back to her guest, who was looking at her in some concern.

"Are you quite well, Mrs Grey?"

"Oh, yes. This is all such a worry, that is all."

"I'm sure it must be," said Lakesby, making no attempt to probe further.

A servant returned with a cup and saucer for Mr Lakesby, and Amanda busied herself with her duties as hostess.

"I have just come from Brooks's," said Lakesby. "I'm afraid there has been some talk about the incident."

"Oh, dear," said Amanda. "Edward will be mortified."

Georgiana reflected that talk at Brooks's was probably the least of Edward's problems at present.

"Ironically," said Lakesby, "Lady Wickerston's appearance there still seems to be regarded as more shocking – and certainly more worthy of speculation – than her husband's death."

Amanda shook her head sadly. Georgiana felt no surprise.

"There is something else," said Lakesby. "I have never heard it mentioned in the past, but since Lord Wickerston's death, I have heard a few gentlemen mention that he had suggested his wife suffered from – er – bouts of instability."

Georgiana stared at him in disbelief. "Instability?" she echoed. "If I was married to such a man as Lord Wickerston, I imagine I might suffer from bouts of instability."

"Georgiana!" reproved Amanda.

"Yes, I know how it sounds," said Lakesby. "Perhaps it was something no one took seriously when his lordship was alive. However, the circumstances of his death have provoked a good deal of speculation."

"Yes." Georgiana grew thoughtful. "Tell me, Mr Lakesby, have you ever heard rumours concerning Lady Wickerston and Mr Morris?"

"Morris?" Lakesby glanced fleetingly towards Amanda, who looked startled at the suggestion. "No, I can't say I have. Why?"

"Oh, nothing. Something I imagined, I daresay," said Georgiana with a smile. "It doesn't matter."

Both her companions looked at her intently.

"It is difficult to believe anything which occurred to you was mere imagination, Miss Grey. What is it?"

Georgiana thought for a moment. "I have once or twice gained the impression that Lady Wickerston was angered when Mr Morris showed me some small attention. I'm sure he was simply being polite –"

"I'm sure," said Lakesby.

Georgiana ignored the interruption, but Amanda's lips twitched. Georgiana continued, "But whatever his motives, why would Lady Wickerston be concerned?"

"An excellent point," said Lakesby.

"Georgiana, surely you are not suggesting Lady Wickerston is involved with Mr Morris as well as –" Amanda could not bring herself to finish the sentence.

"Why not?" Georgiana shrugged. "He has been very attentive to her since Lord Wickerston's death." She turned to look at Lakesby. "I think he was not among the men fighting the fire?"

"No, he was not."

"Nor was he at Lady Bertram's," said Georgiana. "Yet he was at Brooks's that day, and he called on Lady Wickerston the next day, so it is unlikely he was away from town."

"Most unlikely," said Lakesby.

Amanda looked horrified.

"There is something else," said Georgiana to Lakesby. "I have received a note offering to save my brother from the hangman's rope."

Lakesby raised his eyebrows.

"From whom?"

"It wasn't signed. However, it appears my page has been talking more than he should, and I suspect it might be an old friend of his."

"Ah, yes, the young highwayman. Do you intend to do anything about this note?"

"My page will speak to his friends and let me know what he finds out."

"Can you trust him?" asked Lakesby.

"I think so," Georgiana nodded. "In any case, it has to be explored."

"Yes." Lakesby looked thoughtful. "Are you proposing to meet the author of this note yourself?"

"I am not sure. I thought I would wait and see what Tom has to tell me," said Georgiana.

"Very wise," he approved. "But if it should come to a meeting with one of these... questionable individuals, I beg you will let me undertake it, or at the very least accompany you."

Amanda interjected before Georgiana had an opportunity to respond. "Thank you, Mr Lakesby. I have to confess, I am very uneasy about Georgiana meeting this person. We don't know who it is, much less anything about him."

"Amanda, I have already promised I will take no risks," protested Georgiana.

"Then it is settled," said Lakesby. He turned back to Amanda, preventing further discussion on this subject. "I fear there is little to be gained from my visiting your husband again."

"No," Amanda said in a resigned tone. "What can be done?"

"Emily spoke to the Bow Street Runner," said Georgiana. "It seems he is not convinced of Edward's guilt."

Amanda and Lakesby looked at her in surprise.

"If Edward is being framed," continued Georgiana, "the person responsible has planned it very carefully and will not make it easy to find out the truth."

Amanda was looking more crestfallen by the moment. "Oh, dear."

Georgiana smiled. "Not easy, Amanda, but not impossible." She looked at Lakesby. "If both Sir Anthony Dixon and Mr Morris visited Marpley Manor on the day of Lord Wickerston's death after Lady Wickerston left, one of them must have taken the opportunity to administer the arsenic. That is the only time it could have happened."

"Well, I can't imagine it was the servants," said Lakesby. "Since both of these gentlemen appear to be friends of yours, Miss Grey, it should be a simple enough matter to approach them."

"And ask if they murdered Lord Wickerston?" said Georgiana. "Of course, a very simple matter indeed."

Amanda offered no comment though she was closely

watching her guests.

Georgiana's glance strayed to the window. Dusk was drawing in, and it occurred to her that she ought to be going home. She rose to take leave, and Mr Lakesby offered to escort her. Georgiana accepted graciously.

She embraced Amanda, adjuring her not to worry too much, and followed Lakesby to the front door. He assisted Georgiana into her carriage, and stepped in behind her. Silence hung between them for a few moments.

"Was there something in particular which made you ask about Lady Wickerston and Morris?" Lakesby said at last.

Georgiana told him of her ladyship's sudden departure when she had made a reference to Mr Morris's concern for her.

"That does sound like a jealous reaction," he mused. "Morris as well as your brother. Well, well." He shook his head.

Georgiana hesitated before continuing. She decided his efforts to help Edward and Amanda entitled him to the whole truth, regardless of its delicate nature. "There is something even more odd." She described the proposition – threat, even – that Morris had made to Amanda.

Lakesby's eyes darkened. "The fellow deserves to be called out. How dare he try to blackmail your sister-in-law! What did she say to him?"

"She asked him to leave. However, she is clearly worried. He said he had evidence."

Lakesby was astonished. "What evidence could he possibly have?"

Georgiana shrugged. "I can only imagine he has more arsenic," she replied.

Lakesby's astonishment grew. "You can't be serious. Where on earth would he get…?"

"You said yourself, Mr Lakesby, it is an easy enough matter to claim there are rats in the cellar and sign the apothecary's poison book." Georgiana saw no need to mention that she had also seen Morris obtain arsenic from a less conventional source.

Lakesby sighed. "I daresay your friend Dixon has some stored away as well."

"I don't know, though my cousin did see him at the apothecary's."

"So it would appear one of them is the guilty party."

"Or Edward."

"Or Edward."

They fell silent, mulling over this possibility. When the carriage arrived at Georgiana's front door she did invite Lakesby inside for refreshment. Lakesby accepted, and as the two entered the drawing room, they found James filling the wine decanter. Georgiana stopped dead.

"Begging your pardon, miss. I had thought to have this finished before you returned. I won't be a moment."

"That's quite all right, James," she said, staring at him, transfixed.

"Miss Grey?" Lakesby looked at her in some concern.

James paused, and set down the decanter, exchanging glances with Lakesby.

"Miss Georgiana?"

Georgiana looked at each of them in turn. "Was there a decanter in the room when you found Lord Wickerston?"

Both men looked surprised at the question. James turned towards Mr Lakesby, allowing him to answer first.

"I don't recall seeing one. Come to think of it, I don't believe there was. Cooper?"

James shook his head. "I'm sorry, miss. I really didn't notice. We were more concerned about getting his lordship out."

"Yet you noticed the glass?" said Georgiana.

"Yes," said James. "But you could hardly miss it, lying on the hearthrug like it was. And that big red stain too."

"Tell me, if you were a servant of Lord Wickerston, would you leave him with one glass of wine and no decanter?"

"No indeed, miss. No disrespect intended but from what I've heard of Lord Wickerston, he'd not look kindly on it."

"He certainly wouldn't," said Lakesby. "So if there was no decanter in the room?"

"It seems likely someone removed it," said Georgiana, "to prevent anyone discovering the arsenic in it."

24

The three stared at each other in silence for a moment. Georgiana glanced at the clock, trying to determine how much time had elapsed since she had despatched Tom to the Lucky Bell. Would he come back with anything useful?

"The poison was in the decanter?" James said at last, his own hand resting on Georgiana's decanter.

Lakesby looked doubtful. "But if that were the case, whoever put it there had no way of knowing when Lord Wickerston would die."

"Beg pardon, sir," said James, "but it is possible to have a good idea when the decanter will need filling. It might vary between households, but most establishments have their own pattern."

"And the remainder would be disposed of once Lord Wickerston was dead," said Georgiana. "That could only be done by someone in the house. And I think we can discount the servants."

"Lady Wickerston?" said Lakesby.

"Her brother, miss?" suggested James.

"Possibly," said Georgiana, aware of Lakesby's eyes on her.

There was a tap on the door and Emily entered the room. Her surprise was evident, and she said nothing until Georgiana signalled encouragement.

"Mr Rogers didn't recognise the hand on either of the notes you gave me, miss, but he'd had information from the newspaper. They had passed on a note that was sent to them – and it was in the same handwriting as yours. The one that wasn't signed," she added.

To Georgiana's surprise, Emily then produced the scrap of

paper which had been among the items the Crimson Cavalier had taken from Mr Morris.

"Mr Morris must have dropped this when he escorted you home, miss," she said tonelessly. "I found it outside. Mr Rogers showed me the note he'd had. The writing was the same as this."

Georgiana accepted the paper held out to her and glanced at the writing. She looked back at Emily, a question in her eyes.

"I took the liberty of showing it to Mr Rogers, miss. We both looked at it, and we're sure it's the same writing as the one he received and the one sent to the newspaper about your brother."

"Mr Morris?" Georgiana looked at the paper in wonderment.

"I can't imagine Morris in league with Dixon," said Lakesby.

"No," said Georgiana.

"I hope I wasn't out of turn, miss," said Emily. "Mr Rogers has gone to speak to him."

"What about the note you received?" Lakesby asked Georgiana.

"Poor quality paper, simple writing." She looked at the clock again. "Oh, where is Tom?"

As if in answer to her thoughts, there was another knock on the door. Tom entered the room, and blinked at the sight of so many people, but addressed Georgiana when she beckoned him forward.

"I spoke to Harry, miss. He don't know anything about this note."

"I see."

"His mate, though…" Tom looked hesitantly at the other occupants of the room, then continued, "Harry spoke to him. He and some girl thought they could make a bob or two.

Harry told 'em, no. He said you'd been good to me and they should find another pigeon."

Lakesby raised an eyebrow. Georgiana wondered whether the enterprising souls were Len and Polly, but knew better than to ask.

"Really? Thank you, Tom."

"One more thing, miss, something Harry thought a bit odd."

"All right. Go on," she said.

"The night of the fire, Harry was working. He said the road was quiet but he saw a cove out on the Toby, riding alone. Thought it was one of the nobs, didn't pay him much heed."

"He didn't hold him up?" asked Lakesby.

"No, sir." Tom shook his head. "Harry don't deal with lone riders; too much trouble, he says."

"Never mind that," said Georgiana. "Please continue, Tom."

"Well, miss, seems Harry didn't recollect until he saw the cove again, in the tavern, doing some business. Then he remembered hearing the bells, just a few minutes after he saw the cove. So the cove must have been near the house where the fire was."

"Your friend Harry saw this man in the tavern he goes to?" Georgiana wanted to be absolutely clear.

"Yes, miss. Said the Crimson Cavalier saw him, too, only he wasn't there today for me to ask him."

Georgiana was aware of Lakesby glancing towards her. She ignored it.

"The thing is, miss, Harry said what he looked like and I remembered, I seen him too. Not at the Lucky Bell, though. Here."

"Here?" It was Lakesby's turn to look closely at Tom.

"Yes, sir." Tom drew himself up to his full height. "It was the man what visited you, miss. Not the one what came with the lady. The other one."

"Mr Morris." Georgiana drew a deep breath and glanced towards her companions. "All right, Tom, thank you. You've been very helpful."

Tom accepted his dismissal and departed. James closed the door behind him. No one else moved.

It was Lakesby who broke the silence.

"So it was Morris who notified Bow Street and the newspaper that your brother might be involved in Lord Wickerston's murder."

"So it seems," said Georgiana.

"Presumably to cover his own guilt," said Lakesby.

"He could not have acted alone," said Georgiana. "He certainly could not have disposed of the decanter." She looked at her three companions. "What better way to prove one's innocence than to confess to a killing which someone else then proves impossible?"

Emily's eyes widened. "Seems an awful risk."

"Perhaps," said Lakesby. He looked at Georgiana. "My curricle is outside. Shall we ask her ladyship?"

"Yes," said Georgiana, "though I think some assistance from Bow Street might be useful. If Rogers has already gone to speak to Mr Morris –"

"He might have found a way of warning Lady Wickerston," finished Lakesby.

"I'll go," said James, "unless you'd prefer me to come with you?"

Lakesby smiled as Georgiana sent Emily to fetch her cloak. "I imagine your mistress would prefer to address this matter herself. I cannot suppose that her ladyship will need much restraint." He held out his hand for the cloak when Emily returned, and dropped it around Georgiana's shoulders before leading her to his curricle.

They waited in Mrs Hobbs's hall as her butler undertook to ascertain whether her ladyship was receiving visitors.

"She may refuse to see us," said Lakesby.

"I think it likely she will," said Georgiana. "Her manner when she last took leave of me was less than warm."

"Miss Grey. Mr Lakesby," came Sir Anthony's voice as he approached them. "Is something amiss?"

"I'm afraid so, Sir Anthony," said Georgiana. "May we come in?"

Sir Anthony hesitated. "My sister is not feeling her best. She and our aunt are taking tea. I'm sure Theresa will be glad to see you on another day."

Georgiana thought that unlikely.

"I'm afraid it will not wait. I assure you, Sir Anthony, we would not consider disturbing your sister if it were not extremely important."

"Very well," he said, stepping back to allow them to enter the drawing room.

Lady Wickerston's fair countenance took on a mask of hostility at the sight of Georgiana.

"I'm sorry, Miss Grey, I am not up to receiving visitors. I'm afraid you must excuse me."

"My dear," said Mrs Hobbs.

Lakesby closed the door once Sir Anthony was in the room, and stood with his back to it.

Lady Wickerston looked accusingly at her brother.

"Anthony, I do not wish to be disturbed. Please let me go to my room." She rose from the table and began to move towards the door.

Lakesby did not move.

"I'm afraid you will be further disturbed," said Georgiana. "Someone from Bow Street is coming to speak to you about the murder of your husband. The murder you carried out."

"What?"

"Oh, dear me!"

"This is preposterous," blustered Sir Anthony.

"I could not have killed my husband," said Lady Wickerston. "You said so yourself, Miss Grey." She looked towards Lakesby. "You found the overturned glass."

Lakesby nodded and spoke for the first time. "The glass we were meant to find. Please let Miss Grey continue. She has not finished yet."

"You put the poison in the decanter, didn't you?" said Georgiana. "Your husband was already dead when you left the house."

"No," said Lady Wickerston. "We quarrelled. He was drunk but he was alive." She looked at her brother. "Anthony, you called on him."

"I didn't see him, Theresa."

"The servants..." Lady Wickerston said, desperation creeping into her voice.

Georgiana shook her head. "They would have accepted your word that he was drunk."

"His clothes smelled of alcohol when we found him," said Lakesby. "It did not occur to me until Miss Grey suggested it that you could have splashed him with wine."

"No," Lady Wickerston said. She smiled, a frozen, hysterical smile. "Mr Morris. He called on my husband. He will tell you he was alive after I left."

"I'm sure he would," said Georgiana. "There is a Bow Street Runner on his way to Mr Morris's lodging." She turned to Sir Anthony. "I'm afraid Mr Morris has been your sister's lover. I believe he started the fire."

Sir Anthony's expression took on increasing horror. "But - but – my sister tried to kill herself. She would not have done that if she had planned her husband's murder to be with a lover. Only genuine distress could cause such an action."

"Or remorse," said Georgiana. "Though I don't think that is the case here."

Lakesby shook his head. "Dr Masters said she had not swallowed enough arsenic to take her own life. It was either carelessness, ignorance or an attempt to throw suspicion away from herself, which could also be done by a confession later proved false."

"Oh, good gracious." Mrs Hobbs was fanning herself, looking ready to faint.

Lady Wickerston was glaring at Georgiana in open hatred. "You! You!"

Lady Wickerston rushed forward, hands extended like claws. Sir Anthony moved to stop her but Lakesby was quicker. He took hold of both Lady Wickerston's arms and pinned them together, forcing her backwards into a chair. Her resistance ebbed away, and she was sitting there sobbing as the Bow Street Runner entered.

25

Georgiana gazed out of the window of her front parlour at the grey morning. Edward had been released but was not at home.

Amanda had thrown herself into her sister-in-law's arms with sobs of gratitude, but her relief at seeing her husband's life saved did not block out the memory of his association with Lady Wickerston. Edward and Amanda had had an uneasy reunion and a long talk, after which he had agreed to stay at his club until his wife felt more settled about their future. He had thanked his sister for her part in his release, and even confessed to being a fool for allowing himself to be taken in by Lady Wickerston.

Georgiana heard the front door. A moment later James entered.

"Mr Lakesby, miss."

Georgiana turned and gave her visitor a small smile. He was dressed in black and carried a pair of black gloves in one hand.

"I see the weather is appropriate for the event," she said with an attempt at lightness.

"You do not have to do this," he said.

"I do. She asked me. After everything, it is the least I can do."

"You owe her nothing."

Georgiana smiled brightly. "If you would prefer not to come…"

Lakesby shook his head. "You know I am not happy for you to make this visit alone. Shall we go?"

James was in the hall, holding the grey cloak Georgiana

planned to wear over her matching gown. She thanked him quietly, in accordance with the subdued mood.

The coach was waiting outside and the yawning coachman hastily begged pardon when he saw Georgiana. She smiled and reassured him. An early start was part of a servant's life, but it was not often Georgiana asked for her carriage to be ready shortly after sunrise. Lakesby assisted Georgiana up and took the seat opposite her. The steps were quickly put up by the attendant groom and the horses began to move.

There was no conversation for some minutes; they were each immersed in their own thoughts, wrapped in an air of solemnity.

"How did you know?" Lakesby asked eventually.

Georgiana smiled. "I didn't, not until I saw James filling the wine decanter. It was only then it occurred to me that the poison could have been in the decanter rather than the glass. How likely is it that anyone else would have drunk it, especially after her ladyship stormed out?"

"Most unlikely," Lakesby acknowledged, "and, of course, you were quite right; Lord Wickerston would have expected to have more than one glass available to him."

"Everyone at Brooks's would remember Lady Wickerston's arrival, and the great commotion she made looking for Edward."

"And she made sure she was seen with him later, after your footman and I had established the contents of the glass couldn't have killed Wickerston."

"Allowing Edward to take the poison from her helped place the blame on his shoulders. Poor Edward. I'm still not certain if it was Lady Wickerston he trusted or the justice system."

"Both, I imagine. Whereas you trusted neither." Lakesby glanced towards her. "I saw Edward yesterday. He thanked me for trying to help."

"I'm glad," said Georgiana.

"Had he gone back to the Wickerstons' on the day of the fire?"

Georgiana nodded. "Some under-housemaid let him in. He didn't give his name, so no one could confirm he was there. He went into the study to check if Lord Wickerston was really dead. It seems he thought Lady Wickerston imagined it in her hysteria. The glass had already fallen on the floor. Lady Wickerston had left it near the edge of the desk with that intention."

"Proving her innocence."

"Yes. With all the attention on the glass, who would think about the decanter? It was really very clever."

"More clever to have solved it," said Lakesby. "You are a remarkable woman, Miss Grey."

"I don't feel very remarkable at the moment."

They fell silent again as they approached the grim, imposing grey walls. The gates were opened immediately and the carriage slowed, threading a way through the crowd which jostled around it on all sides. When the coachman pulled up, Lakesby leapt out and turned quickly to help Georgiana alight. She was aware of his closeness as he guided her through the throng to the doorway.

"Thank you for coming, Miss Grey." Sir Anthony stood in the corridor, pale and dignified. Nearby stood a clergyman and a tall, imposing figure whom she took to be the prison governor.

It was he who led her through the corridor, rather than the guard she had previously seen. Lakesby remained with Sir Anthony.

The governor stepped back to allow Georgiana to enter the cell, saying apologetically that he could only allow her five minutes. Lady Wickerston was seated at a small table, similar to that in Edward's cell. Her hands were folded, her face calm. Her hair was tied back, without ornamentation. Her gown was simple.

"Thank you for coming, Miss Grey."

"I am sorry for this."

Lady Wickerston shrugged. "It does not matter. Richard was taken yesterday; today is my turn. He did not really love me anyway. I was his second choice after your sister-in-law refused him." She looked intently at Georgiana. "Or perhaps his third. Still, he cared enough to help me when I decided to kill my husband. He even started the fire for me. However, I did not ask him to put the blame on Edward. That was all his own doing." She smiled. "You are very clever to have worked it out."

"Well, I…"

"Very clever." Lady Wickerston fell silent again, then said, "Please apologise to Amanda for me, for all I put her through."

"If you wish."

"I do. And Edward too, of course."

"Very well."

"I wish you well, Miss Grey."

"Thank you. I wish you peace."

"Oh, I have peace. I have it." Lady Wickerston grew distracted then stretched out a hand. "Goodbye, Miss Grey."

After the briefest hesitation, Georgiana accepted it "Goodbye."

Georgiana and Lakesby followed the governor and Sir Anthony to the front of the throng. Some seats had been held for them in an area roped off from the main crowd Georgiana was aware of Lakesby's eyes on her. She knew he was concerned for her, but she was determined to see thi through.

As Lady Wickerston appeared, a gasp went up from the crowd. Neither pallor and fragile appearance nor the dignity with which she held herself appeared to belong to a killer.

She spoke briefly.

"Thank you for coming to bid me farewell. Please pray for me. I wish you all the peace I have found."

Lady Wickerston stood still as the hood was positioned and did not flinch as the noose was placed about her neck. Georgiana thought she heard a sob in the crowd. She glanced towards Sir Anthony. He looked straight ahead at the scene on the scaffold, his face expressionless.

The lever was pulled.

MEET GEORGIANA GREY IN
THE CRIMSON CAVALIER

MARY ANDREA CLARKE'S DEBUT
PRE-REGENCY MURDER MYSTERY

London in the 1780s: a hotbed of robbers, ruffians and imposters…

A girl might as well put her faith in a highwayman!

Georgiana Grey is a sore trial to her upright brother Edward: independent, outspoken and determined to follow her own path.

When Sir Robert Foster, a prominent but unpopular citizen, is murdered close to her home, apparently by the Crimson Cavalier, a colourful and infamous highwayman. Georgiana has her own reasons to be certain the Cavalier is not to blame, and to Edward's chagrin, sets out to track down the real culprit.

Georgiana discovers plenty of people with good reason to wish Sir Robert dead, but her quest for the truth is obstructed on all sides. As the net closes on the Crimson Cavalier, her own life could be at stake.

Also available in unabridged audio and large print.

Praise for The Crimson Cavalier:

… sparkling period crime fiction with lively touch that Georgette Heyer would have appreciated.

– Andrew Taylor, winner of the 2009 Diamond Dagger

An entertaining novel, which has a very unlikely heroine… Plenty of surprises, and an ingenious plot line

– Angela Youngman, Monsters and Critics

Clarke captures the flavor of the period and the hypocrisies of the socially prominent…

– Publishers Weekly (USA)

ISBN: 978-0-9551589-5-7   **£7.99**

You can also meet the Crimson Cavalier
and Georgiana Grey in

CRIMINAL TENDENCIES

a diverse and wholly engrossing collection of short
stories from some of the best of the UK's crime writers.

£1 from every copy sold of this
first-rate collection will go to support the

NATIONAL HEREDITARY
BREAST CANCER HELPLINE

*She lay on her face, as if asleep. I turned her over and saw the deep wound
on her brow...*
– Reginald Hill, John Brown's Body

*Her mouth was dry and she was shaking badly. Terror was gripping her;
the same terror she previously experienced only in her dreams...*
– Peter James, 12 Bolinbroke Avenue

*His lips were thin and pale. "She must be following us. She's some sort of
stalker."*
– Sophie Hannah, The Octopus Nest

*When he thought he was alone, he squatted down and opened the
briefcase. I was interested to see that it contained an automatic pistol
and piles and piles of banknotes.*
– Andrew Taylor, Waiting for Mr Right

Published by Crème de la Crime
ISBN: 978-09557078-5-8   **£7.99**

MORE GRIPPING TITLES IN 2009
FROM CRÈME DE LA CRIME

SECRET LAMENT   **Roz Southey**

18th century musician Charles Patterson investigates when an intruder and a murder endanger the woman he loves.
Who is the man masquerading under a false name? Are there really spies in Newcastle? Why is a psalm-teacher keeping vigil over a house? And can Patterson find the murderer before he strikes again?

ISBN: 978-0-9557078-6-5   **£7.99**

DEAD LIKE HER   **Linda Regan**

It seems like a straightforward case for newly promoted DCI Paul Banham and DI Alison Grainger: the victims all bore an uncanny resemblance to Marilyn Monroe. But they soon unearth connections with drug-running and people-trafficking.

ISBN: 978-09557078-8-9   **£7.99**

BLOOD MONEY   **Maureen Carter**

Personal tragedy has pushed Detective Sergeant Bev Morriss into a dark place. But there are bad guys to battle as well as demons – like the Sandman, a vicious serial burglar who wears a clown mask and plays mind-games with his victims.
And Bev is in no mood to play…

ISBN: 978-09557078-7-2   **£7.99**

THE FALL GIRL   **Kaye C Hill**

Accidental P I Lexy Lomax is investigating a suspicious death in a decidedly spooky cottage. Kinky, her truculent chihuahua, hates the place, but he seems to be in a minority.
She's hindered by her obnoxious ex, and a mysterious beast dogs her footsteps. And dark forces are running amok…

ISBN: 978-0-9557078-9-6   **£7.99**

INNOVATIVE INDEPENDENT PUBLISHERS CRÈME DE LA CRIME WOULD LIKE TO OFFER YOU A CHANCE TO SOLVE A MURDER MYSTERY.

Everyone loves a puzzle, and ours present a real tangled web. Teams of crime fiction fans can test their powers of investigation on a choice of three scenarios. An ideal party or fundraising event.

Fatal Exit
Crème de la Crime's best investigative minds are agreed about one thing: Luke Weller the sleazy theatre odd-job man had it coming. But days into the investigation they're baffled.

Fit to Drop
Murder at the health club! Gym instructor Rob Harkness is found dead in his own exercise studio – and everyone has a motive!

Dance of Death
The Hon Hector Bonham-Ware is discovered with an ornamental dagger in his neck during a ball at his in-laws' country house. The question is, who disliked him most?

PIECE together the clues and discover who took a hammer to Luke's skull, attacked Rob with an exercise weight, or stuck Hector with the paper-knife..
EARN points for every element of the mystery you solve – and points mean prizes…

For further details e-mail us at info@cremedelacrime.com

MORE GRIPPING TITLES FROM
CRÈME DE LA CRIME

by Maureen Carter:

WORKING GIRLS	ISBN: 978-0-9547634-0-4	£7.99
DEAD OLD	ISBN: 978-0-9547634-6-6	£7.99
BABY LOVE	ISBN: 978-0-9551589-0-2	£7.99
*HARD TIME	ISBN: 978-0-9551589-6-4	£7.99
BAD PRESS	ISBN: 978-0-9557078-3-4	£7.99

a series which just gets better and better
– Sharon Wheeler, Reviewing the Evidence

by Adrian Magson:

NO PEACE FOR THE WICKED	ISBN: 978-0-9547634-2-8	£7.99
NO HELP FOR THE DYING	ISBN: 978-0-9547634-7-3	£7.99
*NO SLEEP FOR THE DEAD	ISBN: 978-0-9551589-1-9	£7.99
*NO TEARS FOR THE LOST	ISBN: 978-0-9551589-7-1	£7.99
*‡ NO KISS FOR THE DEVIL	ISBN: 978-0-9557078-1-0	£7.99

Gritty, fast-paced detecting of the traditional kind
– Maxim Jakubowski, The Guardian

by Penny Deacon:

A KIND OF PURITAN	ISBN: 978-0-9547634-1-1	£7.99
A THANKLESS CHILD	ISBN: 978-0-9547634-8-0	£7.99

a fascinating new author with a hip, noir voice
– Mystery Lovers

by Linda Regan:

BEHIND YOU!	ISBN: 978-0-9551589-2-6	£7.99
PASSION KILLERS	ISBN: 978-0-9551589-8-8	£7.99

... readable and believable... extremely well written...
– Jim Kennedy, Encore

PUTTING THE MYSTERY IN HISTORY
Crème de la Crime Period Pieces

by Roz Southey

BROKEN HARMONY	ISBN: 978-0-9551589-3-3	£7.99
CHORDS AND DISCORDS	ISBN: 978-0-9551589-2-7	£7.99

Southey has a real feel for the eighteenth century...
– Booklist (USA)

by Gordon Ferris

*TRUTH DARE KILL	ISBN: 978-0-9551589-4-0	£7.99
*THE UNQUIET HEART	ISBN: 978-0-9557078-0-3	£7.99

... a hero that will appeal to readers as much as Richard Sharpe
– Historical Novels Review

SPARKLING CONTEMPORARY CRIME
TO THRILL AND CHILL YOU

IF IT BLEEDS
Bernie Crosthwaite   ISBN: 978-0-9547634-3-5   £7.99

A CERTAIN MALICE
Felicity Young   ISBN: 978-0-9547634-4-2   £7.99

PERSONAL PROTECTION
Tracey Shellito   ISBN: 978-0-9547634-5-9   £7.99

SINS OF THE FATHER
David Harrison   ISBN: 978-0-9547634-9-7   £7.99

Titles marked * are also available in unabridged audio.
Titles marked ‡ are also available in large print.